# Primal Instincts

# SUSAN SIZEMORE

**POCKET STAR BOOKS**

New York  London  Toronto  Sydney

Pocket Star Books
A Division of Simon & Schuster, Inc.
1230 Avenue of the Americas
New York, NY 10020

Copyright © 2010 by Susan Sizemore

All rights reserved, including the right to reproduce this book or portions thereof in any form whatsoever. For information address Pocket Books Subsidiary Rights Department,
1230 Avenue of the Americas, New York, NY 10020

First Pocket Star Books paperback edition September 2010

POCKET STAR BOOKS and colophon are registered trademarks of Simon & Schuster, Inc.

For information about special discounts for bulk purchases, please contact Simon & Schuster Special Sales at
1-866-506-1949 or business@simonandschuster.com.

The Simon & Schuster Speakers Bureau can bring authors to your live event. For more information or to book an event contact the Simon & Schuster Speakers Bureau at 1-866-248-3049 or visit our website at www.simonspeakers.com.

Cover illustration by Gene Mollica

Manufactured in the United States of America

10  9  8  7  6  5  4  3  2  1

ISBN 978-1-4165-6214-6
ISBN 978-1-4391-7695-5 (ebook)

*For Micki Nuding*

# Acknowledgments

With thanks to Brenda Novak for sponsoring her annual auction to support diabetes research and Kea Barnica for her generous contribution.

# Prologue

"Do you know the legend about the selkie? It's not really legend but true, in a way."

He wished the vampire would keep quiet. But the damned creature wouldn't and always expected answers to its inane comments. And since they were working together, he had to put up with it.

He lowered the binoculars and glanced at the vampire called Dr. Stone standing in the shadows at the edge of the pine forest just up from the black rock beach. Heavy clouds scooted by overhead and it was close to sunset, yet the creature was still cautious about light. Odd. He'd been told that it took the drugs that gave it resistance to light.

"What legend? Selkies are creatures that can change from human to seal shape." They were waiting for one right now.

The wind off the water was cold. The raucous noise and fishy smell from the seals frolicking in the waves and on the isolated beach would have thrilled a nature lover. He wasn't a nature lover. And standing there talking to a vampire while waiting for a slimy shapeshifter to emerge from the water made his skin crawl.

Of course the vampire knew this and was relishing his discomfort, though he pretended to merely be friendly, conversing to pass the time.

"According to mortal folktales, a selkie can be controlled by anyone who steals their sealskin. Without their animal skin, the selkie is trapped in human form and cannot return to the sea. Mortals generally get the details wrong when it comes to the supernatural, but those old Celtic grannies got some things right about the watery shapeshifters of the British Isles. Selkies are not all that high on the intelligence scale, or even on the food chain. It's very easy to steal their sealskins."

He turned to face the vampire. "What the devil does that mean? Shapeshifters are in either human form or animal form. Selkies do not have sealskins that can be taken off and stolen."

"I know that. You know that." The vampire

came out of the woods. It moved so lightly past him that he couldn't hear any disturbance of the loose stones. The vampire's gaze was fixed on a sleek dark body moving toward land through the surf as it spoke.

"Selkies—all shifters, really, but selkies more than most—are psychically vulnerable. If I had a dual nature, and probably dual DNA, I'd likely be half-crazed myself. Selkies are the only shifters that are at home on the land and in the water. They are very rare."

"There are raptor shifters," he reminded the vampire. "At home on land and in the air."

"And they are even rarer than the selkies." The vampire gave a low chuckle. "But I don't know of any vampire that would willingly touch the mind of a wereeagle. We're mammals, as are selkies. That's why we've chosen to use a selkie to set our plan in motion."

He'd thought it was because they knew what the seal creature did in its day job.

"Stop thinking of her as a thing," the vampire told him. "Remember that you're going to be her handler. Soon you'll be as close as lovers."

# Chapter One

"You realize that the purpose of terrorism is theater," Tobias Strahan said to the Clan leaders. "It's not so much what our enemies have done to hurt us that they care about, but how we react to it that they're counting on."

Francesca Reynard smiled at the Prime's superior tone. She wondered if the Matri Council was going to let him get away with lecturing them or if the commander of the Dark Angels was about to get his ears boxed. She waited in the council room to see what would happen next. She wasn't supposed to be there and this wasn't a conversation she was supposed to hear. A small rebellion, but she'd take any kind she could get.

*Petty, aren't you?*

The telepathic voice in her head was Strahan's, speaking even more arrogantly to her than he had to the respected Clan leaders.

Primes were supposed to be arrogant, and she normally found them easy to ignore.

But not this one.

*It's a hobby,* she thought back at him.

*Along with petulance and pride, but then everyone knows Flare Reynard's hobbies.*

She'd learned to accept the nickname and had earned the reputation that went with it. *I am reputed to be bitchy,* she pointed out, then raised the mental shields that kept polite vampires out of each other's heads.

She saw the faintest of shrugs from him. Though she could ignore his mind, she *was* female, so she couldn't help but run her gaze appreciatively over the fine figure of an overgrown Prime that he was. He certainly was a big boy. Big hands, big feet, very tall. Muscular, with a tight ass and narrow waist in perfect proportion to his extra-wide shoulders. He was considered the best-looking Prime of his generation, but she liked that the perfection was slightly marred by ears that stuck out a little from a back view.

The Matris bridled and glared at the Prime; most were as offended as he'd intended for them to be.

But Lady Juanita Wolf laughed. "We've been involved in deadly games with the hunters for generations," she reminded Strahan.

"But they've never publicly attacked us before," Lady Anjelica Reynard said. "Never set us up to be found out by the media."

Strahan nodded. "We can't afford to react in the classic manner. They're counting on that. They want to post videos of your people on YouTube, to get news crews camped outside your homes. Because outing us is the best way to destroy us."

"I can almost understand mortal vampire hunters attacking like this," Lady Cassandra Crowe said. "But you haven't convinced me that one of our own is a traitor, that information is being passed from inside our own community. There is absolutely no reason."

"I think I know the reasons," Strahan said.

"We've heard enough on the subject already," Lady Serisa Shagal said firmly.

Los Angeles was Shagal territory, this was her Citadel, and she felt that the defense against the threat to her Clan should be hers to handle. But she had agreed to Strahan's demand to cede emergency powers to the Dark Angels since the attacks were on all supernatural groups, not just Clan vampires. There had been arson and bombings committed against vampires and werefolk all over Southern California, including trouble at the medical clinic here in Los Angeles. The Angels were a multispecies special forces group who answered only to Strahan, who had formed his unit in anticipation of these sorts of attacks.

Francesca admired his confidence in the face of so many Clan Matris. He'd walked into their meeting, taken over, and convinced everyone to do things his way.

Francesca admired his ability to bully Matris but resented that he'd interrupted her own effort to save the day when her friend Sidonie Wolf faced execution for bonding with a werewolf member of the Dark Angels. Francesca and other vampire females had been attempting to start their own revolution as well as save Sid, but now Strahan's power play had forced that effort to the sidelines. She did not admire him at all for interrupting her bid for freedom, even if he had achieved her objective of saving Sid.

He turned his head slightly, giving her a view of his sharp profile and hard expression. A woman couldn't help but think of a male like that as tasty—even a woman like herself who hated the vanity and total jerkhood of the males of her species. Luckily, she'd had years of practice at ignoring the instincts that reared up in her as she watched this Prime. She'd paused to watch him lecture the Matris, not to get all tingly and warm.

It also helped that a squad of Primes came pouring in through the doorway. She stepped aside to give them plenty of room to get to their various Matris.

"The arrangements are all made," Barak Shagal told his Matri and bondmate. "Everyone's cars are waiting. Guards are placed, and the pilots of your private planes have been alerted."

The plan was for all vampire females in California to be whisked away to safety, but Francesca had no intention of going back to the Clan Citadel in Idaho. She'd come to California with a purpose and wasn't leaving until she'd accomplished it. She was glad she'd kept quiet and in the shadows. It made it easier for her to slip out the door before she could be noticed and called back.

# Chapter Two

*Where do you think you're going?* Tobias wondered as he saw Flare Reynard sneak away. Watching the sway of her hips as she walked was a joy. But the stiffness of her spine and proud lift of her head told him she wasn't heading for her mother's limo. She obviously had plans of her own.

But he was in charge here, and the thought of showing her that brought a brief smile to the hard line of his mouth.

"Brat," he muttered under his breath.

He knew he should mention Flare's leaving to Lady Anjelica and let the proper people take care of it, but he couldn't resist tracking her down himself. If anyone needed a public lesson in discipline, it was the Clans' most adored and spoiled female.

Finding Flare wouldn't be difficult for a Prime of his skills. Even with her shields tightly drawn around her, he thought he could pick up the unique scent of her perfume, which had permeated his senses the moment he walked into the tense meeting. Or at least he could track her by the stunned looks she tended to leave on the faces of any Primes she encountered.

Tobias's cell phone rang and he paused in the mansion's entrance hallway to answer it. Personally, he preferred telepathy, but not every member of his Crew could communicate mind to mind, not to mention the regular mortals who needed to get hold of him. So, he carried a phone, an elaborate device with multiple functions—which interrupted him at inconvenient times and places, such as now. He stepped outdoors to the side of the wide staircase at the front of the house as he put the phone to his ear.

"How's Joe?" was Dee McCoy's first question.

"You could have called him and asked," Tobias said to the mortal witch.

She snorted. "I can picture him standing in front of a firing squad as his phone rings and hearing, 'Wait a moment while I take'—BANG!"

"Vampires don't use firing squads. The Joe

problem is settled, and his lady Sid will be joining the Crew. Set up orientation for her."

"You got us a girl vampire?" It took a lot to impress Dee McCoy, and Tobias smiled at the awe in her voice.

"Yes, I'm good," he said. "Also, the L.A. op has been authorized. The locals will be staying out of our way, and all is right in my world."

"Except for Saffie . . ."

Tobias looked around as he waited for Dee to go on. Joe and Sid were standing near the bottom of the stairs and moved closer so he could talk to them once he was off the phone.

After a significant silence, Dee told him, "I've gotten a couple of *sips* from her that give me the impression she's having some trouble at school."

This wasn't the time or place to ask for details, but he was grateful as always for the witch's reminder that he had more important things to deal with than saving the world. "I'll call Saffie as soon as I get the chance," he said.

"Tonight," Dee answered.

Tobias grunted and ended the call just as Sidonie Wolf said to Joe, "And there's the Prime responsible for setting this whole mess in motion."

She was talking about him. He gave her an acknowledging nod and walked past the couple, all the while shamelessly listening to the female vampire explaining to the werewolf the deeper game Tobias played by reuniting the two of them.

*I put their lives at risk in an effort to help the cause of female liberation,* he thought. The supernatural world had to change before it was destroyed and he'd do whatever he had to to save everybody—vampire, werefolk, faefolk, the creatures even immortals had trouble accepting. Every sentient being deserved freedom and equality—except maybe ghosts, but they were ex-humans and not really any of his concern.

While his thoughts circled around the problems of his peoples, he circled alertly around the front of the mansion, aware of all movement. He noted the evacuation of Matris and other females by their concerned Primes, identifying who occupied each limo and the direction each car took as it left the gate. Neither Reynard female was among the exiting groups.

"Someone needs to shake some sense into that spoiled princess . . ."

Tobias paused to laugh at his response. *I've already got one teenager to deal with,* he reminded himself. Besides, Flare Reynard was no child. She was a dangerously beautiful female, and more than the scent of her perfume called to him. *But she does that to any Prime with hot blood in his veins,* he told himself. *I want that glorious body* beneath me in bed and the taste of her blood on my tongue. But I won't let lust make me stupid like it has every other Prime who's ever gone after her and failed. If I want her, I'll have her.*

Awareness made him turn, and he caught furtive movement out of the corner of his eye. He was standing in front of Flare before she reached the side door of the multicar garage.

"Flare, my dear," he said with a blatantly false smile. "What are you doing here?" He leaned against the door, his arms crossed.

He expected an imperious order to get out of her way. Instead she looked puzzled. "Dear?"

She crossed her arms. He appreciated what this did for her breasts, and she obviously knew it. Primes were far too easy to seduce, which was why they were taught self-control, and the lessons from the crèche were reinforced by the Angels' discipline and training. Which Tobias momentarily thought was a shame, because, damn! Flare was one fine female.

Francesca was delighted when Strahan's gaze focused on her breasts. She knew he wouldn't fall for this distraction for long, but she enjoyed the flutter of warmth caused by this Prime's sexual interest.

She looked into his big brown eyes and said, "The Bat Signal is flashing. You need to go save Gotham now."

"I appreciate the comparison to my favorite vigilante, but you can't insult me and you're not going anywhere but back to Idaho."

She grinned at this challenge. "I don't take orders from you."

"The Matris would disagree. I am in charge of this territory."

"I have an appointment at a secure facility."

"I see you're using this young Prime for tongue-sharpening practice," her mother said, standing suddenly behind her.

*Damn!* She'd tried to leave the Citadel unnoticed and somehow she'd ended up the center of the attention of the very people she was trying most to avoid.

"Lady Francesca and I were merely exchanging pleasantries, Matri," Strahan said to her mother.

"Yes. I know how *pleasant* she can be at times."

"She's witty, ma'am, and sharply direct. As is proper for a vampire female."

"What are you talking about, Strahan?" Francesca asked.

Lady Anjelica went on. "Don't you have somewhere you're supposed to be?"

Francesca wasn't sure who her mother was talking to, but Strahan picked up the conversational ball. "We all do. Let me escort both of you to your car."

"That's a good idea," Anjelica said. She looped her arms through theirs and led them out of the shadow of the garage.

"I'm not going to the airport," Francesca said when they reached her mother's car. She threw an annoyed look at Strahan, waiting for his protest. She would have avoided the coming family argument if he hadn't sneaked up on her by the garage.

But the protest didn't come. Apparently he'd decided to let her mother deal with her.

The driver held open the passenger door for them.

*Go ahead, wash your hands of me.* She was annoyed at her resentment of the Prime's attitude. Of course he was going to leave her to deal with her mother. He wanted her out of town and she couldn't blame him for that. Shouldn't, at least. She shook her head and made herself stop looking at tall, muscular, gorgeous, overconfident Tobias Strahan. Something about him brought out the most petulant part of her. She didn't want to ignore him the way she normally did Primes. She wanted to—

*Provoke the hell out of me until I kiss you senseless?*

Francesca fought down the urge to laugh at his arrogance. Laugh. Not turn on him in scathing fury? Now, there was a new reaction for her to Primal arrogance.

*I only deal in facts, ma'am. Arrogance is for the unsure.*

*Oh, do be quiet, Strahan. I've got more pressing business than dealing with you.*

*But you would like to be kissed.*

*By the right person. I'm not dead, but I am picky.*

Their telepathic conversation was so rapid, the driver had just finished opening the car door when her mother replied to her, "You most certainly are not going to the airport with me."

# Chapter Three

Expecting an argument, a stern command to return to the safety of the Citadel from the ruler of her Clan, Francesca was left with her mouth hanging open.

She wasn't the only one.

Strahan said, "Lady Anjelica are you—"

"You heard me correctly," Anjelica said. "My heir has accepted her duty to give the Clan children, and I am not getting in the way of her giving *me* grandchildren. I'll drop you off at the clinic, Flare."

Francesca shot a triumphant look at Strahan, grinned at her mom, and got into the backseat. "Turkey baster, here I come," she murmured happily—but a sudden wistfulness colored her mood.

She knew what was required. She knew the way she'd chosen. But being so close to Strahan's potent masculinity reminded her that there was another way for a female to become pregnant. The sooner she was away from his pheromones, the better.

Tobias frowned at Lady Anjelica's decision. "You are undermining my authority, Matri."

"I know it seems that way, Prime, but the continuation of our species is imperative."

"More imperative than the safety of our females?" He shook his head. "I don't think so, ma'am."

"Of course you shouldn't think so, Prime. Your rightful concern is the security of our females and your mission. A Matri's concerns must take in a broader outlook." She gestured. "Join me on the ride to the clinic. I believe you're planning on going there anyway."

He was. But he'd had a few other things he'd planned on doing first. He didn't like this, but if his riding along to Dr. Casmerek's helped get one more Matri on her way to safety, he'd bite down on his annoyance and do as she asked.

"Thank you, Lady Anjelica." He would have handed the Matri in beside her daughter, but she gestured for him to take the center seat.

Seated so close to Flare, he couldn't help but come into contact with her; the way their thighs brushed drove him crazy. Her warmth flooded into his body. Once again her scent enveloped him. And despite the fact that they were both fully clothed, he could feel skin sleek as satin against him. The whole trip was delightful agony. He gave no sign. He'd been commanding a mixed bunch of species and raising a mortal daughter, and this had caused him to develop different habits about privacy and propriety.

When the car arrived at the clinic, Tobias and Flare entered and went their own ways. He was disciplined enough to control himself despite the distracting temptation she presented, but he did take one last appreciative glance at her magnificent backside before she disappeared behind an office door.

Francesca leaned against the door, closed her eyes, and gritted her teeth, even though that forced her slightly extended fangs into her bottom lip. She was quivering with arousal as well as anger, and the anger just made her more aroused. That last hot look he'd given her when he didn't think she was looking had just about done her in.

She didn't blame Strahan. He hadn't made a move, said a thing, or let his shields down one little bit. She didn't blame herself, either.

Her mother had done that to them on purpose!

Francesca didn't even blame the Reynard Matri for her unsubtle attempt at matchmaking. It was what Matris did, what she'd likely do if she ever took over the job.

*But it's not going to work on me, Ma.*

Would the mating-receptive chemicals roaring around in her body have any effect on the fertility tests she'd come in for? She didn't want to waste her time or anyone else's. Well, there was only one way to find out. She took one more calming breath and walked to the examination room where the lab techs were waiting for her.

"Hi, Chiana, hi, Kea." She'd gotten to know and like both women during her visits to the clinic. "I know you're ready to get started, but I'm not quite myself. Are you up for a few minutes of gossip while I calm down?"

Chiana was a small woman, supple and slender with gloriously thick dark brown hair. She was a wereseal—*selkie* was the old-fashioned term. She didn't talk much, but she was incredibly easy to talk to. This made her popular with nervous vampires afraid of needles and other medical procedures.

Kea was far more outgoing; a tall redhead, she was the daughter of a Prime and a mortal woman. She'd provocatively informed Francesca of this the first time they met, expecting the wicked Flare to sneer at her lineage and prepared to sneer back at vampire shortcomings.

"Nice to meet you," Francesca had said. "Do you want to go out to lunch when we're done?"

They'd gone out together for lunch and shopping several times, and Francesca had introduced Kea to her book club.

"You look all hot and bothered," Kea said now. "Did one of the new boys in town catch your fancy?"

"Unfortunately," Francesca answered. "Caught my libido, at any rate."

She sat on the exam table and crossed her legs, then quickly uncrossed them because that just made the ache worse.

"Which Dark Angel caught your fancy?" Kea asked.

Francesca gave a self-deprecating laugh. "Strahan himself."

"That makes sense." Kea looked relieved to hear that information, then blushed.

"Oh, no," Francesca said. "Don't tell me *you're* interested in one of the Angels? They're all so ridiculously macho, they make regular Primes question their masculinity."

Kea's eyes sparkled with amusement. "That's rather the point, isn't it? I'm used to fending off the local boys, but . . ." She fanned her face with her hand. "There are a couple of Primes among the Dark Angel guards around the place who have my attention."

"I thought you had a crush on Tony Crowe," Francesca said.

"Yeah, but now that he's bonded I'm out of the running."

Chiana spoke up quietly. "You were never in the running. None of us ever were." She sighed romantically. "I wish all of us could have a love story like that."

Francesca had seen Crowe with his mortal bondmate at the Shagal Citadel but didn't know the details of the romance.

Before she could ask, Kea said, "Dr. Casmerek has issued a need-to-know order on the medical details, but apparently Tony's lady was experimented on by the bad guys and Tony saved her."

"Very romantic," Francesca said. "Very Prime." She turned a teasing look on Chiana. "Please tell me you aren't longing to be rescued from a horrible fate by a big, bad vampire boy."

She didn't know if vampires and selkies would be compatible, but her best friend Sidonie had just hooked up with a werewolf. Who knew what combinations were possible?

"Chiana's already got a boyfriend," Kea said.

Chiana looked uncomfortable. "I don't like to talk about him."

"That's because he's a mortal," Kea said. "She's been seeing him for a couple of months now. They met on a beach when she was on vacation."

The shy selkie was blushing. "I wish I'd never mentioned him to you."

Francesca decided it was time to change the subject. "I think you should stick some needles in me now," she said.

# *Chapter Four*

After examining damage from the attack on the clinic, Tobias's next task was to interview a witness. Since Tony Crowe was cooperating with the Dark Angels taking over security for every immortal outpost in the city, Tobias was surprised to find Tony waiting for him outside Rose Cameron's room with his arms crossed and an attitude that said there was no way anyone was getting past him to talk to his lady.

"Rose is taking a nap," Tony informed him before Tobias could ask. "And she will be taking a nap or otherwise occupied any time you or your Angels show up. She's been through hell and I'm not letting you make her relive it."

"I need to ask her a few questions."

Tony shook his head. "You want to ask those questions telepathically, don't you?"

"That would be the most efficient way."

"You have prisoners from the house where she was held before we rescued her."

"It's never good to send a werewolf in when you want to take prisoners," Tobias said.

"Sidonie was in on the rescue, too. I know for a fact she tied up some of the bad guys. Too bad," he added. "I would have loved to rip out the throats of the people who hurt my Rose."

"I'd be happy to give you the chance. You can help hunt down the ones really responsible."

"I intend to."

"Crowe, the Matris have agreed to conduct this war my way. You'd be great working with the Angels. But I won't let you go off on your own. You will not get in my way. May I see your lady for a few minutes? Please?"

Tony smiled again, a bit of fang showing. "I'll consider the Angels' offer, Tobias. But you can't see my Rose."

"You're being—"

"A Prime protecting his new bondmate."

Tobias automatically took a step back. Of course Crowe would oppose another Prime going near his mate, especially one who wanted to make telepathic contact. He was going to have to think of a way around this development. Biology and culture got in the way of doing things sensibly far too often.

Tobias nodded gravely. "Your point is taken, Prime. My apologies."

Crowe clapped him on the shoulder. "Glad you see it my way. You're a good kid, Tobias."

Tobias couldn't take offense; compared to Crowe he *was* a kid. He walked back down the hall, saying over his shoulder, "Just don't let any of my people hear you call me that."

When Tobias reached the clinic reception area, he came to an abrupt halt. "What are you doing here?"

It was no way to address a Matri, and Lady Anjelica's haughty expression told him so.

He bowed. "Pardon my rudeness. But why aren't you on a plane for Idaho?"

"I will be." She gestured toward an office door. "Come with me. I want a private word with you."

Tobias never expected anything to go exactly as planned, so he always had contingencies worked out. Only this time he hadn't foreseen problems involving females popping up to disrupt his strategy. Between his daughter, Rose Cameron, and a couple of Reynard women, the day was spiraling out of his control—which both amused and annoyed him. How typical for a Prime that it was women who were the distraction.

He showed no emotion as he followed Lady Anjelica into the private room, then stood in front the closed door and waited for her to tell him what she wanted. The slight nod she gave told him she appreciated his protective gesture, even if it was as automatic as breathing.

"Of course you know I tricked you into coming here with us," she said. It wasn't an apology.

Tobias answered with a slight shrug.

"I've been observing you and my daughter and wanted the chance for closer observations."

"She's hot. I want her. Nothing surprising in that."

"Every Prime wants her, and she doesn't generally give a damn, but she responds to you." Lady Anjelica gave the kind of dangerous smile only vampires could give.

He *so* did not like where he suspected this was going.

"Attraction isn't relevant."

Her smile only got wider. "You said *attraction*."

"I meant arousal."

"Nope, you can't take it back. You are attracted to my daughter. I can see that the two of you are an obvious match. I've been waiting for this for a long time. So has our entire Clan."

Her mentioning Clan ties upped the stakes of this game from personal to political. *Damn! What is Flare Reynard getting me into?* "Flare's a pleasure to look at. A pleasure to touch. It would be a pleasure to have her. But I can forgo that pleasure."

Anjelica was totally unimpressed by his stern tone. "Are you sure? Think about her, Prime, and tell me what you feel."

He didn't intend to go there, but his blood suddenly sang with fiery hunger. He swore to himself and pushed away the knowledge, the need.

"What do you want from me?" he asked the Matri.

"Don't pretend to naïveté. You know very well what I want."

He looked at her, his thoughts guarded and his features totally blank. *Maybe she won't say it outright.*

"I want you to sire my grandchild."

Arranging stud services was perfectly natural for a Matri, so the proposal should have sounded perfectly natural to him. Maybe it would have if she'd been talking about anyone but Flare. He found himself wanting to defend the female. Flare might not have been likable, but he admired her spirit.

"Flare's already made her choice. You approved it."

"I've never liked it. Until a few hours ago I didn't believe there was any other way to get her to do her duty."

She looked him up and down in the carefully assessing, appreciative way of a vampire female scrutinizing a Prime, making him more embarrassed than pleased. It was a bad sign when a Prime didn't respond to every female out there. It came at a point in a Prime's life when he responded to only one woman. Wanted only one woman.

*Please, goddess,* he prayed. *Not now. Not her.*

He wondered if he should inform Lady Anjelica that there was a one in three chance he would sire Flare's child without their having any physical contact. The sperm donors for the fertility clinic had to come from somewhere, and the Dark Angels' Primes were forward-thinking enough to offer their services when the Clan and Family Primes Casmerek dare to approach had been outraged. But telling Anjelica this would be a violation of Flare's privacy, his own, and that of the other volunteers, and he couldn't do that.

He said, "Lady Anjelica, there's a war on. We don't have time for this."

She just kept smiling. "A war. I'm glad you mentioned it."

*Uh-oh.* There was an unmistakable threat in her eyes.

He gave her a narrow-eyed glare. "What are you up to?"

"Not everyone shares your paranoid outlook. Quite a few don't believe the Dark Angels are a good idea, either. I can help you with that."

He waited. She waited, still smiling.

He broke the silence. "So you could help—or you could hurt."

"I was thinking more like destroy."

A Matri as wealthy and influential as the Reynard Clan leader opposing him? Destroying everything he'd built to protect all supernatural groups? Oh, yeah, she could do it.

"Now I know where Flare got her personality."

"I'm far more of a harridan than that sentimental child could ever be."

"You would actually jeopardize our future for the sake of getting your daughter knocked up?"

"What future do we have if the younger generation refuses to find bondmates? What's next? Cloning? What future do we have if more and more of us depend on the daylight drugs? Aren't we going to lose ourselves by blending in more and more with the mortals?"

"That blending in is for our own safety."

"We're vampires! We don't need to be safe, we need to be—" Lady Anjelica caught herself, and her lips curved into a serene smile once again. "There's no need to argue over it. My point is this, Prime: Sire a Reynard child and have my full support, politically and financially, for the Dark Angels. Refuse and I'll destroy you."

"That's quite plain, lady."

"Decide. Now."

Tobias held up his hands in front of him. "I'll do it!"

She gave an imperious nod. "Good."

He'd do it. He'd have a great deal of pleasure doing it, and he'd thought of a couple of other reasons to keep Flare at his side that had nothing to do with saving his team. Reasons that might just help save his world. Even though having her around was going to be a pain in the ass.

# Chapter Five

"You don't look happy."

"Is that any of your concern?" Francesca snapped at Strahan. His large presence took up a lot of space in the reception area, directly blocking the exit. "What are you doing here?"

In a way she was glad to see someone she could snarl at. She'd just been told she'd have to wait at least a week for the results of yet more tests. She'd been warned the procedure might not work for her. It had also been strongly suggested that she stop using the daylight drugs that gave her parity with mortal humans. But even if she did that, it would be *months* before the drugs were completely out of her system. Wait, wait, wait.

She was *not* a patient person.

And here, blocking her way, stood Mr. Perfect Prime himself. Everything always went this great warrior's way.

She wanted to bite him.

Strahan had no trouble catching that thought and answered her with a show of fangs. The fierce display sent her back a step. Even worse, her body responded with a flood of tingling warmth.

"I didn't mean bite you like *that*!" she yelled at him.

He came to her in a blur of movement. His arm came around her waist. Her body melded too perfectly against his. Hot skin, hard muscle, masculine scent. *Damn.*

"Yes, you did." His voice was a whisper, a promise.

Francesca kicked him in the shin, which only made him smile. His smile made her laugh, something a Prime hadn't managed to do in a long time.

"Yes, I did," she admitted. "But we won't take it any farther and you *will* let go of me now."

"You started it," he said, ignoring that she'd conceded.

"I always do."

"Do you ever apologize?"

"Rarely."

Strahan stepped away from her, but he didn't

stop blocking the exit. "I'm here to take you to safety."

Francesca began to regret having turned down the offer to take up residence in the well-guarded clinic. She knew being imperious or totally nasty wouldn't get her anywhere with the Dark Angel commander.

"I'm not going back to Idaho," she said, wondering how many times she'd have to repeat this while he slung her over his shoulder and carried her onto an airplane. Not that the idea of being slung over his broad shoulder was in and of itself repulsive—far from it.

Strahan held up a hand. "I've already discussed this with your mother. She wants you to remain in Los Angeles."

Francesca was immediately suspicious. "Really?"

"I've agreed to personally see to your security during the crisis. You're coming home with me, Flare."

"Home?"

"To the Dark Angels' base of operations."

Hang out with the Dark Angels? She fought off the temptation to jump up and down with delight. "You've agreed to personally look after me. You're a busy Prime. What did she offer you?"

"Her support for the Dark Angels," he answered immediately.

She gave an evil laugh. "You're willing to put up with me for a little money?"

"For a lot of money."

She was willing to accept this answer for now, though he was bound to have other reasons. Her mother certainly did. But she'd work around, through, or over whatever schemes came at her and be in the middle of the action instead of safely locked in a tower for once.

"You're going to earn your fee, Strahan."

He ducked his head and scratched his jaw, then looked back at her with a smile that tried to melt her bones. "I'm sure I will."

*You are made of asbestos,* she told herself. "What are we waiting for, Strahan? Let's get to this headquarters of yours."

He paced around the small apartment, nervous, annoyed by the sound of waves crashing on the nearby beach. Of course the damn selkie had to live near the ocean. He'd hated moving in to keep a constant eye on her, but he did what was necessary.

Someone was playing Christmas music in a nearby apartment. It was almost as irritating as the repetitive pounding of the surf. Peace on Earth? Not likely. Not as long as monsters roamed it and tried to rule it.

She was late. Why? Had the monsters decided it was best for all of them to hide inside the clinic? Had she somehow managed to break free of the mental conditioning that bound her to him? She hadn't shown any sign of rebellion but the creatures were clever . . .

He rushed from the kitchen into the living room the instant the door opened. "Where have you been?" he demanded.

The creature flinched at his harshness. She looked like a small, frightened woman, but he knew what she really was. He wouldn't let himself have any dangerous, soft emotions about her no matter how vulnerable she pretended to be.

"Where have you been?" he asked again.

"Christmas shopping," she answered. "My friend Kea asked me to go. A Dark Angel came along. He and Kea talked a lot when they weren't flirting."

Christmas shopping? Flirting? He was constantly disgusted at these monsters' parodying of real people. In the deep past they'd stayed hidden in their dark lairs instead of mingling with their victims. Part of the reason for this operation was to drive them back into the dark where they belonged. Where their influence on humans would once again be minimal.

If he and the other hunters had their way,

they'd destroy the night creatures altogether. But they had their uses, so leaving a minimum number of the monsters alive was part of the devil's bargain they'd made.

"What did your *friend* and the vampire talk about? It better be important."

She'd been obedient about bringing him information ever since the vampire had brainwashed her. He still reinforced the fear constantly to make sure the creature continued to be of service.

Her shoulders slumped and she wouldn't look at him when she spoke. "Rose Cameron is still staying at the clinic."

"What's her condition?" he demanded.

"I don't know. I couldn't get in to see her today. Tony won't let anybody into her room. The Prime told Kea that even Tobias wasn't allowed in and he's been put in charge of everything."

"Is she aging rapidly?"

The vampire would want to know, as would whoever was behind the vampire. He'd been told the layers of secrecy were in place to keep everyone safe, but he didn't feel at all safe here, at the level closest to their informant inside the monsters' stronghold.

"She was fine when I saw her this morning. She's been with Tony since they returned from the Shagal Citadel."

He stepped closer to her, lifted her chin. She still wouldn't look him in the eye. "What was that meeting about? Did your talkative vampire friend tell you?"

Was that a hint of a smile? A brief flicker of satisfaction?

He shook her. He wasn't allowed to beat her. "What?" he demanded.

She didn't answer until he let her go. "They were all there at the Shagal Citadel—the Clan females. There and gone. Tobias got them away from you."

He swore. The Hunters and their monstrous allies all wanted to get possession of the Clan and Family females. The Hunters had killed many vampire females in the past and wanted to do so again—it was the surest way of wiping out the race. Of course the Tribe vampire had other plans for captured females. A compromise had yet to be worked out, but the females were sought-after prizes.

"All the females have been evacuated? You're sure?"

The selkie was programmed never to lie to

him. "All but two of them. One's joined the Dark Angels. The other one is under Tobias's protection. That's all I know."

She'd given him some things to think over. Not that he was supposed to think. He was supposed to report, and only to his vampire contact.

"One more thing," he said. "You didn't mention to this Prime that you had a human boyfriend living with you, did you?"

"Of course not! I'd never tell a vampire about you."

She glanced at the door as though expecting it to crash open. He'd been worried about that himself.

"You haven't told anyone about me, have you?"

Tears leaked from her eyes. She whispered, "I—no."

The pain in her voice was most satisfying. "Good. Go to your room."

# Chapter Six

An incoming call on Tobias's earpiece demanded his attention before he could escort Flare out the door. He paused, one hand on the smooth skin of her arm. While he gave his attention to the call, his senses absorbed silky warmth and heady female scent.

"Go," he told the caller.

"Need your opinion on a possible lead," Joe Bleythin answered.

"I'm listening."

Joe's reply was succinct and toneless. "Sid and I were involved in the discovery of the Hunyara werewolf tamers. The bad guys then were a group of feral werewolves. I killed a couple of ferals that were guarding the place where Rose Cameron was being kept. This tells me we didn't get the entire feral group when we cleaned out their den up in the Northwest. But the lead Sid and I would like to follow here in L.A. involves a feral pack that attacked a Hunyara some years back. Those three ferals are dead, but tracing them might lead to the origin of the feral connection with our current bad guys."

"We have some stuff on the incident in the database." Tobias had been collecting seemingly random facts for a long time. "Have Sasha look it up."

"Will do. Sid's also got a call in to the Hunyara who was attacked—she's bonded with a Family Prime—to check her memories. I'd like to take a look at those ferals' den."

"You're my best nose, Joe, but do you think you can sniff out any information after all these years?"

"I'd like to give it a shot. And Sid's telepathy might come in handy asking around the ferals' neighborhood."

Tobias considered the request and the best uses of manpower. "Have your look. But do it fast. Don't get any locals involved." The protocol for this op was to unobtrusively protect the people being targeted while keeping them out of the action no matter how much this annoyed the local Primes and werefolk.

"Understood."

Francesca wanted to break the contact with Strahan. She wanted to step away, to deny the contact with him. But it was the permeating awareness that kept her in place as the connection went deeper by the second. He paid her no attention and she was glad of it.

Strong. Ruthless. Leader. Completely focused and disciplined. Driven.

The Perfect Prime, he'd been called. The Perfect Warrior. Francesca felt the truth of it permeating his spirit. His spirit thrilled her. It also terrified her, because this was just the sort of male she was strongly attracted to.

Primes weren't the only men who were perfect warriors.

She'd known such a man and lost him and wasn't going through that hell again. She didn't have to. The hell was always going to be part of her.

Francesca swore viciously and pulled away from Strahan. The emptiness that washed through her was easier to live with than the connection.

"This is way too emo," she muttered, angry

with herself, and stared out the glass door at palm trees and colorful flowering bushes until the threat of tears passed. She'd lost all enthusiasm for spending time among the Dark Angels by the time Strahan came up to her.

He took her arm again. "Let's go."

Francesca jerked away but managed to squelch the impulse to shout at him to leave her alone. Her Matri had ordered this. She'd agreed to it. She couldn't argue, but she didn't have to take defeat gracefully.

"Fine," she said. "Let's just get it over with."

He ignored her pouting and tilted an eyebrow sardonically at her. "I'm delighted to hear you say that."

He reached out again, but she walked out the door ahead of him toward a black SUV parked in front of the main door. Wanting his touch far too much to allow it, she projected haughty pride to cover how shaken she was.

*Flare's mercurial. That's what Flare is. One moment I think this might be a pleasant experience. Then she snaps at me, and there's no fun in having my pride bitten.*

Tobias drove in silence while his thoughts raged and physical awareness of the ice princess beside him fueled the heat of his mood. He ran his tongue over his slightly extended fangs, which ached to sink into Flare's throat, her wrists, her thighs. He wanted his tongue on her nipple and his teeth in—

*Calm down! Eyes on the road. Mind on the op. No biting. I will not taste her. I'll have her, but without blood. I will not take or give a single drop if I know what's good for me.*

His aching fangs told him that tasting Flare would be the most erotic experience of his life. But he'd plenty of experience in ignoring his anatomy's opinions. He'd worked through pain and fear and every other intense thing a body could go through. He'd even died once, and if a baby hadn't been crying nearby he would happily have stayed that way. Intense attraction to one snotty beauty wasn't going to conquer him after everything else he'd been through.

Embarrassment was the main thing he had to fear at the moment. He was glad no one had called him and that Flare sat beside him in surly silence. He would not have enjoyed the obvious sign of arousal if he had to open his mouth. As it was, Flare was no doubt aware of all the heat coming off of him. She was no doubt wallowing in her famous power over every Prime in the universe.

"Just how many Primes are there in the universe?" she asked.

His gaze cut her way for an instant before he looked back at the busy freeway. He counted bright lights coming toward them from the opposite lanes of traffic, but he saw an afterimage of her curious look and the lush curve of Flare's lips in a faint smile.

*Goddess, she is beautiful!*

And she was a far better telepath than he'd realized.

*It's the beauty and the bitch people see, not the brains. I like to keep it that way. Besides, you've been shouting into my head for hours.*

*We haven't been on the road for hours.*

*Seems like it.*

He knew how good his shielding was. How had she gotten around it?

"Not on purpose," she said. "How many Primes are there, do you think? If anyone's done a census, it would be you Dark Angels."

He concentrated on the opportunity she was offering him, to get his mind off wanting her. He was almost grateful, although he wondered what she was up to.

"Three hundred and twelve among the Clans and Families in the U.S. We don't have an accurate count of young males currently in crèches.

I don't know how many Primes there are in the world," he told Flare.

"You don't know officially, you mean," Flare said.

She caught on quickly. He nodded. "But if I asked Sasha Corbett, she'd know. She's our data miner."

"You've got one of the Corbett twins working for you?"

He was surprised at how impressed Flare sounded. "You've heard of them?"

"Hell, yes. If you want something found, hidden, or changed, Sasha and Ana Corbett are the people to go to."

He wondered how a sheltered Clan female found out about the Corbetts' very specialized skills. More importantly, what had she wanted found, hidden, or changed? Were there secret depths to Flare Reynard? He made a note to ask Sasha about it.

He wondered if maybe he should ask Flare.

She said, "You're driving toward Malibu. If you're heading where I think you are, it's not much of a secret hideout."

# Chapter Seven

"Where I'm taking you is totally safe," Tobias told the spoiled female. He resented her comment deeply. "I'm not going to risk your pretty hide."

"I didn't say it wasn't safe. Security is your business. I said the location isn't exactly secret."

He turned the car into a long driveway that went downhill to a cliffside house overlooking a long stretch of beach.

"You can't possibly know where we are," he said as he stopped the SUV.

Flare sat very straight and tense. Her aggressive posture triggered a primal instinct in him. There were times when a Prime absolutely had to put a female on her back and make her accept his dominance. Flare was close to driving him over that edge.

Tobias forced himself to look around, to assess their surroundings and precautions. The grounds were lit by strategically placed floodlights. Dark Angels stood guard in shadows to keep out immortal intruders. The house's state-of-the-art security system would alert them to most mortal trouble, and he knew the owner's gun cabinet was well stocked.

Flare leaned close to snarl, "What do you mean 'You can't possibly know where we are'? This is my sister-in-law's grandfather's house."

The distinctive scent filling Tobias's awareness wasn't perfume, it was her. She was as receptive as he was aroused, even if she didn't know it. It was too bad he'd managed to get himself under control.

"This is Ben Lancer's house," he said calmly. "He's an old friend of mine."

"And Ben is family."

Tobias calculated the kin relations of the Reynard Clan. Flare had two brothers. One of them, Alexander, was bonded to a mortal woman named Domini, who was also related on her paternal side to the Corvus Clan. Domini's mortal father's father was—

"Ben Lancer," he said again.

"Small world we live in," she sneered.

"Getting smaller all the time," he snapped at her.

The space between them was certainly small. Primitive lust still burned between them. He saw that Flare was finally aware of it when she turned sharply away from him, her hand shaking when she reached for the door release.

The door was opened for her by an Angel and a hand was extended to help her out. Tobias barely stifled a jealous snarl but didn't try to stop his triumphant smile when Flare's glare sent the other Prime hastily back a step. She stalked off alone toward the front door.

Tobias got out of the vehicle and watched her walk away. The other Prime watched with equal appreciation. "Don't you dare even think, dream, or fantasize about her, Ali," Tobias told his subordinate. "She's all mine."

He knew the truth of it in his blood. He followed her to the house, unsure where the truth was going to lead them.

*I hate fighting all the time. Why do I have to fight all the time? Strahan started this one and—*

The fight had gotten her so turned on she

could barely walk. And so embarrassed she never wanted to face Strahan again.

*I have to do something about my temper.*

How many times had she been told that? By how many people? Especially by herself. They called her Flare for a very good reason. Anything could set her off. Her temper was frequently useful for keeping horny Primes at bay, but not tonight. Oh, no. Blowing up at Strahan had the opposite effect, and she still wanted to claw his clothes off, to taste his hot blood in her mouth.

Didn't they call that "truemating" back in the old days? "Bloodfire" was another translation from the old language they all learned but never used. Did Primes and females still practice it behind closed doors? She'd never experienced that kind of intensity with a Prime lover. Maybe you had to be bonded first.

"Oh, no," she muttered as she reached the door. "That's not going to happen."

She could feel Strahan coming up behind her. At least she was distracted from the shiver of anticipation by the door opening before she could knock.

"Francesca!" Ben greeted her.

She gladly stepped into the offered hug. He was

still large, solid, and strong. Despite the mortal's advanced age, Ben Lancer was a sexy old dude. A lot of it had to do with his deep, whiskey-rough voice. That a vampire female had loved him when he was young and let him go was a shame.

He released her as Strahan came up behind her. "What's the most beautiful woman in the world doing here?" Ben asked.

Francesca peered past his shoulder. "Domini's not here, is she?"

"She is."

"Then cut out the most-beautiful-woman-in-the-world crap. It's taken years for her to get over our first meeting."

Strahan put his hands on her shoulders and shoved her inside the house.

"Hey!"

Once the door was closed, he ignored her to confront Ben. "Domini should be safely out of the area with all the other females."

The old man was not intimidated by the suddenly fierce Prime. "She's not a vampire yet," he answered. "You told the locals to go about their business. Domini's business is her weekly gaming night with her granddad."

"Arkham Asylum?" Francesca asked eagerly.

Ben nodded.

"I want in on that."

"Hush," Strahan told her, his attention focused on Ben. Who glared right back.

After a few seconds of alpha male staring, Ben said, "Come on into the kitchen. Your witch wants you."

Strahan gave up and followed the mortal. Francesca followed him. Along the way Strahan's *Why doesn't anyone ever listen to me?* leaked to her.

*Because civilians don't think like you,* Francesca answered before she could stop herself. He gave her a puzzled look over his shoulder.

"Oh, were you expecting me to reply, *Because you're an asshole?*"

She chuckled as his very strong determination to ignore her from then on came back to her.

"That's not going to happen," she said.

*I know,* he thought. *But we can both give it a try.*

# Chapter Eight

The rich, dark smell of strong coffee permeated the large kitchen. Tobias noticed a half-full carafe sitting in a chrome coffeemaker, but Dee McCoy was standing by the stove, stirring a large copper pot, and that was where the coffee scent originated.

"If she offers you a cup don't take it," he whispered to Flare.

"Why? Did she flunk potions class?" Flare whispered back.

Dee gave them an arch look. "I can hear you."

"I've given up caffeine anyway," Flare said.

This reminded Tobias that she wanted to have a baby, and of his role in the procedure.

"I'm not making this for you," Dee said. "It's

a special brew for a couple of recalcitrant Purist homeboys. No offense, Ben."

"None taken," Lancer answered. "I haven't been one of those loons since I was a teenager."

Tobias gave Flare a quick look to see how she took the references to Benjamin Lancer's vampire-hunter past and saw that she wasn't appalled or offended. But then, she seemed to already know the mortal fairly well. Tobias found this hard to fathom. Flare Reynard was the ultimate vampire female, right? Far too superior to associate with mere mortals, except possibly to hand store clerks credit cards while shopping on Rodeo Drive.

Domini Reynard came into the kitchen. She smiled and ran forward. "Francesca!"

Tobias fumed at all this domesticity while the sisters-in-law hugged. They then stood in front of the refrigerator conducting a whispered conversation full of such devastatingly boring homey information that eavesdropping would have put him to sleep.

Two more of the Dark Angel Crew entered, a werejaguar named Joaquin and the newest Prime recruit, Yacov Piper, known as Jake. Dee also referred to him as "that pain-in-the-ass Tribe boy" and glared at him as he walked past her to take a seat at the kitchen table.

Jake didn't glance her way. After all, she was

mortal, and a female at that. Jake had been a member of Tribe Manticore but had come over from the dark side a few years back and been sponsored by Family Piper. He'd signed on with the Angels to fulfill the vow he'd had to make to protect others against the Tribes. But he hadn't yet absorbed the notion that such protection extended to all people, mortal and immortal alike.

Tobias trusted him. Dee didn't. Jake seethed over the mortal female's outranking him. As long as they both obeyed orders and didn't cross any disciplinary lines, Tobias was leaving the pair to work their dynamic out on their own. No rule stated that members of the Crew had to like each other. Work together, yes. Die for each other if necessary, yes. Hugs and kisses not required.

Tobias wanted to shoo the civilians out, but since he also planned to keep Flare with him at all times, he decided to get on with the meeting while her attention was on Domini. Besides, it *was* Ben Lancer's house, and the old mortal had insights he could contribute.

Dee turned off her concoction and took a seat as far from Jake as possible.

Tobias sat at the head of the table. "Telepathic interrogation didn't work on the prisoners?" he asked the witch.

"My questioning of them was a partial

success," Jake answered. "But they have been worked over by a very talented Prime—and yes, there was a strong Tribe feel to his technique. The Purists' memories only go back several days. I got the impression that they've been wiped and reprogrammed several times."

"Nasty," Joaquin said.

"Clever," Jake replied.

Francesca glanced toward the table as the Prime spoke, in time to see the witch tense up. The Prime had the most world-weary eyes Francesca had ever seen and a totally ruthless attitude. A personality very much to Strahan's tastes, she supposed, but without the civilized veneer the mortal felt comfortable with. The blond male had the feel of a shapeshifter, but Francesca wasn't any good at detecting the nuances separating the different types of werefolk if they weren't wearing their fur coats. She knew a few werefoxes, because they were affiliated with her Clan, but hadn't spent time with any other type of shifter. Well, there was the sweet selkie at the clinic.

"We can't get a clean look into their heads until they have all of their memories back," the witch said.

"We know they were working with a Tribe," the Prime said. "What more do we need to know?"

Francesca spoke up. "Whether or not it was voluntary. Did they make a deal with creatures they consider mankind's worst enemy, or were they forced to help vampires? The hunters will want to believe the worst."

She came closer to the table as all gazes shifted her way. She ignored all but Strahan's curious dark glance. Curious but not contemptuous.

"You'd like to have the help of the sane members of the vampire hunters. Getting them to cooperate will be easier if you have proof their fringe Purist movement is voluntarily working with Tribe vampires. If they think the Tribes are coercing mortals, suspicion falls on all vampires. Better to have the hunters help go after their own crazies."

She smiled with a bit of fang showing for all those watching her, but her gaze never left Strahan's.

"Military matters aren't my department," she said. "Politics I get."

She hoped that Strahan understood she was offering to help and not just mouthing off in infamous Flare fashion. As Reynard Clan heiress she couldn't openly give her support to the Dark Angels. Anything she did could affect her mother's position on the ruling council. Her being allowed to have a child with the help of the clinic had already caused Lady Anjelica some political trouble.

But if Strahan wanted to ask her opinions . . .

He gestured for her to sit beside him at the table. "Tell me, Lady Flare, what's really going on with these attacks?" he asked when she took a place beside him.

She could detect no mockery in his attitude or his mind, though he'd pounce on her least mistake.

"As you have already said, terrorism is theater. The attacks have been done to get a response. The intention is to use the response against us. The enemy wants us to out ourselves. I'm sure that the Purists involved have finally abandoned the secret game mortals and immortals have always played. They want to finally destroy us by making the general public aware that monsters really do live among them. They're playing along with Tribe vampires because they're certain mortals will kill all of us once they know we exist. They are thinking that they are only giving the appearance of being manipulated while really using the Tribes. Of course, that's not what is happening at all."

"What is happening?" Strahan asked.

"Probably more than I can guess at, but I'm certain of several things."

"I'm listening."

His concentration on her was so intense that Francesca forgot about everyone else in the room. She'd never seen anyone with eyes as darkly compelling as his.

"I know that the Tribes have united with each other for the first time in centuries to destroy the Clans and Families. They're putting aside their differences temporarily to face a greater threat. This alliance is something they should have done a long time ago and we've grown complacent thinking that the Tribe mentality wasn't capable of it."

The voice of the other Prime at the table chimed in. "Amen."

Francesca continued talking to Strahan. "The Tribes have grown weaker and weaker while our cultures have prospered in the modern world. We have been trying to destroy their culture and can't blame them for hating us."

"Even if they deserve it," said the witch.

"So, they're conspiring to bring down the Clans and Families by getting us to out ourselves by responding to the recent attacks. They want the media spotlight all over us. They're used to living in hiding, while we're living more and more among mortals. They are certain they'll survive while the villagers will take torches and pitchforks to the rest of us. And that's still not all that's going on."

"Are you about to agree with my personal conspiracy theory?" Strahan asked.

"That there is someone behind the scenes manipulating the Tribes who are manipulating the Purists? And that the conspiracy started decades ago? Oh, yes, I quite agree."

"Who? Why?" Strahan asked.

"The usual suspects. The usual reasons for war—we have what they want."

"You think we're really fighting mortals who are hiding behind the more obvious enemies?"

Francesca nodded. "Mortals with the resources to finance research to provide the Tribes with knockoff daylight drugs. Mortals with the resources to create a private security force of feral werefolk. Mortals with contacts in the very secretive Purist community. Mortals with the resources to recruit disaffected offspring of mortals and Primes."

"There are too many of those dwelling in the trusting bosom of the Clans and Families," the other Prime said. "The Tribes are right not to allow that sort of breeding. The population explosion of half breeds is a big mistake."

Francesca ignored him. "I think there's a

secret master out there somewhere pulling all the strings. You've been preaching it for years, Strahan. It's always sounded like a crazy conspiracy theory, but I believe you're right."

Strahan beamed at her. "You think I'm right."

*Oh, Lady, a Prime with deep dimples!*

He took her hand in his.

She enjoyed the warmth and latent strength in his touch and didn't try to pull away. She said, "I may agree with you, but that doesn't mean we're dating."

The witch sitting next to her gave a snort of laughter, and Francesca finally broke away from Strahan's penetrating gaze.

She looked around the table and focused on the blond shifter. "I'm guessing that right now, the area werefolk are meeting to argue over whether or not to go along with this plan to keep the locals out of the fight. Their leader was furious at the stunt the Matri pulled trying to execute a werewolf. That's going to make the shapeshifters leery of following any vampire's orders."

"They are meeting," the shifter said. He looked to Strahan. "I did my best to soothe the situation, but you need to talk to Shaggy Harker again, Tobias."

"It's already on my list."

"Maybe you should make him an honorary

Dark Angel," the witch suggested. She tapped her watch conspicuously. "You do have a date this evening, Tobias."

He glanced at his own watch. "It's getting a little late out on the East Coast." He held up a hand as the witch frowned at him. "Just saying. A promise is a promise."

"It's not like Saffie's going to be in bed just because she's supposed to be. I'm sure Saffie's up doing homework," she added.

"Speaking about flunking potions class . . . ," he muttered.

The witch gave him a shrug and an unconvincing innocent smile.

Strahan focused on the group around the table. "Let's wrap this up. Joaquin, let Shaggy know about Joe's investigation into the ferals. The local werefolk can help in the hunt if anything turns up," he said to the shifter.

Joaquin nodded. "That will make them happier."

"Make the rounds of everywhere we're guarding, Jake," he said to the Prime. "Get a personal feel for individual situations."

Jake stood. "Understood." A second later the Prime was gone.

Strahan turned his attention to the witch. "How soon before you can dose the Purists, Dee?"

She went over to the stove and sniffed the steam rising from the copper pot. "It's ready, boss."

"Then do it. I'll want Sid Wolf to interrogate them when they've gotten their memories back. She was recruited for her telepathic talent; this will be a good test of it."

Dee dipped fragrant dark liquid into a thermal container and turned to leave the room. "I'll give Sidonie a call as soon as they drink this."

Francesca couldn't repress a stab of jealousy at the fact that her friend Sidonie had a purpose among the Dark Angels, a role in protecting the immortal community, while she remained—Flare, Fantasy Lust Object To All Primedom.

Boring.

Ben and Domini had left the kitchen and had probably gone back to playing Arkham Asylum. Francesca started to get up to see if she could get in on their game night. A thought from Strahan stopped her.

*Stay. There's something I want to discuss with you. But first . . .*

# Chapter Nine

He dialed a stored number on his cell phone, then put the phone to his ear. He smiled in anticipation.

As the phone rang Francesca stared at him in surprise. *What the demons could he want me for? Other than the usual.*

When the phone was answered his anticipation turned into a glow of pleasure. "Working hard or hardly working, Saffron, my love?" Tobias Strahan said after a young female voice said hello.

"Daddy!" An enthusiastic squeal carried to Francesca's ears.

*"Daddy"? A daughter? Wait a minute.* Francesca was almost viscerally aware that Strahan

wasn't bonded. But only bonded Primes took any part in rearing their female offspring.

Well, Sidonie's sire had been involved in her life, but Sid Wolf and Tony Crowe never did anything like other vampires.

Strahan had been born Tribe even though he was raised Family, and as Jake had so recently pointed out, Tribe Primes weren't exactly loving parents of mortal offspring. And this girl must be mortal.

But there was love in Strahan's voice as he spoke to the girl and love in his thoughts and feelings toward this Saffron even as he began to lecture her about some trouble she was in at school.

It looked like he was a hard man with a soft center.

She smiled at the thought, but only for a moment. Until she realized seeing this side of the Prime threatened to bring down the necessary walls she'd built up.

His caring emotion was so strong it twisted Francesca's heart. She almost ran from the room but refused to be so cowardly. She wanted to hate Strahan, but her grief wasn't the Prime's fault. Probably it was only biology. She loved a mortal but was attracted to an alpha male of her own species.

Alpha female to alpha male was the natural order of things. *Damn it.*

She got up and walked to the patio doors, rested her forehead on the cool glass, and concentrated on the sound of the nearby ocean instead of the telephone conversation behind her. Seeing the reflection of the back of Strahan's head in the dark glass didn't help. There was something . . . *appealing* in the way his ears marred his perfection just a little.

She closed her eyes and remembered—Patrick. She hadn't let herself think his name for a while, or think about the way his gray eyes could go from bright with laughter to an icy warrior's stare. A shiver went through her and a fist tightened around her heart.

He was dead.

Lately she'd been more obsessed with the idea of her love for him than loving him, hadn't she?

She wanted to remember the touch of his lips on hers, the feel of his hands on her, but those tactile sensations were lost to her even though her body ached with growing longing.

Strahan's suddenly raised voice drew her attention back to the conversation. "No, I will not call Mrs. Palmer. If you were given detention, you know better than to try to get out of it."

"But it's not fair! I should be able to read whatever—"

"What does fair have to do with it, Saffron Strahan? Weren't you raised to take responsibility for your actions?"

After a stubborn silence the girl said, "Yes, sir."

"Good. What lesson will you take away from this?"

"Not to get caught if I want to study magic."

He sighed. "All right, I won't argue with you on that one. Make sure to keep up with your academic studies."

"Can I come home, Daddy?"

It was Strahan's turn to be silent for a few seconds. "Your winter holidays are coming up soon."

"I want to come home now. I miss the Angels."

"The Angels miss you too. You're safer where you are right now. Your friend Kelsie's mother contacted me about your going to London for Christmas with their family," he said rushing on. "You'd enjoy that."

"I wouldn't."

"Think of all the old bookstores with arcane magical texts."

The girl gave a loud sigh. "I can order that stuff online, Dad."

"Christmas in London with your best friend," he said. "Think about it."

She muttered a grudging, "I will."

"Good. I have to go now."

"Ass-kicking in L.A.? Dee's been keeping me up on the op. I could help."

"I have to go now," he repeated. "I love you. Go to bed."


Tobias put away the phone and sat thoughtfully considering his daughter for a moment. It had been easier when she was little . . . but how was a Prime supposed to deal with a mortal teenager? Dee did her best to help and was the closest thing the girl had to a mother, but the ultimate responsibility was his. *How the hell did I ever get myself into this?*

*Oh, yeah, I walked away from a plane crash with an orphaned baby in my arms.*

And now he was being blackmailed into purposefully siring a vampire child. Imagine how surprised Lady Anjelica and Flare were going to be when he insisted on helping to raise *his* child, even if the baby was a sacred, shielded daughter.

When he looked around he found Flare standing with her back to the kitchen, her tension palpable. He moved silently up behind her and found his hands massaging her knotted shoulders. She leaned into his touch and her head came back to rest on his shoulder. Tobias didn't think she was aware of anything at the moment. Her reaction was as automatic as his had been. As she began to relax, Tobias found his concentration narrowing down to awareness of the pulse of her throat, so vulnerably exposed to his fangs.

An offer? A tease, more likely. This was Flare after all.

If he took her up on the temptation to taste her and she rejected him outright, it would get in the way of the seduction she surely knew he had planned for later. No way was he letting her play him.

He made himself step away. She shivered and shook her head, as though coming awake, and spun to face him. "Where—? Oh, it's you."

He barely stopped himself from a sarcastic comment when he saw the unshed tears in her eyes. "What's the matter with you, woman?" he demanded instead.

"None of your business, Strahan," she shot back.

Animosity crackled between them, hot as lightning. The scent of her blood permeated his being. For a moment he could taste it, heady and life giving.

How could any Prime deny himself . . . ?

Tobias stepped back, putting his hands up before him. His claws were fully extended. Fangs throbbed in his mouth. He'd never been so close to losing control, and his response to Flare was as much a need for combat as it was a need for sex. He'd never reacted so strongly to a female before.

Her fangs and claws were as sharply evident as his. Fire glowed in her eyes.

The thrill of the hunt coursed through him.

And he didn't like it.

It must be a trait of his Tribe ancestry, he thought. Tribe Primes mastered their females. *Even if they have to tie them down to do it,* he added ironically.

He wondered if there was anywhere he could get his hands on pure silver bondage equipment in Los Angeles.

She felt his amusement and demanded, "What's so funny?"

"Me," he answered.

# Chapter Ten

Francesca knew what was happening between her and Strahan, but she didn't think he did. His simple answer to her angry question helped calm her down. He was embarrassed as he got himself under control. That was a good sign.

She wrestled her body back into its mortal form as she struggled to remember how they'd come to be standing like a pair of horny gladiators ready to rip into each other. He'd been on the phone. She'd been trying to meditate. Then—he'd touched her. A simple touch.

But nothing was simple about what was happening to them. Or maybe bonding was the simplest thing in the world. Struggling against it was the complicated part, but battle it she would.

Strahan couldn't want it either, not with his obsessive need to fight the good fight leading his Dark Angels. A bondmate would only get in his way. Especially useless spoiled princess Flare.

"Wait a minute," she said, remembering suddenly. "You wanted to talk to me about doing something." *Before the world went weird.*

The flicker of amusement from him told her that Strahan picked up her thought and agreed with it.

"I can't help it," he said apologetically.

"I know. Maybe it's the weather," she added. "That raging storm outside must be messing up our electromagnetic signals."

He glanced out the patio door at the clear night sky and nodded. "Yeah. All that thunder and lightning must be messing with our telepathy."

She was pleased that he went along with her fiction.

He gestured, and she followed him back to the table. They sat across from each other, the width of the table offering some distance between them.

"What can I possibly do for the Dark Angels?" she asked before he could say anything. "You don't want anything personal from me, I hope?"

His dark gaze roamed over her hungrily, but he said, "Nothing personal. You've heard of Rose Cameron."

"Would that be the red-haired mortal who was with Tony Crowe at the Citadel? The one who reminds me of an old-time movie star?"

"That's her. And she is an old-time movie star, *the* Rose Cameron."

"But Rose Cameron would be ancient for a mortal. Shouldn't she be dead? Or at least in a nursing home?"

"I think she may have been both."

She looked at him suspiciously, but he didn't seem to be the joking type.

"I'm not good at guessing mortal ages, but the person I saw was very young. And there was bond energy arcing between her and Tony," she recalled after scouring her memories. "Just a beginning thread of it."

"Yes. The beginnings of the bond is the problem I need your help to get around."

Francesca prepared to be indignant. "Don't tell me you want me to seduce Tony Crowe away from this woman?"

A dark shock of jealousy washed over her, quickly cut off by Strahan's tightening his shielding. "You think far too well of your charms if you think you can break a bond."

"I would never try to!" she shot back. "But it's the damn fool sort of thing somebody might think I would try to do. Femme fatale Flare, Flare the vamp—wait, I am a vamp. But I'm not a home wrecker."

Strahan held his hands in a T sign. "Time out, lady. Let's start over."

His gesture was another reminder of Patrick, of the type of sports-loving jock her mortal warrior had been and Dark Angel Strahan was.

"Do you like football?" she asked.

"Who doesn't?"

"You military types are all alike."

"No, I think it's just a man thing."

"I like football. Basketball. Hockey."

"Baseball?" he asked hopefully.

"Best of all."

"But you're—"

"Yeah, yeah, snooty bitch princess Flare. There's more to me than getting my claws manicured."

"Really? For example?"

"I don't get polo and I've never been on a yacht. I have a pilot's license and—" She decided it would be self-serving to tell him about the charity she worked for.

Strahan eyed her with solemn curiosity for a moment. Then he laid his big hands flat on the table and took a calming breath. "Meanwhile, back at Tony and Rose . . ."

She repeated his gesture and fought off the temptation to reach across to him. Fortunately, the table was too wide for that. "What do you want me to do about them?"

"Rose was a captive of our bad guys. She was experimented on by them. Tony, Sid, and Joe rescued her last night. I haven't had a chance to talk to her yet. I need to know what she knows, and I need to know it from her, especially the information she doesn't know she knows. But Tony won't let a Prime near her."

"Of course not, he's bonding with her."

He nodded. "But he would let her talk to a female vampire. Allow one into her head."

"That's why you recruited Sid Wolf," she said. He gave her a speculative look that told her he was waiting for her to figure it out. "Ah," Francesca said, "you're not willing to risk Sid's relationship with her sire."

"There's no reason to make trouble within a family if it can be avoided. You're a female telepath."

"And if Tony Crowe ends up angry with me what difference will that make to anyone?" *Except maybe to my friendship with Sid.*

"Precisely," Strahan answered. "Will you talk with this mortal woman?"

"Will I mess with her head and bring you everything inside it?"

"I believe that's what I implied."

"And interrogate her in such a way that no one will suspect the Reynard heiress did it for the Dark Angels?"

"Do it in a way that no one knows you did it at all. And be gentle with her. She's a good guy and has been put through hell by the bastards we're after."

*Does he think I'm inept enough to leave burn marks all over some nice old lady's mind?*

"You have to spend time at the clinic anyway," he added. "It should be easy for you to find some private time with Rose. Will you do it?"

It was a straight-up question, no puppy-dog little-boy pleading in his big brown eyes. Most Primes she knew were more the cajoling type when it came to getting what they wanted out of females. His method of simply asking worked far better than anything else would have.

"All right," Francesca said. "I'll give it a—"

*Boss! Situation developing!*

The shout came out of nowhere, not from the earpiece Strahan had put away or the phone in his jacket pocket. It was simple, effective telepathy, aimed at Strahan, but Francesca heard the alarm as well.

*Attack on the Prime actor's house,* the Dark Angel added.

*On our way,* Strahan answered. He rose to his feet, shouting, "Dee!"

Then he grabbed Francesca by the wrist and dragged her along.

# Chapter Eleven

"What are you doing here?" Tobias asked Flare.

Dee spoke up from the backseat. "That's what I've been asking."

"She has," Flare said from the passenger's seat. "You haven't been listening."

It hadn't been a long drive from Lancer's house to an even wealthier part of Malibu. Tobias had concentrated on getting to their destination with the greatest amount of speed while dealing with the developing situation telepathically. If Dee had said anything in those few minutes he hadn't noticed, which he didn't understand and didn't like. The ability to multitask was essential in his job.

And how had Flare Reynard sneaked into the car with them?

"Sneaked?" She held up a bruised wrist. "You did this, Strahan."

"You did," Dee said in agreement. "You dragged her along, boss. Can't you stand to have her out of your sight?"

It was not a facetious question, and Tobias didn't like the answer that sprang instantly to mind. That he *couldn't* bear to have Flare out of his sight. Away from his touch. To be away from constant intimate awareness of her mind, her body, and her blood.

*Damn instinct!* Didn't it know he had an op to run?

"Stay here," he told Flare. He ignored her flash of annoyance. "Let's go, Dee."

He filled the mortal woman in on his telepathic communications as they walked toward the actor's gated mansion two blocks away. He'd parked far enough back not to draw the attention of the attackers. It wasn't an attack yet, but the Purists were gathering for one, cautiously avoiding any contact with the police and private security teams that patrolled the streets of the wealthy community. One by one mortals were slipping through the shadows, massing for an assault.

Of course, the point was that the Purists

wanted the mansion's security system to be triggered. They wanted all those police and private security people to head straight for the house. They wanted the alerted media to rush to the scene. They wanted to draw attention to the supernatural community, just as they'd tried to do with their other attacks over the last several days.

"Theater," Tobias muttered.

What were the bad guys really up to with these distractions? He'd find out eventually, but he had all these little fires to put out first—before some of his own kind really got burned.

Jake and Jerame were stationed on the estate's grounds, monitoring the approach of the enemy. His Crew was spread thin tonight.

"I had only Jerame guarding the house because it's the last place I thought would be attacked," Tobias informed Dee. "When I told a movie star to go about his business I thought he'd spend his off hours out partying, safe in the embrace of pretty girls and watchful paparazzi."

"I thought he had a reputation for drunken brawls and sexual excess."

"Turns out he's a domestic sort. His bad rep's a product of his publicist's imagination and media manipulation by our very own Corbett twins."

Dee tsked. "Is nothing sacred anymore? Young movie stars are supposed to be bad and reckless."

"So are young Primes."

"And what is a virile Prime doing lolling around his home? Please tell me he has a live-in harem. And if so, how do I join it?"

"Don't let Jake Piper hear you talking like that. Our ex-Tribe boy may believe you. As for our actor friend, he told Jake he's having a business dinner."

Dee was disgusted. "I bet his name's not even James Wilde."

"I don't know of any vampires named Wilde. He lives too out in the open to be anything he seems to be."

"Purists busting in on an orgy would be more fun."

"It would be. But Purists busting in on a meeting of powerful Hollywood types is far more dangerous."

"I'm sure they only believe in vampires at the box office."

"For now," he said in agreement. "But there's a fine line between rumors and reality in these parts."

"Better not to get vampire rumors started. What's the plan, boss?"

"The Purists' attack will be planned to start when the gate opens for the guests to leave. Putting film executives in danger will not endear our boy to the moguls, even if they don't believe he's a vampire. However, they'll be much more understanding of pretty girls and watchful paparazzi."

"I think I see where this is heading, boss. Want me to call Sasha Corbett, then get naked in front of the gate?"

"Call Sasha," he said, "but you'll be too valuable in a fight." He glanced up the street where the seething energy of a pouting princess radiated from the darkness. "I've got another pretty girl in mind for the diversion."

*Mom's going to kill me if she finds out about this,* Francesca thought as she pranced up the street—and prancing while barefoot, swinging her shoes in her hand, wasn't easy.

But since she'd been wearing flats, which were decidedly not sexy, bare feet looked better. Her black skirt was hiked up nearly to her hipbones. She'd been wearing a lacy black sweater over a cami. Now she was wearing only the lacy black sweater. Her nipples were not appreciating the cool night air, but she was sure the watching males were appreciating her nipples peeking out through the sheer lace.

She carried a champagne bottle in her other hand. How the witch had gotten her hands on the wine at such short notice was a mystery. When she'd asked, Strahan had grinned proudly at the red-haired mortal and said, "Delilah McCoy is the most resourceful woman you'll ever meet."

"I am, you know," Dee said, grinning back at Strahan.

The pair's camaraderie ground against Francesca's shield of indifference. Strahan and McCoy liked each other; maybe it was more than liked. They certainly shared a purpose. They were Dark Angels and she would never be. She was an outsider Strahan only turned to for a moment's help.

*Jealous much, are you?* Francesca asked herself as she strutted up to the closed gate. *Yes,* she admitted. *But not going into the who or what.*

*Heads up, woman!* another voice said in her mind.

She could sense far more than Strahan's attention on her, but his were the thoughts touching hers. She recognized the sparks of Dark Angel minds in the darkness but could also pinpoint the hostile attention of other watchers as well.

She had an audience. It was time to play to it.

Francesca smiled into the eye of the security camera to the side of the gate, dropped her shoes, and coyly waved her fingers. "Hello, Jimmy!" she called. She pressed the buzzer. "Jimmy Wilde, come out and play! I'm here!"

She heard cars approaching and caught the glow of headlights from the corner of her eye but carefully kept her back turned to the street. In a moment there was more to the light than head-lamps; she was illuminated by glaring flashbulbs and the click of cameras at her back. The media sharks had come looking for blood—the poor dears had no idea—and it wouldn't be long before the police and rent-a-cops pulled up to join them.

*A riot is a terrible thing . . .*

*Pay attention!* Strahan's order was stern, but she could feel his amusement in her head. . . . *to waste,* he added.

"What are you doing here?"

The disembodied voice this time issued from a speaker beside the security camera and had a rich Irish accent.

"Jimmy!" Francesca bounced up and down and waved the champagne bottle while cameras clicked and recorded. "You told me to stop by, remember? Let me in! Or come out and play."

"Oh, I'm coming down all right." The angry Irish voice issued loudly from the speaker.

He'd been telepathically briefed to play along with this nonsense.

There was a solid wall of hungry anticipation behind Francesca. The paparazzi's excitement almost overlaid her awareness of Angels and enemies alike.

Soon the gate swung open and two dark cars pulled out into the street before James Wilde stepped into the firing line of flashbulbs and shouted questions.

She hadn't expected him to grab her and kiss her in front of the crowd, but it made sense for dragging out the diversion a little longer. The kiss looked fierce and hungry, but there was no passion in it. Francesca barely remembered to lean against him and put her arms around his neck. She did remember to drop the champagne bottle.

Which was when the fight between the Dark Angels and Purists started.

She had no idea what sort of potion the witch had put in the bottle, but the fumes from it kept the media bloodsuckers' attention on her and Wilde instead of the fight—even after Wilde spun her through the gate and closed it behind them.

# Chapter Twelve

"Stay here," the actor Prime ordered her before rushing off to join the fray.

*Of course.* It was an order she was getting used to hearing. This time she didn't mind obeying it. Let the boys have fun without her. Francesca knew just how far she dared go in helping the Dark Angels, and the last few minutes had come very close to crossing that line. If any of the photos about to hit the tabloids showed her face she would be in very deep trouble with her Matri.

Then again, her mom was enthusiastic about the prospect of having a grandchild from her. So even if she was going to get locked away in Idaho for the foreseeable future it wouldn't be until that deed was accomplished.

She was not perturbed when a scream issued out of the darkness near the house. The sound did make her fingertips tingle, claws wanting to come out. A faint scent of blood perfumed the air and she ran her tongue over her slightly extended fangs.

What a shame the boys got to have all the fun.

Francesca kept her instincts under control by nursing her resentment against the whole of vampire culture and stayed put. She adjusted her clothing, leaned against the gate, and waited.

Eventually Joaquin, the blond werewhatever, came up to her and said, "Boss told me to take you back to the safe house."

*I don't want to be safe.*

No answer came back to her.

*Typical Prime bastard. Strahan brought me here, used me, and now abandoned me to go hunting.*

She knew this was not completely true and was annoyed with herself. She was a pro at pouting—shouldn't she be able to come up with something better than that to keep her interest in Strahan under control?

"Welcome back," Ben Lancer told Tobias as he opened his front door.

Tobias had a key and knew all the security codes, so he was surprised to find the old mortal waiting up for him.

"You do know our needing permission to enter somewhere is only folklore, right?"

Lancer didn't take this as a joke. "Not at my house it isn't," he said.

Tobias hadn't been in contact with Lancer for many years, but he trusted their old friendship. "What's up, Ben?" he asked.

Lancer moved aside to let Tobias enter the house, then led him into the kitchen before he spoke. "I hear you had a pretty good time tonight."

Tobias wondered where Lancer'd gotten his information. "I did," he answered. Except for watching Wilde kiss Flare and being unable to stop it, the last several hours had been most satisfactory.

Lancer opened the refrigerator and handed Tobias a beer. "Unless you'd prefer something stronger," he said. "Scotch?"

Tobias had already twisted the cap off the beer bottle. "I'm good." The old mortal's emotions were . . . not angry, exactly . . . more like tense and worried. "What's the matter?" Tobias asked him. "What have I done that you don't like? Was it bringing Flare here?"

Thick silver brows lowered over bright blue eyes. "Why would that bother me?"

Tobias didn't know. Flare had been the first thing that came to mind—hadn't been off his mind since the beginning of the day. Had they been together for only one day? It seemed like forever.

He shrugged. "It's been a long day, Ben."

"A fun one for you," Lancer said. "You've been hunting Purists, protecting vampirekind. Taking prisoners?" he asked, the tone and tilt of his head skeptical.

Tobias knocked down the rest of his beer before answering. "I take it you want a full report on the Dark Angels' activities."

"I think I deserve one."

"Because you're my host? Because I could be putting your household at risk?"

Ben Lancer snorted. "My household consists of professional bodyguards. I deserve an explanation as your self-appointed mortal conscience. There's a whole city full of mortals out there uninvolved in your war. I want to make sure you remember the innocents and try to keep them out of your battles."

"I noticed you said *try*."

"I understand the nature of combat. But you

damn well better keep collateral damage to a minimum."

Tobias knew that if he didn't stop the attacks in Los Angeles, mortals were soon going to know of his kind's existence. Then the war wouldn't be with only Purists and hired guns. Who would be the innocents then? Who would be the targets? Vampires and werefolk, that's who. But for now, Lancer's concerns about mortals were legitimate.

"Several mortals did die tonight," Tobias said. "Mercenaries working for the bad guys."

"I have no problem with that. Pros know the risks. What about the Purists?"

"Taken prisoner. Every Purist we manage to snatch is being held. For now."

Lancer didn't ask about later. He knew the old rules between vampires and the mortals who hunted them. The Purists would eventually be brainwashed and freed, turned over to the hunter authorities to deal with, or killed. Their fate depended on the truth about how they'd become involved in the attacks.

"What about the cops you ran into tonight? What about the security patrols?"

"Are you worried about how we treated the paparazzi, too?"

"Even them," Lancer said. "More or less."

Tobias smiled. Many of Lancer's clients were celebrities. The bodyguards who worked for him would probably cheer any news of bad things befalling the packs of paparazzi they spent time fending off.

"No permanent damage was inflicted on any innocent mortal we encountered tonight, Ben. We messed up some memories, but nobody was hurt."

Lancer gave a sharp nod, satisfied. "Make sure you keep it up."

"Keep what up?" Domini asked, coming into the kitchen. She glanced at the kitchen clock, then at her grandfather. "Weren't you going to bed?"

"Weren't you going home?" he growled back.

"Not until Alec picks me up." She jerked a thumb at Tobias. "He's"—her eyes glazed over briefly—"going to have a baby." She blinked. "Damn. I hate when that happens."

Tobias stared at the woman.

"You do know she's a seer?" Lancer asked.

"Don't mind me," Domini said. "I see real things, but I'm pretty sure it's Francesca who's going to have a baby. My sixth sense is having directional problems this evening."

"I have every intention of having a baby," Tobias admitted.

Domini looked him over from head to toe. If he hadn't been aware of her bonded status, he might have leered back at her. "Good luck with that," she said after she'd assured herself of his masculine gender.

"That does it," Lancer said. "This time I really am going to bed." He kissed his granddaughter's cheek, gave Tobias one more stern glance, then walked out of the kitchen.

"What was that all about?" Domini asked, eyeing Tobias with protective suspicion. "You aren't trying to get him to do more than host this little party of yours, are you?"

What was it with the Lancer family? Tobias wasn't used to being questioned. Nagged, yes. Dee was an expert at it. But the first rule among the Dark Angels was absolute, unquestioning obedience. Not that it wasn't good to be questioned sometimes, at least by competent outsiders. He needed reminders that he wasn't omnipotent.

Such as Flare? Oh, yeah, she was a major reminder.

She'd looked sexy walking up the street dressed like a tramp. And he couldn't do a damn thing but stand there and want her.

Domini glanced at the wall clock again. "I'd really love to get home, but my bondmate is working late tonight. Who do you have on my house?" she asked casually.

"A couple of werecoyotes," he answered. "Stationed on the hill above your place."

She nodded. "Good choice. There are coyotes in the neighborhood. No one will notice a difference if they see them."

It was so nice that this professional bodyguard was comfortable with the idea of being protected herself. Unlike, say, Flare.

"What is wrong with that female, anyway?"

He hadn't meant to speak and the words came out as a low, growling complaint. The mortal woman still picked up on them.

"Francesca's really a sweetie," she said.

"How do you know I mean Flare?"

Domini chuckled. "You're a Prime, and she's the one you all want. Not that any of you have the faintest idea of how to go about it."

Oh, he knew how to go about it—but the proper method for taming a vampire female wasn't something he could talk to a mortal female about. Especially not one bonded to a civilized Clan male.

"Care to give me some advice?" he asked. "Lancers seem determined to give me advice tonight."

Domini shook her head. "My name is

Reynard, remember? Francesca is family. You'll have to work it out with her." She turned to go, then glanced back at him. "One thing, though: she absolutely loathes, hates, and despises anyone but her brothers calling her Flare."

# Chapter Thirteen

"Francesca." His whisper was hoarse with need.

"Hmm . . . ?" the female lying flat on her stomach murmured. Awareness of him had not yet really intruded on her peaceful sleep.

"I'm a dream," he whispered. "A good dream. The best dream you'll ever have."

He leaned forward from the chair beside her bed. Her bare back was covered by a bright red sheet, only her shoulders visible, a tumble of shining black hair obscuring her elegant profile. He appreciated the outline of her body beneath the clinging satin for a moment, licking his lips. But the gift wrapping didn't hold his interest for long.

He enjoyed the anticipation, the curl of desire tightening at his groin, the fire growing in his blood. The pulse of stirring fangs was pleasant in his mouth, not yet the driving ache he wanted. The inside of his mouth was warming, taste buds preparing for the feast. His acute sense of smell honed in on the sharp tang of female scent.

Her unique scent.

He tugged on the edge of the sheet, cool satin caressing his fingers. He watched it caress her skin, knowing exactly how it felt to her as it slipped down her back, revealed a slender waist and the smooth mounds of her buttocks.

He paused to appreciate her beauty. His vision adjusted as he watched. He took the time to savor the changing view. The red of the sheets darkened to near black. The lush body laid out before him grew clearer, white as alabaster, the pulsing blood beneath running in warm silver rivers. The scent of flesh was sweet in his nostrils and in the back of his mouth. Her body heat rose up in a heady mist, calling to him.

His claws shredded the cloth in his hand, making him smile and bringing on a compulsion impossible to resist. He moved to sit on the bed. For a moment he held his palm over her back with his eyes closed. Close enough to be warmed by her heat but not touching.

*Anticipate. Anticipate. Hunger. Was there ever anything so sweet as hunger?*

*Satisfying it.*

*He touched her. Only one finger. The tip of one diamond-sharp claw.*

*One small prick. One bead of blood. Another. Another. A thin line of blood down the long length of her spine. Silver of life emerging the scarlet of sex. The sweet heated scent merged with the tang of hot copper.*

*His fangs grew over his bottom lip, craving.*

*He gave a low, animal growl.*

*Hunger, need, and pain merged into a deep answering groan from her throat. Her spine arched up toward him.*

*Lie still, he ordered.*

*She answered with a snarl. Her muscles tensed, but she didn't move.*

*Obedience deserved reward.*

*His mouth came down, the tip of his tongue flicking. He tasted each scarlet drop, savored, licked hot silk skin, moved on. Her orgasms shot through him—into his mind and down to his cock. Her blood intoxicated him.*

*She turned over when he reached the base of her spine. Sinuous and swift, she came at him with raking claws and gleaming fangs. Her predatory beauty sent a shock of intense heat through him, leaving him vulnerable for a fraction of a second. Long enough for claws to swipe across his chest. Pain and pleasure sang through him.*

*She sucked the wounds, licked, and sank her fangs deeply into one of the cuts. He howled in ecstasy.*

*Even as his mind shouted,* Control! Keep control! *he threw her down onto her back and held her there. She thrashed and snarled while he forced a kiss on her. They tasted each other as blood mingled from their lips and on their fangs and tongues.*

*She swore when he pulled his mouth from hers, breaking the connection before the blood bond could build to the point where their tastes, their very essences, became one.*

*He held her slender wrists locked in his large hand and held her down with his heavier body while he sank his fangs into her throat. Her breasts were crushed against his chest and his cock pressed against her belly. Awareness of her softness, her heat, excited him. Her awareness of him echoed back into his mind. She was just as excited, a little afraid, angry at his dominance. But pleasure at it, longing for it, flickered into flaming life in her soul.*

*She couldn't give in to this! Wouldn't! Wanted to.*

Your soul is mine, *he told her.*

Fuck you!

*His mouth covered her nipple. His fangs sank into soft skin. His tongue stroked the already hard bud.*

*Blood and sex. Necessary. The same.*

*Nothing ever like this before.*

*She was strong and fierce and fought like a demon while he gave her the arousal she craved. Arousal and satisfaction that rocked through her and back into him in building, blinding explosions.*

*He lost track of everything. Not knowing when holding her down became holding her to him, never wanting to let her go. Not knowing when her struggles turned to insistent writhing beneath him.*

*Her hips arched against his. Her legs clasped his waist. His cock moved toward welcoming wet heat.*

"What are you doing here?"

Tobias took in a gasping breath. He opened his eyes to find that he was seated in a dark bedroom with a painful erection. Flare Reynard was sitting up in bed glaring at him.

"I'm not sure," he said.

She was wearing an oversized Lakers T-shirt. The royal purple and gold colors suited a princess, but he had preferred her naked.

It had been a dream?

She sat up, leaning back on her elbows, which made her breasts arch up. Her nipples were puckered beneath the cloth. She ignored his hungry stare.

She ignored his crotch but still gave him a searching look. "Would you mind taking off your shirt?" she asked.

"Why would I do that?"

He'd been naked in the dream—at least he had no memory of clothing. He'd been concentrating on *her* nakedness.

"Because in my dream, you had black angel wings tattooed on your back."

He shook his head. "No tats."

So, she'd dreamed, but not exactly the same dream he'd had. Was that good or bad? Was the sex good or bad? He had no doubt there'd been sex. He could smell the sharp tang of her arousal, knew she was aware of his.

She was also taking this remarkably well—so far. He waited for her to spring a trap, at least a tantrum, but offered honesty of his own.

"In my dream you were naked on red satin sheets," he told her. The bed was actually covered in pale blue bedclothes.

"Isn't that just typical sexual fantasy material?"

"Tattoos?" he countered.

"Tats are very sexy."

"Shameless wench."

She shrugged. He couldn't help but notice the way her breasts moved beneath the cotton shirt. This didn't help calm his hard-on any. He took slow, deep breaths and thought about unattractive things.

"What are you doing in here?" she repeated.

"Here" was a small guest bedroom in Ben Lancer's house. He ran a hand across his short hair while he searched out how his steps had led him to Flare's bed.

She reached over to a bedside table and switched on a small lamp. They didn't need this extra light, but maybe it made her feel more normal, less psychically vulnerable—less connected. Nothing could help or change his awareness of the unconscious, unwelcome connection.

"I was in the kitchen," he recalled. "A few of my people reported in. Then—I went looking for you."

She sat up straight and folded her hands on her stomach. "You planned to sit by my bedside to keep me safe all night?" Her tone was dangerously sweet.

"No. I wanted to fuck you."

She threw back her head and laughed. *Goddess, what a lovely throat!*

"Don't think about it, big boy," she said.

"Can't help it," he answered.

"Primes."

"Any man in the world would be turned on by you."

She frowned but accepted this as her due and not as a compliment. She had no modesty.

And why should she? Primes had none. Why expect it?

"The thing is, I don't remember coming in here," he said, returning to the subject. "What I remember is—"

"The dream," she said, glaring at him.

He wasn't going to be intimidated or apologize. "You had it too. It was a shared fantasy. We're telepaths. And we're—"

"Don't say it!"

# Chapter Fourteen

" 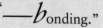onding."

Francesca leapt out of the bed. She was tempted to leap on him but told herself the urge to scratch and bite was residual arousal from the dream. She wanted his blood—the dream her wanted his blood.

The real her denied what tasting him would bring.

Never. Never. Never. She'd never get that close to a Prime. To a soldier.

"I told you not to say . . . that word, Strahan."

"Not exactly."

"You knew what I meant."

He stood, towering over her, and came very close. His size, the male heat and scent of him, his arousal, all of it surrounded her. He was so very dangerous to her—so very attractive.

He put his hands on her shoulders. Warm, strong hands. "We can't deny it."

"We can ignore it," she snapped back.

Even as she spoke, she fought the urge to press her body against his. Softness to hardness. Female to male. Memories of the dream swirled around her, burned through her. She was too tempted to make the dream real.

She pulled away from his touch and fell onto the bed when she turned around. "Totally undignified," she grumbled as she rolled across the bed and got to her feet on the other side.

"As flouncing away in a huff goes, that was pretty pitiful," he agreed.

She put her hand across her mouth to stifle her laughter, and he smiled with shared humor.

Strahan made her want to laugh, and that made him far more dangerous to her hard-held defenses than a typical Prime's arrogant attempts at seduction.

"I can be arrogant," he said.

"I know you can." *But . . .*

Just how closely were their thoughts already meshed together? This was only surface communication, right?

"We don't want to be part of each other," she told him.

"You should not make pronouncements concerning what other people want. That makes you arrogant."

"Everyone knows I'm arrogant." She put her hands on her hips. She considered tossing her hair back over her shoulder but thought that was probably a bit much. "You don't want spoiled arrogance in a mate."

He shrugged. "You can be tamed."

This should have made her angry but sent a dark thrill of excitement through her instead. "Now, that's a ploy no Prime has tried on me before."

His hot look told her he wasn't bragging. He wasn't joking. There was no ploy to get her interest involved. If he wanted her interest, he'd take it.

"You have an army to run," she pointed out. "You don't have time or need for a bonding in your life."

"There aren't enough Dark Angels to call it an army," he said. "It's a defense force."

"There are plenty who call it a mercenary band."

Another shrug. "We accept financial donations upon occasion."

"I am trying to make you angry and disgusted with me," she said. "You are not helping."

He crossed his arms over his wide chest and looked her up and down. She knew she had a great deal of thigh and leg showing, but the rest of her was modestly covered. The way he looked at her, she might as well have been naked.

"There you stand," he said, "the most beautiful female in the world, and you think I'd let a couple of little things like fury and revulsion change my mind about wanting to bed you?"

"Silly me," she muttered.

This conversation was going nowhere. It shouldn't even have been happening. She could accept his wandering in and nodding off, and their psyches entwining in dreamland, without any rancor. She didn't want to recall the erotic details of her own dream and didn't want to know the details of his. It had happened. It was over. Better to pretend that no specifics had been shared.

He should not have uttered *that* word.

"It's time for you to leave," she told Strahan.

"Not yet."

"Oh, for—!"

He was looming close to her in an instant. She hadn't seen him move. *I'm a vampire too; I should have seen it!*

She looked a long way up into those big

brown eyes. "You're good, soldier," she said, conceding.

She hated herself instantly for using the word. A hot knife twisted in Francesca's heart. She used to call Patrick *soldier*. It was a betrayal of his memory—but this Prime *was* a soldier.

*Damn.*

He gently put a finger under her chin. His gaze searched hers. Curiosity probed her shielding. A gentle mental touch rather than a demanding probe, but she still didn't like it.

"What's wrong?" he asked. "What hurts you so much?"

She jerked her head away from his touch. "I am Lady Francesca Reynard." She spoke each word with icy precision. "*You* have no right to question *me*."

This cut direct worked. She really hadn't expected it to. Anger replaced his concern. His dark eyes went hard, and he took a step back. He drew himself up to his full, impressive height.

She still managed to look down her nose at him. It was a matter of attitude she'd had a lifetime to practice. Rank, pride of place, social superiority, the whole heavy history of their kind was her best armor. Ugly though it was.

"You aren't Clan," she reminded Tobias

Strahan. "You're barely even Family. You're the son of a Tribe stray taken in by the Strahan Family. You don't even know who your mother is."

She knew she was laying it on too thick, but she had to stop this Prime from getting through her defenses. She had to stop him from even *talking* about bonding with her. She desperately wanted him not to want it. Her.

*Why?*

*Get out of my head!*

*What about out of your heart?*

*You* are not *in my heart. No one will be. Never again.*

*So that's what hurts you. You don't want me taking someone else's place.*

*Damn!* He hadn't been offended at her aristocratic sneering. He was a better actor than she was.

"Nothing fazes you, does it, Strahan?"

"I'm the father of a teenage girl. Everything fazes me—I've learned not to show it."

He'd done it again, made her want to laugh! And no Prime bullshit about how he was fearless. He was melting her—she who could not be melted.

"Damn!" she spat.

"What?"

*It's gotten too warm in here for the ice princess,* she thought, and hoped to the moon goddess he didn't pick up the thought.

The next thing she knew he was holding her in his arms. "It's going to get a lot warmer," he promised.

# Chapter Fifteen

Tobias was prepared for a slap or her raking claws leaving a blood trail down his back, at the very least a fang-filled snarl. Instead, Flare put her arms around his neck and drew his head down into a passionate kiss, the heat he'd promised generated by her.

He pulled her closer, made the kiss deeper.

This was just what he had in mind. Needed.

His hands moved up under her T-shirt tracing the warm, smooth skin of her belly and waist . . . but he managed to pull away before touching her breasts. He was in complete agreement with her frustrated growl, but being in control of the first time they made love mattered to him. He pulled away from her embrace.

She stood still, breathing hard, with a stunned expression. Then disappointment flashed briefly across her face, hidden quickly by anger.

"What's this about, Strahan?"

No Prime ever turned down a Clan female, and certainly not the legendary Flare Reynard.

"We do this on my terms," he said. "For my reasons."

"Terms?" she echoed. "Reasons? You already said you wanted to have sex with me. I decided that I wanted to have sex with you."

"You still want me."

"The impulse is fading." Her spine stiffened with pride. Her head came up. She looked him over with an arrogant sneer. "I don't know what I saw in you."

"A momentary lapse in good taste?" he asked.

"No doubt."

"Reaction to tonight's incident with Jimmy?"

"What incident with—oh, the kiss." Her smile was vicious. "Jealous?"

"Yes."

He closed the distance between them and grabbed her shoulders. He read the urge to fight in her muscles and the effort it took her to calm the impulse. She stayed still and waited with feigned indifference.

"You're used to Primes being jealous," he told

her. "You're used to being fought over and you revel in causing conflict. That's how females control the Primes."

"Your male squabbles have nothing to do with me," she answered. "The fact that your brains are in your dicks has never been anything but trouble for vampire females."

"I can't afford any conflict among the Dark Angels' Primes because of you. I'm marking you as mine, and that'll be the end of it."

Flare was outraged. "You motherless pig! I never want to have sex with a Prime—and now you are definitely at the bottom of the Dregs of the Universe list."

His hands, his telepathic awareness, and all his other senses told him she was lying. Flare Reynard wanted him as much as ever. As much as he wanted her. He hoped her fury blocked out her awareness of his desire. He projected as much cold ruthlessness as he could.

"Doesn't matter," he told her.

She fought down a brief moment of fear. "Rape for the good of your cause? Even you wouldn't get away with that."

He smiled. "You'll say yes. I guarantee it."

When she started to laugh, Tobias forced a kiss on her.

She ground her claws into his back, but she

didn't try to escape his greedy mouth. It took every bit of discipline he had not to completely lose himself then and there. To touch was to drive each other to the brink of insatiable lust, no matter what either of them wanted.

He pushed her away, held her at arm's length. Her eyes glowed with heat. Her fangs were fully extended. He knew he mirrored her show of arousal. The scent of blood and the tightening of healing skin on his back rushed through him. He hungered to taste—

*No blood!* Flare's thought screamed into his head. *Absolutely no blood tasting!*

Her denial of the most basic sharing angered the aroused vampire and pleased the pragmatic commander in him at the same time. He was glad she too fought to control her instincts.

*No bonding,* Tobias thought back.

Neither of them wanted that.

The hell they didn't, but they would both pretend they had a choice.

Instinct versus will. Could they do it? Should they try?

"For tonight, we'll try," he told her. "Never worry about what tomorrow will bring."

*Easy for you to say, soldier. Females have to worry about tomorrow.*

*Let me do the worrying for you. As far as sex goes,* he added just before the mental shout of outrage washed over him. The angry blast of thought disoriented him for a moment, but he grabbed Flare around the waist and swung her onto the bed as soon as his senses cleared.

He grabbed cloth and relieved her of the Lakers T-shirt, leaving a few scratch marks from his claws on her perfect body. It was hard on his control to catch the aroused scent of her blood and totally fascinating to watch the thin lines of scarlet as they appeared, then healed.

Just as he'd planned, heightened arousal was her reaction to the brief pain. What a pity he couldn't lick the blood marks from her yielding flesh as he had in the dream, he thought. He could only leave her wanting it, dreaming about how it would feel.

Strahan was trying to tame her and Francesca knew it. Every touch, thought, and word was aimed at controlling her. She didn't like it, but she was loving it.

"Insane," she muttered. "I've gone insane."

Strahan grinned. "Wonderful, isn't it?"

For all that she despised the masculine beauty

of Primes, she found herself delighted by Strahan's. That lush full mouth, those huge brown eyes looking into her soul!

"Wonderful," she breathed.

*Damn.*

He brushed damp hair from her temples and forehead. Dropped gentle kisses on her face. "I know. It's not our fault we were born so beautiful."

There he went, making her laugh again, and tasting her mouth when she did. *Dangerous male. Beautiful, dangerous male.*

She didn't notice for a while that he was holding her down just like in the dream. For a while she didn't care. All that mattered was the waves of desire breaking and building—

*Let go of me, you motherle—*

*Hush. You know you're loving it.*

*Loving. Needing. Wanting with every fiber—*
*That isn't the point!* she raged with what was left of her coherency.

*Total control isn't always nec—*
*Then why are you insisting on it?*
*—essary for you.*

He hadn't stopped kissing and caressing her, but for a long, luxurious time she stopped consciously noticing while every other sense overrode her mind. He blocked her every effort to touch him, to actively participate in mutual pleasure.

This was all about what he did for her. To her.

A voice finally rose up out of Francesca's soul.

*Shut up and enjoy it!*

This brief lucidity passed as his fingertips trailed down between her thighs. She was already wet and swollen, aching for his exquisite touch.

All she wanted now was more.


Her complete surrender rolled through Tobias at the exact moment he couldn't hold on any longer. He turned Flare onto her stomach and pulled her hips up to meet his hard thrust into her. He sank into tight heat, fighting off the red tide of blood hunger. He pounded into her, drawing orgasms from her with every hard stroke. Her explosions hit him like lightning that drove straight into his cock.

Her senses were wide open to him, feeding him as he fed her pleasure, looping, twining them together. There was no beginning of him, no end of her, until the final tsunami climax shattered her away from him.

With a cry of pain and completion, Tobias shattered back into himself. And down into the lonely dark.

# Chapter Sixteen

The bruises were already healed by the time Francesca came awake, but she was exquisitely aware of where each and every one of them had been. The fact that she'd been marked was the first thing she was consciously aware of. They were like invisible ink, tattoos only she was aware of . . . delicious secret marks of possession. She lay on her back, savoring these new sensations.

*Who, why,* and *how* were concepts that didn't filter into her head for a long time. But come they did.

Along with a satisfied smile and flesh thrumming with total satiation.

She considered purring.

\*　　\*　　\*

Until sensation turned to vivid memories. Hands. Mouths. Fangs and claws. Blood and sex and a big body covering, claiming—

A will stronger than hers. Wanting that strength. Being made to want it.

Being conquered.

*Damn, it felt good!*

*What the demon is the matter with me?*

Francesca sat up swearing, eyes opening onto a room she didn't recognize, naked on a rumpled bed that had seen a lot of use. There was blood on the sheets. Patches of dried blood on her as well, and the sharp, mingled scents of sex with—

"Strahan!"

"Here," he answered through a nearby doorway.

She swung her legs over the side of the bed, her feet sinking into a thick carpet. She recognized where she was now, a guest room in Ben's house. The curtains were open to the morning light. The ocean murmured close by. The sound of a flushing toilet covered the Pacific for a moment and brought her attention back to Strahan.

"That was an accusing shout of your name. I wasn't asking where you were," she told the Prime as he came out of the bathroom.

"Oh." He scratched the rippling washboard of his naked stomach. "You hungry?"

He looked tousled, barely awake, his hair still damp from a shower. It was a good act, but she didn't miss the way his gaze assessed her from half-closed eyes.

"You are not disarming me," she told him.

He gave her a thorough look that sent tingling heat through her. "If you're armed, you're better at concealing weapons than any of my Angels."

"That's too blatant an invitation to flick my fangs and claws at you, Strahan."

"But they're so pretty," he said, coaxing her. He was looking at her bare breasts as he spoke.

Neither of them made any attempt to cover their body. Her mortal lover would have come out of the bathroom wearing a towel. She would have at least pulled on her nightshirt to hold a serious conversation. But her borrowed T-shirt had been turned into small gold and purple shreds covering the bed and floor. And vampires didn't have the same nakedness taboos as mortals.

"Maybe we spend too much time around mortals," he said, picking up on her thoughts. "Too much time mimicking them, blending in."

"I like quite a few mortals," she answered.

"But do you want to be one?" he asked.

It would have been easier to respond if he'd

been needling her. This was worse; it was a serious question that called for a thoughtful answer. One that it was too early in the morning to come up with.

Francesca shook her tangled hair away from her face. "Go put on your uniform and go save the world."

"I intend to. Should I bring you back a cup of coffee while I'm at it?"

She wanted to fall back onto the mattress and sleep for days. She wanted him out of her sight no matter how grand he looked naked and freshly clean.

He sat down beside her on the bed. He clasped his huge hands around a raised knee and gave her a sideways look that radiated diffidence.

Was Tobias Strahan actually embarrassed?

"I should explain about last night," he said.

She was suspicious of his sudden shift from typical Prime to reasonable being. He'd played her before, and that wasn't an easy thing to do. All her defenses went up against him.

"Just what was last night all about?" she asked.

He raised an eyebrow.

"Besides the obvious," Francesca added. *Several obvious reasons,* she added to herself. "Tell me the ones I haven't figured out on my own."

"You're a very intelligent female, Fla—Francesca."

*Does he somehow consider that a compliment? Oh, well, at least he called me by name.* If he could insult her intelligence, she'd parry with a dig at his origins. "Females are the brains of the species," she pointed out. "That's something you Tribe boys seem to have trouble with—and look where that's gotten you. On the run and in the dark."

"I'm right here," he said, and ran fingers up her bare thigh.

She took a moment to enjoy the shiver that went through her, then said, "Yes, you are. I suggest you don't come any closer at the moment."

His smile struck her in the heart. In a good way. Which was a very bad way, all things considered. . . .

"I don't have time to make love right now," he said.

"Was that what we did, make love?"

"No. But we could work our way around to it without too much trouble."

He was so correct, and there was no reason not to admit it. Francesca nodded. "But we're not going there," she added.

"There will be more sex." He was very sure of himself.

She decided not to argue about future encounters but to work on avoiding them instead.

She returned to her original question. "What was last night about?"

He got up and started putting on clothes. He was mostly dressed before he answered. "You haven't been trained to take orders from anyone but your Matri. I can't have anyone around me who doesn't do what I say, when I say. Last night was to help save your life in case I ever put it in danger. I was also jealous of Jimmy kissing you and got a little mean," he added, once again giving her that heart-attack-inducing smile.

Jealous and possessive was a Prime's natural state, but Francesca couldn't mind it. She normally wasn't pleased by it, like she was this time. Better to concentrate on the original subject.

"You didn't put me in danger at James Wilde's place."

"I still need you to talk to Rose Cameron."

She couldn't see how there was any potential danger in talking to a little old lady mortal. "Do you always use that kind of sex as a basic training exercise?"

"Only with the beautiful ones."

A moment's jealousy of her friend Sid Wolfe, the latest female Angel recruit, shot through her—before she realized he was joking. By the

Lady of the Moon, this Prime truly was a danger to every defense she'd built up around herself. She wondered if she should run off and hide in the Reynard Citadel until the Dark Angels evacuated Los Angeles.

"That would be cowardice," he said.

"A strategic retreat," she answered loftily.

"The time for vampires to run from their problems is over." He gave her a hard look. "For all of us."

She was prepared to argue that he had no business speaking for all vampires. A knock came on the door, and the smell of coffee and frying bacon drifted from the kitchen.

"Now is the time for all vampires to have breakfast," Francesca said.

"Boss?" the witch called from the hallway. "Time to roll. And thanks for keeping everybody up all night."

"You're a brave woman to bring that up, Delilah McCoy," Strahan yelled back.

Francesca laughed at Strahan's momentary discomfort. Being a Prime, his blush faded quickly, then he gave her a proud thumbs-up. She didn't remember a lot of details, but they'd both probably howled like banshees.

"Somebody had to say it," Dee's voice came

through the door. "When shall we expect your exalted presence, oh potent one?"

"Be there in two," he said.

Strahan seemed to totally forget her presence as he put on his shoes. There was a lot more Francesca wanted to talk about, but the Prime was in warrior mode now. Everything about him was alert and focused. She knew that petulantly demanding his attention wouldn't do any good, so she didn't bother invoking her Flare persona.

All business, he marched out and closed the door behind him.

She missed him instantly.

# Chapter Seventeen

Francesca showered and did her hair, then applied the powder and lipstick she found in her purse, a paltry excuse for her normally complex makeup regime. She wasn't sure if her luggage had been flown back to Idaho or was still at the Shagal Citadel, but at the Lancer house she had to make do with scrounging for something to wear. Fortunately, her sister-in-law wore similar-size clothing and kept some there at her grandfather's house.

Francesca made do with what she found, but she didn't have to like it. She and Domini did not have similar tastes. Domini understood perfectly well that clothing was persona in her professional life but didn't have the need for constant armor in her personal life that Francesca did. Francesca would never have picked the pair of skintight jeans and college team sweatshirt for herself. She supposed she could roll up the legs of the jeans and fasten her long wavy hair into a ponytail to try for a sort of sophisticated retro mock-fifties teenager look, but decided this effort would look silly among Strahan's hard-assed commandos.

"Furthermore, I'm a Spartan, not a Bruin," Francesca complained as she pulled the burgundy UCLA shirt over her head.

She followed the scent of coffee and not her awareness of Strahan into the kitchen, though her attention riveted on him the instant she stepped into the crowded room. At least she wasn't alone, as everyone else's attention was on Strahan too. He was talking to Dee and Jake, who were doing a superb job of ignoring each other by concentrating on him.

*Interesting couple,* she thought.

*They're not,* Strahan thought back, letting her know he was aware of her.

"Why Wyoming?" Jake asked.

"Why not?" was Strahan's cold reply.

His attitude brooked no argument. The Prime didn't give him any, though his anger burned close to the surface.

"What about the prisoners?" Dee asked.

"Have you dosed them with the memory drug?"

"Yes, sir."

"Then they're Sid's responsibility now. You have your assignment. Report when you know anything."

Francesca discarded her avoidance of caffeine and took the mug of coffee Ben Lancer offered her but couldn't take her attention off the trio in the center of the kitchen. The Prime was furious, the witch clearly unhappy, and Strahan ignored their reactions. Whatever this assignment might be, they didn't want it, he didn't care, and they didn't argue despite their reservations.

"Yes, sir," they said together.

"I'll send you a postcard from Yellowstone," Dee McCoy told her leader.

"Make it a Christmas card," Strahan replied. "Dress warm," he added.

The vampire and the witch left, physically together but mentally far apart. Why on earth had Strahan assigned them to work together on an op far away from the rest of the Dark Angels when the pair so clearly detested each other?

*To teach them to work together, obviously,* Strahan thought at her.

Of course. Discipline. Authority. He'd used sex on her to assert leadership and was now using isolation on this pair. *You really are a first-class total control freak, even for a Prime,* she thought.

*A female of the species would know.*

She didn't argue; running a vampire Clan was similar to commanding a military unit. She was slated to become a Matri, so maybe she could learn a few tips from this martinet.

There was a plate stacked with toast and a platter with some bacon and scrambled eggs. Francesca made herself a sandwich out of the leftovers, and she leaned against the sink, her back absorbing warmth from the window behind her. The winter sunlight was feeble even by Southern California standards, but she loved the feel of it.

What on earth had it been like to be a vampire before the daylight drugs? It didn't bear thinking about. No wonder the Tribe boys were so mean. And angry about having to do without the miracles of science unless they gave up their own ancient, evil ways.

She ate, sipped coffee, and watched the master of the Dark Angels as he dealt with one after another of his cohorts and sent them on their way. It occurred to her after a while that she was going unnoticed. She'd been so busy appreciating the fine figure of Tobias Strahan that it took her a while to realize she wasn't being watched, leered at, or come on to by any Prime in the room.

Because Strahan had marked her as his? *Oh, please.* But it seemed to be working.

She wasn't the object of anyone's lust. She liked it.

*You most certainly are a lust object,* Strahan thought.

*You don't count.*

*I'm the* only *one who counts.*

She thought about arguing but kept her thoughts and words to herself for now. She respected the command structure of the Dark Angels enough not to challenge Strahan in front of his people, waiting for her chance to get Strahan alone.


Flare didn't like being the center of the universe? Tobias hid his surprise at this revelation. He thought he must have been mistaken at thinking that was what he'd picked up from the most beautiful woman in the world. Who knew she was the most beautiful woman in the world and took Primes worshipping at her feet as her due.

Or maybe he'd just imagined that.

Her relief at being left alone? Or her regal acceptance of being the center of the universe?

He wanted to ask her which was the real Flare and probably couldn't stop himself from doing so even though it would be smarter to leave her alone. One of the problems with two beings trying to meld into a bond was the instinctive compulsion to learn everything there was to know about each other. His curiosity was killing him when he needed to concentrate on more important things.

If he was lucky he'd gotten Flare pregnant last night and she could be sent away to a safe haven. But would he be able to put the need for her aside, for even a little while? He was tough, he'd cope.

Until she came crawling back begging to be with him.

Or vice versa, he admitted ruefully.

They hadn't shared blood. She'd been smart to insist that they not taste each other. That would help slow the bonding. But if she wasn't already pregnant he'd continue to have sex with her until she was. At some point blood was bound to become a part of the equation. He could hardly wait.

*Calm down, boy.*

For a moment Tobias wasn't sure whether the thought was his or hers. He shook his head and forced himself to concentrate on business.

"Tell Ed I want a sweep of the Citadel ASAP, Tsuke."

The Japanese werefox made a note on her PDA. She wasn't exactly a werefox but a *kitsune*.

Tobias wasn't quite sure of the differences. Vampires were vampires, werefolk were complicated.

He pinched the bridge of his nose as he mentally ticked through the assignments and orders for the day. "Okay, that's everything," he told the remaining Crew. "Dismissed."

# Chapter Eighteen

$W$ithin moments he was alone with Flare Reynard. His impulse was to take her back to the bedroom.

"Let's go," he told her.

Her faint smile told him she knew what he was thinking and what he meant. "To the clinic."

He nodded. But the cell phone in his jacket vibrated before he could take a step. "Excuse me." He took out the phone to check the text message.

Flare was standing at his side as he gave a snort of laughter. "What?" she asked.

"From Saffie." He let Flare read the message on the small screen:

> Remember the cheek swab thing?

"Meaning?"

"My mortal teenage daughter."

"That was who you were talking to last night? I thought it sounded like you were talking to a kid. I tried not to eavesdrop but heard some of what you said."

"That's okay." He typed an answering text, which wasn't easy on the tiny keyboard with his big hands, while he explained. "Her science class got involved with a DNA study."

Remember. ??

Mistake?

??

What if results suck?

U don't suck.

U do.

UR adopted.

"I thought it would be a good idea for her to learn something about her ancestry. When this came up she told me she thought the work mortals are doing to trace migration patterns is fascinating." He sighed. "I never thought consenting to a biology project would cause a panic attack."

"She doesn't know anything about her family?"

He was annoyed by the notes of alarm and sympathy in Flare's question. Of course a Clan female would only understand about Clan connections.

"You don't need bloodlines to make a family," he told her.

"I know that. But you must think genetics counts for something, or you wouldn't have encouraged your daughter to—"

"Point taken," Tobias growled.

"I'll take that as an apology." She walked away.

He went back to soothing Saffie's worries, but guilt nagged at him the whole time he typed text messages to his daughter.

He was beginning to suspect that he suddenly had more women in his life than was healthy for a simple soldier Prime.

Francesca looked out the patio door with her arms crossed tightly across her stomach and tried unsuccessfully not to think about how easy it was to become attached to mortals.

If she and Patrick had had a daughter, she would have been mortal. Nothing wrong with being mortal; Francesca would have loved her just as much. Taken pride in her. Raised her to be the best person she could be. Vampires lived longer, were faster and stronger, healed more quickly, but they weren't any smarter than mortals. They didn't have any more spirit or talent or anything that really made their minds different from a human's.

*Damn it, Patrick, why'd you have to go and die on me? We would have made beautiful babies.*

"Sorry. I didn't mean to hurt your feelings."

Francesca hated that she hadn't noticed Strahan come up behind her and that she felt like that was where he was supposed to be. She watched his faint reflection in the glass as he filled the space behind her. For a moment she couldn't recall why he might think he'd upset her.

"I like most mortals I've met," she finally said. "Small ones are especially cute. They take a lot less training to domesticate than vampire children."

His laughter was ironic. It coaxed a faint smile from her.

"Of course, I've never raised one," she added. She thought she successfully hid the stab of pain these words brought her. Never mind the connection she and Strahan were developing, there were some things she needed desperately to keep to herself. "Where is she? I get the impression it's a private school somewhere."

"Very private," he answered. "Very exclusive. Very expensive. Back east. She hates it."

"Well, if she was raised around your Crew—"

"That's the point. I've let her get close to

danger too many times. She needs some stability. She needs to learn how to be a normal mortal girl."

This time Francesca gave the ironic laugh. "She's being raised around vampires and werefolk—and studying to be a witch, I think—so how can she even pretend to be a *normal* mortal?"

"She needs to have the chance."

"Or so you have decided, oh master of all you survey?"

"Don't start. All I want is for Saffie to be happy and safe. That's all I've ever wanted."

His sincerity twisted her heart. She turned to face him, unsatisfied with talking only to his reflection. The look of absolute pain and horror was frightening. And utterly compelling. She had to reach out to comfort—

# Chapter Nineteen

The baby batted her big brown eyes at him again and Tobias couldn't stop the smile. He didn't spring for first class often, so he hadn't been at all happy when the Indian woman with the baby sat down in the seat next to him.

He'd had one of his feelings since he boarded the plane. He expected the baby to add to his irritation. Instead she was proving to be a delightful distraction on the long international flight. He had a lot of thinking to do but played peekaboo with the baby until she went to sleep. The baby's mom didn't mind his attention to her but didn't say anything to him, either. She nodded off a little while after the baby did, though her hold on the child resting against her shoulder never slackened.

Parenting wasn't something he'd ever given any thought to, but he found the example of it next to him quite touching.

As the huge plane plowed on through the night he turned his head toward the window. Every now and then he caught a glitter of moonlight off the ocean far below beyond his own reflection in the glass.

He wondered where the legend of vampires not being able to be seen in mirrors came from. Was it from folklore or the movies? He knew that many of his own kind very deliberately shunned knowing anything about the mythos that surrounded vampires in mortal minds. They were snobs, in Tobias's opinion. Besides, what you didn't know could get you killed.

The problem with both vampires and werefolk was that they weren't paying attention anymore. He had a strong feeling that it was a much bigger problem than even the paranoid few like himself suspected. Oh, Clans and Families kept an eye on the fanatic fringe of mortal vampire hunters. Werefolk were expert at hiding from mortals— even those few mortals who knew they were real thought they'd been hunted to extinction. But Tobias suspected that it was time to keep an eye on more than just the traditional threats.

And what about internal threats? Not all Clan

and Family Primes worked for the protection of the good old U.S. of A. Even though most vampires had migrated to the wider spaces and more open society of America in the last three centuries, those who hadn't had their own loyalties, their own ideologies. Prime fighting against Prime in mortal conflicts had happened in the past. Tobias felt it was coming again.

What about the Tribes? Feral werefolk? The Tribes were keeping too low a profile in his opinion. They were up to something. Getting themselves organized? Finding or forcing mortal alliances?

And feral populations were growing, even though the werefolk councils in America, Asia, and Europe actively and angrily denied it.

He was on his way home from Africa and the tale he had to tell wasn't a pretty one. He'd resigned his army commission to make this trip, to tell his story, to put a plan in action. He was a Family Prime. He hadn't taken any vow to protect mortals, but he'd loved his military career. He knew some of the people he was heading to America to meet would mock his feelings, but they would have to listen to his evidence.

He'd been in West Africa on a totally covert mission. His five-man team had been there as protection for a team of spooks gathering intel on the bad and ugly things mortals were doing to each other in that desperate, unstable, violent, but very mineral-rich part of the world.

He'd seen a lot of death along the way. Mortals killing mortals for ancient grudges, for modern politics, mostly out of greed. Illegal diamond mining was a lucrative way for mortals to fuel trouble all over the world.

It was diamonds that had gotten every living soul in one village they'd come across killed. He'd been the only one who'd truly understood how appalling the sickening sight he couldn't get out of his mind really was. He'd made his mortal comrades forget what they'd seen, what they'd found. He was the only one who could bring this knowledge back to the world. His world.

He'd recognized the villagers for who they'd really been, werefolk. Lion People. It took more than AK-47s and machetes to kill people who could change at will into lions, but every male, female, and child was dead. Why? Because they worked their own small, carefully concealed diamond mine. They'd probably worked it for many generations. The trade was their means of keeping themselves secret from the mortal world.

Who would know about the place? Other immortals.

Who could kill werelions? No one who wasn't

even more dangerous and deadly. Other werefolk, perhaps. Weretigers might stand a chance against werelions. A very large pack of werewolves might be able to do the job.

But Tobias knew damn well from what he'd seen, from what he'd smelled, from what every sense and extra sense told him, that the killers had been vampires.

He didn't yet know who. He didn't yet know why—maybe it had only been to get the cache of diamonds and no other agenda. He knew only that immortals had killed immortals and he had to do something about it.

A sudden hard jolt brought him out of his thoughts. Another knocked the plane sideways almost instantly. The jarring continued. The baby beside him started to cry. Seat belt signs lit. The captain's voice announced, "We've run into some bad turbulence, folks. We should be out of it in a few minutes."

The turbulence didn't last long, but it was wild while it did. The baby didn't cry for long after being startled awake, but Tobias watched her mother's face going paler and paler with nausea, until she'd turned a faint shade of green that contrasted horribly with her bright turquoise sari.

As soon as the seat belt sign went off, he said, "Go."

She handed him the baby. "Saffron," she told him, and ran for the nearest unoccupied toilet.

It was in the center of the plane, between first class and coach. That was where the bomb went off.

The poor woman never had a chance. Nor did anyone in the back of the plane, where the explosion and fire immediately swept through. Those in the front of the plane didn't have a chance either. They had the long fall ahead of them.

# Chapter Twenty

"Oh, dear goddess! How could you . . . ? How did you . . . ?"

Francesca knew Strahan must have been holding her up because she could not have been standing on her own. The horror of the memory was too much. The fear . . .

But at least the voice was her own. She looked out of her own eyes now. She was herself. But the terror was fresh. The falling . . .

His fingers tightly gripped her arms. He held her as close as it was possible for two beings to be without melding into one. His warmth kept her alive.

No. That wasn't right. It was her warmth that

kept him alive—while he fell and fell and the earth came closer and . . .

*At least they were over land.*

*What does that matter when striking water at terminal velocity would be no different than striking . . .*

Francesca made herself look up into haunted brown eyes. His eyes. His eyes, not hers.

She forced her mind away from his direct memories. This time she *would* stay herself. But she had to know!

"How? Even a vampire shouldn't have lived through that. And a mortal baby?"

Strahan nodded. "Shouldn't be possible, but it happened. I can't exactly say we were saved. At least I wasn't. The pain was—" He shook his head. "The cold was worse. The fall goes on for a long time when you're that high. At least the oxygen masks still worked. I made sure Saffie was able to breathe. Wrapped her in my coat, her blanket, her mom's shawl. You couldn't tell there was a kid in the cocoon I put around her. Maybe being bundled up like that helped her, cushioned her. I held her close and curled up around her."

"But how did you survive everyone else's fear?"

It must have been a telepath's worst nightmare, to be bombarded with the emotions of all those people who knew they were doomed.

His face went blank, but his eyes still burned with anguish. "I've been a soldier all my life," he said. Then he bent his head and admitted, "I still have nightmares reliving it."

Francesca nodded. His honesty deeply touched her, made her proud of him. She knew this wasn't the time to hug him, even though she wanted to. "Damn right, you do. You couldn't be sane and not be haunted by it."

"I don't think I *was* sane for a while after the crash. I . . . coped, but because Saffie needed me.

"The pilot was damned good," he went on. "Half the plane was gone, but he still managed to keep the nose up."

"He tried to glide? Like a shuttle landing?"

"Tried, yes. The cabin was mostly in one piece after we hit the ground. But no mortal could survive that landing. I remember—I remember curling myself around the baby and then darkness and—pain."

What he did say was hard enough to express, but Francesca was aware that what he wasn't telling her was worse. Something he didn't want to think about haunted his mind, his soul, even his physical memory. She knew it couldn't just be the recollection of pain. He was a Prime, a soldier. Pain came with the territory.

*It was blood.*

She knew he'd never told anyone else this, yet he couldn't help telling her. Couldn't help trusting her with this secret. She was appalled at this intimacy—and honored by it.

"Mortal bodies fly apart with that kind of impact. Bones are crushed, skin bursts, limbs are torn away, organs—you get the picture."

She swallowed nausea. "Vividly."

"There was blood everywhere, along with every other bodily fluid. The reek of it blended together—goddess, but I didn't want anything to do with blood for a long time after that. I had to get out. Maybe I should have checked for other survivors, but I had to get out of that charnel house."

"Nobody could have survived."

"Of course not, but . . ." His gaze had been far away; now he looked her in the eyes. "I shouldn't be doing this to you."

She wanted to understand him. What he needed was important to her. "Talk as much as you need to. I'm here."

His big hands cupped her face. "Why are you the one?"

Her heart raced at his touch. She fought the urge to kiss him, fought the desire brought on by his nearness. If talking helped heal his wounds from that awful time, it was her duty to listen.

"Damned if I know why you're telling me," she answered. "What happened next?" Francesca coaxed him.

"I remember crawling, but where to and for how long, I have no idea. I was blind for a long time, I think. At least the world was completely dark and my eyes hurt like hell. The air was sweet and fresh, but my lungs were injured and it hurt to breathe until they started to heal. I'm not sure how long I crawled, but we were out of sight of the wreckage when my vision came back."

"The plane crashed in Canada, didn't it?"

She recalled how news of the air disaster had filled the headlines back then. Investigators had found evidence of a bombing but no clues on who was responsible. No terrorist group had ever laid claim to the horrendous crime.

He nodded. "Nova Scotia. Lucky for me. Where we hit helped me to survive."

"How?"

"The Fenris Pack has a sanctuary up there. They were the first to reach the crash site. Saffie would have died if we'd had to trek out of there. I'm not sure I would have made it."

Each of Strahan's individual words made sense to her, except for two. "What's a Fenris Pack?"

He looked at her like she was crazy for a moment. "Vampires don't know very much about other immortals," he said with an exasperated sigh.

"Well, you obviously do."

"The Fenris are werewolves," he told her. "A fanatical pack that spend most of their lives shifted to wolf form. They keep as far from mortals as they possibly can. They showed up to try to help at the crash site and were not happy when all the rescue crews, investigators, and media showed up in their territory. It was months before they had their sanctuary all to themselves again. In the meantime they took in Saffie and me, kept us hidden, and got us out of the area when I was able to travel."

"Why hidden? Why didn't you take the baby back to mortals?"

Why would a Prime adopt a mortal child? She believed that had been her original query before time had disappeared into Strahan's bad memories.

He stepped away from her, suddenly wary. "Her mother gave her to me."

Well, that certainly made no sense. The woman had run to the bathroom; she hadn't meant to get herself blown up before she could come back.

"But what about her family?"

"I couldn't contact her family."

"Couldn't? Or you didn't look for them? Surely you could have gained access to the passenger list." That was the sort of thing the Corbett twins were experts at and charged exorbitant fees for.

"No one survived the crash," he said. "No mortal could have."

"Not even a miracle baby who managed to crawl away—"

"Oh, please. Don't you think there would have been an investigation of how this *miracle baby* survived? An investigation that would have led to the Fenris Pack? The entire immortal community?"

She saw the logic to this argument, even if she thought Strahan used it more as an excuse after the fact to justify the impulse that bonded him to the mortal child. He couldn't have been thinking clearly when he made the decision to keep Saffron. There was no use questioning something that it was too late to change.

Besides, it was none of her business. Even though she was profoundly affected by this Prime's love for a child.

Strahan's attention shifted as a call came in on his Bluetooth earpiece, ending any further conversation. He answered the caller's questions, then took Francesca by the hand.

"Come on," he said. "Time to go to work."

# Chapter Twenty-one

"Contacting me by telephone might not be wise at the moment."

He listened to the vampire's sneering voice issue from his telephone handset and gritted his teeth. "You also told me that it wouldn't be wise to meet. Not being a telepath, I can't think of any other option. Unless you can get e-mail in your coffin."

"I read my e-mail at Wi-Fi hotspots." The vampire's sneer was gone now. "But I'm not checking it at the moment. Our communication lines aren't as secure as our enemy's, but we are working on that," he added.

Sometimes he thought this liaison with the monsters was just plain crazy. The creature was prone to mood swings. Sometimes he could be outgoing and treat his mortal allies like buddies. Sometimes he was sullen. Sometimes the creature's natural arrogance dominated his personality. The monster even called himself by an arrogant name—Dr. Stone. A vampire variation of the eighties term for a drug dealer *Dr. Feelgood*, was how the vampire explained the stupid nickname.

He suspected the knockoff daylight drugs the Tribe vampires used weren't as improved as they claimed. But as long as the Tribe Primes stayed sane enough to carry out the alliance's goals, what did it matter? The Purists would put them all out of their misery eventually anyway. But until that time he had to be patient with the animal.

"I have information from the selkie that Primes might want to act on."

"Is the guinea pig still alive?"

Though he was fully aware of the immortality experiment, he resented the vampire's term for the woman who had been used. Even if she was a vampire's whore.

"That is part of the information, yes. She is alive, and test results run by Casmerek's lab show that she is healthy, so far."

"You do understand how valuable she is, don't you?"

Of course he did! He had money invested in the longevity project. They all did. It was rumored that the Tribe vampires had poured all the profits from their illegal diamond trade into the project—blood diamonds, indeed.

Even if the Purists weren't the main financial backers of the scheme to adapt all the vampires' physical advantages for human use, their motive was to improve humankind. He wondered why no one had ever thought to make a profit from the monsters before disposing of them for good before now. Not that the Tribe Primes saw the project that way.

They were all playing games with each other. But for now he remained the helpful accomplice.

"We need her back," the Prime said.

"An assault on the clinic would not be wise."

"I know that! Did you risk a call to tell me what I already know?"

"Of course not."

"Can your selkie sneak her out?"

"Possibly," he answered. "I'll have her work on it." He paused to relish the response he knew was coming, then asked, "Should she bring the female vampire along, as well?"

"The female—!" The Prime calmed down. "They have a female there? Is that why you called?"

He tried to keep his gratification out of his voice. "Yes. And yes. I thought you'd want to know."

Now, didn't that make him sound like a good, trustworthy ally? It was Purist policy to kill vampire females to keep them from continuing the species. Offering the Tribes a breeder showed good faith, that the Purists had truly changed for the sake of future mutual profit.

At least it mollified suspicion.

"Bring me the female," the vampire said.

"I doubt I can do it alone," he answered. "I think what we need is a plan."


Daddy hadn't gotten it. Saffie had a feeling—a bad feeling. And if anyone should have understood about bad feelings, he should have. But he didn't this time. It was the distance between them, she was sure. Phones and computers were great for keeping in touch, but being able to touch was better. She might not have been a telepath, but at least she understood that much.

It wasn't that she was worried that she'd find out that she was from Mars or something. All she had to do was look in a mirror and know that at least her mother had been Indian—maybe born in Ohio or France, but Saffie knew her genes had

*Indian subcontinent* stamped on them. But her dad—no, the male half of her genetic code? What if he turned out to be a flesh-eating demon or something? Not that she'd ever met any demons, but with a vampire for a daddy, who knew what was possible in her paternal DNA?

She'd had a growing feeling of dread since a couple of days after they'd done the test. Ever since waking up from a dream about the plane crash. She couldn't remember a thing about the crash while awake, but sometimes it snuck up on her in her sleep. She'd woken up from the latest dream wondering for the first time why she'd lived. A voice in her dream suggested that maybe she wasn't mortal.

It had only been a dream, but the dread grew worse with every day closer to the test results showing up.

She had a few minutes before it was time to walk into a class where disaster awaited. She needed some support. Some defense. Someone to offer more than *There, there, there's nothing to worry about.*

Yes, there was. She didn't know what, but she needed a plan B. Even a plan A would have been nice.

"Dee." Her witch mentor had trained Saffie to listen to her feelings. Dee would understand.

Saffie gave up on texting and opened her laptop to send a quick sip for advice to the Crew's witch. All she could do then was head to biology and hope for a chance to check for an answer during the class.

"Welcome to New York," Gregor announced to the pair of slaves as he entered their windowless workroom. "I brought doughnuts."

This got the geeks' attention. His entry hadn't caused them to look up from their computer screens, but sweets did. He handed over the box. "You prove my theory that one should treat pets well."

"Dibs on any chocolate," the female said. "Thank you," she added when Gregor cleared his throat. Young mortals could be so rude.

"Did you enjoy the trip from Los Angeles?" he asked.

"We were handcuffed, blindfolded, and stuffed into an airplane," the female said. "Oh, yeah, it was great."

"Of course nobody bothered to tell us why," the male said.

Gregor gestured around the windowless room. "I thought you'd enjoy the change of scenery. I see your equipment also arrived safely and that you're hard at work. You'll find that the Master here on the East Coast is even more demanding than the one in Los Angeles."

"I thought you were the Master in L.A.," the woman said.

"I am but a humble liaison, transferred here the same time you were." The entire West Coast operation was being dismantled, and they were using Purists' attacks to divert the attention of vampires and werefolk from their move.

"What are you doing here, Greg?" the male asked as he handed the doughnut box to his work partner.

"He's come to mess with our minds—probably make us forget we were ever anywhere but here," the female said. "He telepathically wipes our memories now and then."

"I don't remember," the male said.

"That's the point," the female said.

Gregor moved to loom menacingly over her desk. "And how is it *you* remember?"

She looked up, paling but trying for a brave smile. "Because you told me to?" she guessed.

"Correct answer."

Her quavering smile disappeared. "We've made progress on breaking into Sipher."

"Don't be so modest," the male said. "We're totally into the Dark Angels' network."

"Only the net sips," the woman said.

This pair of mortals earned their continued existence because of their expertise with computers. They were IT specialists, hackers and data miners who gave the Tribe a view into modern communications. It was tricky, allowing the pair access to the Internet and other communications devices yet keeping them from using their knowledge to call for help or plan an escape. Gregor's responsibility was to keep the pair docile and servile. These mortals were his Master's private property even though they were Gregor's to direct. The information they gathered and he reported was shared with the Coalition at the Tribe leader's discretion.

Gregor made very sure the pair were well taken care of. There was no reason such a valuable mortal resource should be subjected to the Primes' usual dominance games. Let them play with each other; it was demeaning for a Prime to abuse anyone but his own peers.

There had been one incident in California where the male hacker had been subjected to a beating by a bored Prime while Gregor had been absent. When he'd discovered the hacker too injured to work for a week, Gregor had forcefully reminded the one responsible that it was unwise to interfere with their overlords' plans in any way and that this delay was not appreciated. The example he made of that Prime had been a valuable lesson to the other Primes. Especially since he'd left the body in the hall outside the slave quarters for several days as a warning.

Since that incident, Gregor had made sure the pair were confined in a room with their computers. They had cots to sleep on, food brought in, and could download any entertainment that suited them. Their lives were not too different from many other nerds.

"Nothing has changed with the move. As long as you do your work you're safe," Gregor assured them now.

"More or less," the male muttered. It was obvious that some part of his subconscious remembered the beating.

"Tell me about these sips—" Gregor turned as the door opened behind him. "No one is allowed—My apologies, sir," he added hastily as the Master Prime stepped into the room.

The Master waved his words away. "I'm told you've added prizes to my collection of weapons. I've come to see their uses for myself."

"No new prize, sir. They've merely been moved to headquarters along with everything else."

Gregor stood squarely in front of the seated mortals but the Master gestured for him to move aside so he could get a better look. He ignored the female, but he gave the male such a fierce glare the mortal began to tremble.

"What have you done to deserve to live?"

The male answered quickly, though his voice shook. "Deciphered the encrypted Sipher social networking—We can now read the messages the Dark Angels send each other."

"Master," Gregor said, prompting the male, as the Master Prime raised a hand to strike the slave.

"M-master," the male added.

The Master looked at Gregor. "Explain this."

"Clans and Families use the Internet for what is called social networking—they send short, private messages to each other via an encrypted program called Sipher. These short messages are called sips."

"What a stupid notion. Why don't they simply use telepathy?"

"Because they mimic mortal behavior," Gregor reminded the Prime Master. "Also, not everyone using Sipher has psychic abilities, or at least compatible ones. This is especially true of the members of Strahan's Dark Angels. The Dark Angels use the Sipher network extensively."

"This foolishness is useful for gathering intel?"

"Not particularly," Gregor said. "The sips are mostly trivial personal conversation."

"Then why did the slave speak of anything so worthless?"

"No! No, Master." The male mortal was visibly trembling. "If we read enough sips we're bound to find out lots of things. People let information slip when they think they can't be hacked. They forget to be cautious. All we have to do is monitor enough—"

"Tell me what Strahan's *Angels* are talking about." The Master's harsh voice cracked across the mortal's dithering.

The male stared at his computer screen. "Um—well—the latest sips are from a pair of mortals and—"

"Read them," Gregor sneered. He understood the mortal's fear but didn't disguise his opinion that this was a waste of time.

"The one called SaffieS says, Dad says not to worry about DNA test. Help! D'Bones answered, Can't. Stopping apocalypse. UR OK, Saffron."

Instead of the fury Gregor expected, the Master looked interested. He smiled. "Saffron . . ." He rubbed his jaw. "Now that's a word I haven't heard in years. Is this Saffron a person? Or is that a coded message?"

"A person," the slave said. "Young, I think. The sips are from a schoo—"

"Answer only what you are asked," Gregor ordered the male.

The Master's smile widened. "A person named Saffron, connected to Strahan." He chuckled. "Dragomir will be interested in that. If . . ." His attention switched to Gregor. "Find this Saffron. Bring her to me."

"Her?" Gregor asked.

But the Prime Master walked from the room without bothering to answer.

# Chapter Twenty-two

"Traffic's a mess," Tobias complained. "Even by L.A. standards."

It was raining, and the radio had reported mudslides closing several roads. Francesca missed the promise of sunlight earlier in the morning and sighed at the wet gray all around them now. The slapping of windshield wipers and barely moving traffic was depressing. She wasn't sure where they were heading and conversation had been nonexistent since they'd left Ben's place. Strahan had been giving off waves of silent brooding.

Now that he'd made an effort to come out of his funk, she tried to keep him going. Normally she welcomed Primes keeping quiet and leaving her alone, but she guessed she was attracted to the sound of Tobias Strahan's opinions. It'd beat the repetitive *swish swish* of the windshield wipers and dull traffic reports on the radio.

"This is not the sort of winter I'm used to," Francesca said, trying out the neutral theme of the weather. "At home it would be a blizzard this time of year."

"In my part of the country too."

Francesca turned her head sharply to stare at the big Prime behind the wheel. *Good Lady, the great wandering warband leader has a home somewhere!* She was suddenly dying of curiosity but curbed it. She closed her mouth on the personal questions and shielded her thoughts from broadcasting them. The less they knew about each other the better, right? Anything to stave off this bonding nonsense.

"I assume the mudslides slowing us up are the end result of the wildfires from last summer."

Strahan nodded.

"I'm told you think that the fires around San Diego right now are arson by the same people attacking us."

"Not exactly," was his answer.

"What on earth do you mean by 'not exactly'? Are they or aren't they? Sidonie said you did your best to convince every immortal in San Diego they were under attack. Of course, this was before she became a Dark Angel, so she was allowed to be skeptical about your motives. Now she says of course the fires were set by renegade immortals."

"When did you talk to Sid about me?"

"Last night before I went to bed."

Francesca groaned as she realized she'd walked into a verbal trap. Admitting that she'd called her BFF to discuss a man totally discredited her cool, sophisticated image. She slumped in her seat, looked straight ahead, and crossed her arms. Maybe she should take out her e-reader and pretend to be absorbed in a book, she thought.

Strahan chuckled.

"I hate you," she muttered.

He reached out and patted her shoulder. "There, there, dear."

She would have preferred if he'd patted her thigh—though she wasn't sure if it was because it would give her a chance to protest his behavior or because she wanted the warm rush of a more intimate touch. Her reactions to him confused the hell out of her.

"Think what your confusion does to me," he said, reading her feelings. He sighed. "I need to keep a clear head. We need to have sex again."

It was Francesca's turn to chuckle as she looked back at him. "That is the best line any Prime has ever used to try to seduce me."

"The truth is always best," he answered sententiously with a wicked gleam in his dark brown eyes.

Even his teasing turned her on. Francesca decided it was time to get the conversation back to safer ground. "Please explain what you meant by 'not exactly.'"

"The people we're up against now are second stringers," he answered. "Dangerous enough, certainly a threat to the local immortal population, but the big boys have already cleared out."

"And you know this how?"

"My certainty frustrates you." He gave her a teasing smile.

She knew it would be rude, and far too suggestive, to bare her fangs at him. Besides, what if someone in a nearby car saw? "Answer the question, Strahan."

"I've got a feeling," he said.

Francesca managed to keep from reacting with the anger that flashed through her. Maybe he wasn't being facetious. Instead of *flaring,* as the dear brother who'd given her her stupid nickname put it, she made herself analyze what Strahan had said.

"You're a precog?" she asked.

"Hell, no! I wouldn't wish precognition on anyone. I can't see the future or anything else; I get strong *feelings* about things, situations—I know that this is right, this is wrong, this is what's going on. It's complicated, but facts fall into place to support my feelings."

"Always?"

"I am Prime," he responded.

Francesca bristled. "Of course. Primes are never wrong."

He shrugged. "Okay, maybe I've been lucky so far."

Ah, the Prime wasn't being typical. He was teasing, being self-deprecating instead of arrogant. Strahan kept behaving in delightful ways she wasn't used to in a male.

Suddenly traffic was moving again. It was also raining harder. Strahan set about weaving in and out of traffic with the skill of a commando NASCAR driver. He grinned like a maniac, and she laughed at the adrenaline rush as well. Much honking trailed in their wake.

Francesca asked, "Didn't you have a *feeling* about the plane crash?"

"Good question," he answered, but he looked pained.

"Sorry. I don't mean to drag up bad memories for you. My curiosity got the better of my—"

He held up a hand. "I meant it. It's a good question. You need to know my weaknesses along with my strengths."

Francesca genuinely didn't understand what he meant by this. Was he talking about lifelong commitment? About bonding stuff? About protecting her as a Dark Angel? She decided it was better not to ask.

"I had a very bad feeling when I got on that airplane," he said. "But my attention was on what to do after finding the murdered werelions. I was already considering how to organize what became the Dark Angels. I knew there was going to be opposition to the idea and that the logistics were going to be a nightmare. Fear of a future pitting immortals against immortals distracted me from my feelings about the present. And Saffie was pretty darn distracting too," he added with a fond smile.

The affectionate look on his face totally melted Francesca. It made her want to grab him and kiss him and rest her head on his shoulder.

"Damn, you're a dangerous man," she complained.

His gaze slid briefly to her, then back to the road. "So I've been told."

She knew all she'd have to do to know if he was reacting to what she really meant would be to relax her guard, to let her consciousness flow with his. He seemed to have no trouble getting past her shielding—she could tell it wasn't even conscious effort on his part. Maybe it was one of the ways his *feelings* worked. Psychic gifts were complex and downright weird. She knew that with anyone else she'd have been furious and spitting viciously at the way she was being read. But with Strahan—it was just the way he was. Correction: it was the way they were together.

*Bonding. Shit.*

"Logistics nightmare?" she asked, trying to keep both their attention on a subject that had everything to do with him and nothing to do with them. "I thought the idea of the Dark Angels spread like wildfire. And why such a dramatic name, anyway? It's so, so—"

"Clan?" he asked, and laughed. "Why would an adopted Family Prime use something that sounds so chivalrous for his special ops group?"

"Yeah."

"Clans name themselves after creatures mortals think of as vermin—when in fact they are the protectors of mortals. The Families are into living between both worlds; their culture is about communicating with both, so we have names like Cage, which comes from the word for 'door' in some old language. And Piper, Bridger."

"What's *Strahan* mean?"

"'Minstrel.'"

He paused, as if waiting for her to tease him.

"I'm a Reynard, named after vermin," she reminded him. "Go on."

"The Tribes name themselves after mythological monsters—Manticores and Grendels and Hydras and such."

She wondered what Tribe he'd been born into but didn't ask. She'd mocked him quite enough about his Tribe origins and wasn't going to bring up a subject she hadn't apologized for yet.

"Tribe boys revel in thinking of themselves as rough, tough, evil demons. So, of course they think of other vampires as weak and wimpy—angels to their demons. And angels have no dicks, right?"

"So you wanted to show them that angels have dicks."

"And fangs, and fighting skills. I wanted a name that I could make Tribe Primes fear."

"Hence, *Dark* Angels."

He nodded. "Besides, there was this television show with an incredibly hot heroine called—"

"You named your Crew after Jessica Biel?"

"Alba. Don't tell anybody, okay?"

"Oh, I won't," she promised solemnly.

He went on. "Finding recruits for the Angels turned out not to be the hard part. Finding battles to fight hasn't been the hard part. It's been finding out who's behind the war that's been driving me crazy since the beginning."

*Okay, this makes no sense.* "Our people in this city are under attack. You've been put in charge of the counterattack. Isn't this what your group is all about?"

"Yes. We're the best defense our kind has against this sort of attack. The problem is, the enemy knows that too. We have to be here right now. Meanwhile, something else is going on I haven't found out about yet."

"You believe these attacks, designed to out if not destroy the Los Angeles immortals, are a simple diversion?" Francesca asked in astonishment.

Strahan nodded.

"Good for you. You understand intrigue almost as well as a Matri. And you are also the most paranoid person I have ever met."

"I take that as a compliment."

A hard jerk of the steering wheel took them onto an exit ramp. Francesca peered at passing scenery through the heavy rain.

"Are we headed for the clinic?" she asked.

"The Shagal Citadel first," he answered. "I have a feeling."

Francesca grinned rather than question his emotional turmoil. "Good. Maybe I can find something decent to wear there."

# Chapter Twenty-three

"What's this feeling about?" Francesca asked as they rushed up the wet stairs to the Citadel door.

Strahan's arm was around her shoulder, tucking her head protectively under his open jacket. Yesterday she would have refused this bit of gallantry; today she just went with it and tried not to acknowledge that she liked it.

*The mighty have not fallen yet,* she promised herself. *I'm relaxing and going with the flow.*

Except that she wasn't the least bit relaxed being this close to Tobias Strahan. At least it took only a few seconds for them to reach the mansion's door.

Her surprised gasp wasn't at seeing a naked

man open the door but at the fact that the Citadel door wasn't opened by a Prime of the Shagal Clan.

Strahan took her reaction the wrong way. "Cover your shame, Ed."

Ed looked confused. "I don't have thumbs when I'm wolf shifted, boss, and I had to answer the door."

Ed had silver gray hair and a young face. He also had absolutely nothing to be ashamed of. Francesca hid her smile at the realization Strahan was having a jealous reaction to another male's presence. She felt him go still and tense beside her as he realized it too. Strahan demanded absolute control of himself, and around her he wasn't achieving it. She understood his dilemma and decided to help him out—because the Dark Angels and the nasty situation really needed his complete focus more than she did.

That didn't stop the instinctive pang at losing the attention of her bonding partner as she ducked out from under his arm and into the house.

Strahan stepped in and stood behind her, not quite touching but oh-so-close. She caught the heat of his body, the scent of rain in his hair.

"Found anything yet?" he asked Ed.

"I just got here a few minutes before you," the werewolf answered. "Traffic's a mess. This city stinks," he added. "I hate it when we get into urban warfare shit."

Francesca was caught by a sudden craving to mate. She was a nanosecond away from turning around and kissing Strahan before she caught herself. She wanted to grab him and hold on tight. She'd known Strahan for a couple of days and she went hot around him, cold with dread at the notion of not being around him. Here she stood, a puddling column of quivering lust, when the Prime had work to do.

"Damn!" she muttered, and stomped out of the foyer, leaving the Prime and werewolf to their business.

She had to stop and rub her shivering arms once she was out of sight of Tobias Strahan—sight, scent, touch, aura. Francesca fought the urge to be immersed in all of them. She so needed to get her attention on something besides bonding reactions.

*I'm going to have a baby,* she reminded herself. *My way,* she added as images of Tobias Strahan flooded her mind and body.

She wanted to get her mind on anything else, but her quiet surroundings didn't help. The Shagal Citadel was a huge house and she shouldn't have been surprised not to see anyone as she passed through it toward her guest room, but the place had a deserted feel to it. Not that she didn't pick up telepathic sparks of people in the place, it was just—

Oh, of course, this was a sanctuary for Shagal females and the Matri and her daughter weren't there. Odd how that one small difference totally changed the psychic feel of the house. She doubted her own reaction was the same as Strahan's *feeling*. Maybe she should have stayed with him to find out firsthand what his intuition was all about.

Catching a glimpse of herself reflected in a shiny copper sculpture as she passed it convinced Francesca that her own mission was more important than whatever danger lurked for the Dark Angels in the place.

"I have got to get out of this outfit!"

She let out a delighted laugh when she entered her room and discovered it was just as she'd left it—had it been only a day ago?

The UCLA sweatshirt was pulled over her head and dropped on the floor before she swung open the walk-in closet door. Almost every item on the hangers was black, but Francesca chose a dark purple cowl-neck cashmere sweater. She buried her face in the soft material for a moment, then let it slide sensuously over her bare skin. She gave a delicious sigh once she was properly wrapped in luxury once more. The sweater was enough for now. Her sister-in-law's borrowed jeans hugged her bottom and thighs quite attractively and would be practical in case she got to have some sort of Dark Angel adventure at some point.

"It could happen," she told her reflection as she checked her look in the full-length mirror on the closet door.

A few minutes in the bathroom and her hair and makeup were arranged to her satisfaction. She came back into the bedroom feeling much more like herself—Flare Reynard, armored against the world.

She heard footsteps and animal paws padding down the tiled hallway as she came back into the bedroom and glanced curiously toward the slightly open door. Her heart rate picked up and longing tugged at her soul.

Francesca gritted her teeth and turned her back to the door.

Nope. She wasn't going anywhere. It was none of her business. She wasn't going to inquire, even if she did recognize Strahan out there.

She spotted a black leather messenger bag she'd packed a couple of days ago lying on a table. It was ready to go, and she thought it might be a good idea to take it along to keep her feeling civilized on her wanderings in the City of Angels.

She jumped when the door banged open and turned to defend herself with fangs and claws extended as the silver beast rushed into the room. Instinct told her to rip out the werewolf's throat. It leapt. She sprang forward to meet it.

Only to be dragged to the floor by a big body that moved too fast for even her to see. She went down hard, pinned beneath a heavy weight. She caught a glimpse of gray and a soft brush of fur on the top of her head as the beast jumped over her and her attacker.

She fought and sank her fangs into hard muscle, stopping only when the taste of hot blood sent desire flashing through her.

"Don't stop now," Strahan said in response to her biting. He gave a growl of pleasure deep in his throat.

Francesca went very still, forcing down both the fury and the arousal. She'd tasted him! Never mind that she'd given in to the instinct to protect herself—she had tasted Tobias Strahan's blood. Maybe no more than a drop, but—

She didn't realize her fangs were still in his flesh until he eased away from her.

"Actually, continuing this fun would be a bad idea." He got up and pulled her to her feet. "What was all that trying to kill my sniffer about?"

By this time she'd completely resumed her

human shape and the heat that blazed through her to fuel her temper was all embarrassment rather than survival instinct. She glared at Strahan, but he was looking over her shoulder.

"I thought it was attacking me," she said. She remembered that *it* was named Ed. She turned her head. Ed was also in mortal form now, and he was looking at her leather bag. He might not have been in his werewolf form, but she could practically see his sensitive nostrils quivering. It was a wonder he wasn't on point.

"What the hell is going on here?" Francesca demanded.

"Stinks to high heaven, boss," Ed said.

Strahan gave her a sideways glance, and she knew he was expecting some sort of Flare-like protest that her very expensive designer bag certainly didn't stink.

She said, "What sort of bomb did I bring into my hostess's Citadel?"

*You're no fun.* Strahan's pout filtered into her head.

There was also a glow of pride mixed with the teasing. For her?

*That's not what you thought a moment ago,* she thought back.

Ed looked at her. "Sorry I startled you, ma'am.

Didn't know anyone was in here. The C4 covered your scent."

"Sorry I tried to kill you," she replied.

She appreciated the play of muscles in Ed's naked shoulders when he gave a dismissive shrug.

"Stop distracting my sniffer." Strahan moved between her and the werewolf.

# Chapter Twenty-four

Tobias's head still reeled with the rush from Flare's fangs piercing his skin. That she'd been in fighting mode made it even more arousing. What a brawl they could have had before she finally ended up beneath him! She hadn't meant to arouse him, he couldn't blame her for arousing him—but he wished she hadn't gotten her teeth into him right here and now.

That she'd reacted to defend herself pleased the hell out of him, even though there had been no threat. Primes spent so much time protecting vampire females it was easy to forget how dangerous they could be in their own right.

It took all his concentration to recall that there was a threat. The bomb he'd had a feeling was planted in the citadel was in this room. She did need his protection from this threat.

"Get out of here, Flare," he told her.

Of course she only moved a step closer to the case holding the explosive device. "That . . . *thing* is my responsibility. How did it get in here?"

"You tell me."

He felt her thoughts whirling through possibilities before she said, "I had it with me at the clinic two days ago. I brought a change of clothes with me because I thought I might be staying overnight, but it didn't work out that way. I left the bag in an examining room. Anyone could have put something in it."

"You didn't look inside it?" Ed asked. "Did you place it in this spot? No one's moved it?"

"No," she said, "And yes. And no."

"Then it's likely set to go off when it's opened. Right, boss?" Ed asked.

"I thought you were the bomb expert, Ed," Flare said.

"I just sniff 'em." Ed jerked a thumb at Tobias. "He's our demolition man."

*Lady, I'm going to get him killed!* Francesca's heart pounded with sudden panic. She'd brought that thing into the house and put him in danger. Tobias Strahan was going to die . . .

She moved between him and the bomb. "I'm not letting you get killed because of me."

"What are you talking about, woman?"

She gestured toward the satchel. "Let's get out of here. Evacuate the house. Let it go."

"Can't do that," he answered.

His tone was laconic, his attitude and expression every inch that of the dutiful soldier. *Goddess damn all soldiers! Damn their call to duty, their acceptance of danger as a way of life, when it's just the opposite.*

"Why the hell do you people have to put yourselves in harm's way? Do all soldiers have a death wish? Is that it?"

She was crying. She wanted to beat against Strahan's chest. She wanted to drag him away to safety the way she hadn't been able to do with Patrick.

"Let the damn house blow up. It's just a house!"

"That bomb was set to take at least one person with it. I can't accept that. Besides, our brief is to keep mortals out of this fight. The bad guys want explosions, remember? They want to bring in the authorities and media."

"I know that, but—"

"I've disarmed all sorts of explosives all over the world," Strahan informed her. "I do know what I'm doing."

"I bet you enjoy it too. You get that old Prime rush right to your cock every time, don't you?"

"Yes." He gave the faintest of shrugs. "I am what I am."

She was strung out with terror, which came out as vicious contempt. "Fine. But I'm not going to stand here and watch while you get off."

"Of course not. I already told you to get to safety."

"Here's your kit, boss," Ed said as he came into the room carrying a large metal case. A dented black helmet with a clear face shield dangled by its chin strap from his other hand.

She hadn't noticed the werewolf leave. She didn't think Strahan had either, judging by the annoyed look he gave Ed for bringing in gear without being ordered. *Control junkie.*

"Thanks," Strahan said grudgingly. He flipped open the case, which Ed had set well back from the bomb bag, and began methodically unloading equipment and padded protective clothing. He didn't look up again, just said, "Out now. Both of you."

For a moment Ed looked like he wanted to take her arm, but a toothy sneer from Francesca made him think better of the gallant gesture. He settled for walking beside her as they left the room.

"He'll be fine," Ed reassured her after gently closing the bedroom door behind them. "He's the best at what he does."

"So's Wolverine," she said. "And look at the horrible things that happen to him."

The poor werewolf stared at her in confusion. He didn't have a clue what she meant. He must have thought she was talking about a werewolverine—were there such critters?—and not a Marvel superhero. Or possibly a Clan Wolverine Prime.

Francesca patted his bare shoulder. "Never mind. We have our orders. Let's get out of here."

She let Ed walk ahead of her but didn't follow him very far. She knew she should stalk angrily out into the safety of the garden, but she couldn't do it. Strahan didn't want her around. She didn't want to be around when he blew himself up. But how could she leave him when he was in danger?

*One man I loved has already died alone—*

She gave her head a hard shake and scrubbed blinding tears out of her eyes. And how the hell had that *L* word gotten into her head? Lust, yes, she couldn't help that. But she wasn't falling in love with anybody.

She knew damn well all this sentimental

nonsense flooding her senses was simply the bonding process in action and that she ought to fight it. Where was her pride? Her strength?

Turned to mush by a big beautiful bruiser with the heart of a father and the soul of a warrior. It tore out her own heart to know he was in danger.

Strahan was in danger. She needed to be there.

"Never mind daylight drugs," she muttered. "What we need is something to keep our hormones in check."

No matter how much she tried, Francesca couldn't find the will to do anything but be where he was. She walked back to her bedroom. Not that she went inside when she got there. You didn't barge in on someone disarming a bomb. Or bang on the door and beg him to get out before he blew himself to pieces.

Oh, no, all she could do was sit down with her eyes squeezed shut, her back pressed against the door, and her arms wrapped around her drawn-up knees. She prayed to the moon goddess for his hands to be steady and his luck to hold and hoped that if there was an explosion, it would all be over fast enough not to hurt. She prayed that they would be together.

Because if they ended up dead, she was going to make Tobias Strahan's afterlife anything but pleasant.

*        *        *

Tobias was not nervous, but Flare sure as hell was, and knowing it wasn't making his dangerous job any easier. She was also angry. What the hell did the woman have to be angry about? And what was she doing there, right outside the bedroom door? Her heart hammered in his ears; the blood racing through it called strongly enough to make his sheathed fangs pulse. His own heart wanted to keep pace with hers. Blocking her out of his awareness was impossible.

He'd told Ed to get her out, and when it came to werewolf against vampire, didn't the vampire always win? Okay, he couldn't blame Ed if the female didn't do as she said she would and get out.

He was on his knees in front of the booby-trapped leather bag, dressed in protective gear, tools and chemicals laid out beside him. He kept his physical attention focused on the job. But his awareness of Flare was something on an entirely different level.

He couldn't ignore her. He couldn't go to her.

"Go away!" he shouted.

"No!" she shouted back. "Just . . . do . . . whatever, Mr. Demolition Man."

He laughed. The sound was muffled by the shield protecting his face. "You are such a—"

"Bitch. I know."

"I was going to say *nag*."

On the other hand, he was steadied by the knowledge that she was nearby. She was waiting for him. She was depending on him to get them out alive. And would be totally pissed off if he didn't manage it. He liked that about her.

He could not disappoint the lady.

His lady.

Was going to have to get over her objections to his profession.

All he could think to do was to drop every bit of mental shielding and let her in.

*Watch this*, Tobias thought. *And keep out of my way.*

# Chapter Twenty-five

Francesca held her hands up, staring hard to see through the fading images of the bomb being dismantled. These were *her* hands. Long fingered, graceful, elegant, soft skinned, the nails beautifully manicured. She recognized them, but they were not large, competent, and sure. There was no purpose in these hands. No strength. These hands didn't hold the memories of scars healed and lovers caressed.

Lovers—

"Goddess damn him!"

Fury brought Francesca surging to her feet. Just as the door behind her opened.

She stumbled backward. Strahan fell forward. She found herself tangled up with him on the floor once more. This time she was on top. She grabbed his shirt front. She would have shaken him, but how do you shake a mountain?

"What the hell was that all about?" she demanded. "What the hell did you do to me?"

Strahan was totally unfazed. "Was it good for you too?" he asked.

"That wasn't funny! It was—"

*The question is whether to take it slow and careful or go for speed. Caress it or take it hard and fast . . .*

The thought had come while her/his hands hovered over the leather case. At the time it had seemed perfectly normal, but now Francesca marveled at how close those big, sensitive hands had been to the case without actually touching it. She/he had been exquisitely aware of the softness and suppleness of the leather, almost sensing the molecules of the oblong packet of explosives beneath the thin surface of the material.

"It's a tactile awareness," Strahan said now. He gave a cocky grin. "It comes in handy making love too."

*Hard and fast.*

What Francesca had then experienced through Strahan's senses had been accomplished in a blur of speed faster than even a Prime should have been able to manage.

"I've had a lot of practice."

The explosive was removed and slathered in a cool chemical goo before the wiring even knew it was missing.

She'd been there—felt and seen it all. It was over, and she was still scared—with him, for him. Reaction burned through her.

She pounded a fist on his chest. "Damn you, Strahan! How dare you mess with my head like that?"

He blinked. Opened his mouth to say something—

Her mouth came down hard and hungry on his, tasting that he was alive and burning just as fiercely as she was.

And, oh, those hands were indeed skilled! He had her sweater and jeans off her almost as fast as he'd snatched the bomb out of its case. She was naked on the cool tiles, but she was anything but cold.

His lips and tongue moved down her breasts and belly and between her legs. She clawed at him, ripping through his shirt, scoring his shoulders.

*Should have left on the Kevlar,* he thought.

She needed blood and came as soon as she caught the scent of it. And laughed at his thought. The amusement only increased her pleasure.

*What are you doing to me, Strahan?*

*This.*

His fangs sank into the soft flesh of her inner thigh.

Her world went white hot with pleasure.

*Banshee.*

*What?* Francesca responded to the thought that brought her back from overwhelming sensation.

*You're screaming like a banshee.* The shape of Strahan's thought was laced through with smug satisfaction.

*I suppose you know a banshee?*

*Several. But I've never bedded one before.*

She heard a maddened howl and knew the sound was her own primal response. As if she'd never been bitten by a vampire before.

In fact, she hadn't.

*You're a blood virgin?* Strahan projected absolute male pride and delight at this revelation. She'd never been anyone else's but his! His being was aglow.

She should have been repulsed. She was pleased instead.

*But I bit you first!* she thought, teasing him.

*But I bit you more,* he responded, teasing back.

*Even more would be better.*

But his fangs were no longer piercing her skin. Pleasure still pulsed out from the spot where he'd tasted her, feeding into her growing desire to share herself with him in every way possible.

Strahan moved to cover her mouth with his. She tasted the tang of her lust and blood. Their tongues played around each other's fangs, teasing, stimulating.

*Woman, you taste of moonshine.*

"White lightning becomes you," he whispered in her ear. Then he bit her earlobe and sent another fiery orgasm shooting through her. She bucked beneath him.

And one of his many communication devices sounded.

"Damn!" they swore as one.

"Is it too much for you to turn those off?" she demanded.

"Don't nag me, woman!" he shouted back.

Then he thrust hard into her. His hips ground hard and fast and deep. Francesca met each rough thrust with joy. And if she continued to scream like a banshee into his ear—well, maybe that was partly in revenge for being called a nag. And partly to drown out the sound of his phone calling him back to duty.

And mostly because she'd never felt anything as wonderful as his rough-and-tumble way of making love to her before.

# Chapter Twenty-six

"As you know, we can trace ancestry from your mother's side through mitochondrial DNA. But what I want you to take a look at on your individual results screens are those lines that look like bar codes. Those are called bonding patterns, and that's what was used to trace your paternal descent . . ."

Saffie's biology teacher went on talking about variable-number tandem repeats and other stuff she might normally have found fascinating, but Saffie's attention was riveted on the blotchy black dash patterns on her laptop screen that told her who her father was.

Or maybe what.

She'd had a bad feeling coming into this, and if

there was one thing she'd learned from her adoptive father, it was to trust her feelings. To double-check her feelings, she tilted her laptop so the girl seated on her left could see it. She got a look at the other girl's DNA information in turn. This got a giggle from Pattie, who was on her right, so she and Pattie exchanged views as well. Saffie was *so* not reassured by what she saw.

Students weren't supposed to access the classroom's Wi-Fi without getting permission and a password from the teacher, but a Dark Angel wasn't going to let minor details get in her way.

Saffie was still careful to slowly tap out her message when she sent an e-mail and a couple of sips, so the soft clatter of keys and hand movements wouldn't give away what she was doing. Frustration at being stuck in the mortals' world boiled in her while she surreptitiously tried to make contact with her own.

Holiday vacation was coming up very soon, but not nearly fast enough for her. She had to get away from this place, these people. Maybe the DNA evidence, whatever it meant, would be enough to convince her father of what she'd been telling him all along. She didn't belong there.

Saffie got no immediate replies from the messages she sent, so she was forced to wait for the end of biology class to make a phone call. She hated bothering Tobias or Dee while they were on an op, but this was *important*!

She'd known going into it that it was important, but had they listened to her? Why did they still treat her like a mortal kid with no psychic gifts of her own? Well—not completely. At least Dee agreed she had a talent for magic, which kept her from being a complete washout for the Crew.

Magic.

A smile spread across Saffie's face, and her worry eased a little. Maybe that was what was wrong with her paternal DNA profile. Maybe she'd inherited some sort of magic-enhancing mutation from her biological father. He was a great and terrible wizard and that was the cause of the conclusion at the bottom that read:

Sample not consistent with human DNA.

Saffie held on to this reassurance until class ended.

Before she could leave, the teacher stopped her with, "A word, Ms. Strahan."

Having spent her life around soldiers, many colorful and profane responses came to Saffie, but she managed a meek, "Yes, sir." While she slowly made her way to the teacher's desk her mind raced, trying to find plausible excuses for what she knew she was going to be asked.

"Your reputation as a troublemaker has reached

a new height," the teacher told her. "I don't know how you tampered with your saliva, but this example of your witchcraft isn't funny."

"Sir?"

"I really believed you were interested in the genetics project."

Saffie managed not to point out that she *was* interested. It looked like she was about to be given an out. She'd been afraid she was going to be told she was being sent to specialists for medical testing, but if her teacher thought this was a prank, it was better to let him think so.

"How did you manage to fake these results?"

"I don't know what you mean," she answered, trying not to sound convincing. Oh, if only she had a vampire's talent for altering thoughts. She had to rely on cleverness and acting talent, and she wasn't sure how much she had of either.

"You're going to make me prove that you're pulling a practical joke on me, Saffron?"

He didn't wait for an answer but took a fresh gene-testing kit off his desk and handed her a cotton swab. "Give me some spit."

She wondered if she should protest that this was an invasion of privacy but decided not to argue about it. Being retested would buy her time to come up with a plan.

The teacher watched her carefully as she

rubbed the swab around the inside of her mouth. "You can go now," he told her when she handed it back.

*Oh, I'll go, all right.* She'd come up with the only plan that was really viable: she was getting out of there and going back where she belonged.

How hard could it be to run away from a fancy high school?

"I've traced the sips sent by this Saffron kid to a private high school in upstate New York," the male hacker told Gregor.

"I so do not care," Gregor said.

"But the Master said—"

"I know I need the information, but the whereabouts of teenage girls doesn't interest me."

"He prefers real women?" the female slave muttered under her breath.

"If by *real* you mean mortal females, the answer is no." He hadn't fought his way high enough in the Tribe hierarchy to win a vampire female, but it was well known that was in his plans. "I don't settle."

Gregor saw the male looking jealously at the female. Perhaps the male thought his fellow slave was interested in Gregor when he wanted her for himself. Gregor knew the female to be more willing to stand up to her vampire overseer but sensed no attraction from her. He noted the mortals' interaction but would interfere with them only if their behavior jeopardized his own agenda.

These thoughts were useless and unproductive and Gregor realized he was only trying to put off concentrating on yet another assignment he didn't want. Doing the Master's bidding was the name of the game, the only way to get where he needed to be, at the top tier of the Tribe hierarchy.

Who was Dragomir? Why was the Master interested in a high school student? If he was being sent off to fulfill some private vendetta he was going to be very annoyed.

"I live to serve," Gregor grumbled. "Tell me about this St. Sebastian's school."

"Secluded place," the male answered. "Set in a hundred wooded acres on a lake near the town of Cageville. It's surrounded by a wall with a guarded gate and covered by the latest in electronic security. There are dogs."

"Sounds like they're watching over a lot of rich people's little darlings."

"Exactly."

"Won't be a problem."

The male's fingers flew over his keyboard. "Weather.com says there's a blizzard blowing in over that area. That ought to help."

Gregor had just spent a year in Southern California. He did not see how snow could be anything but a nuisance. He turned to leave the hackers' cell.

"Do you want me to download the school's location for you on Google Maps?" the male called after him.

Gregor paused long enough to show his iPhone to the slave. "No need. I've got an app for that."

# Chapter Twenty-seven

Tobias rolled onto his back and wiped hair out of his face. He stared at the ceiling and murmured, "I really didn't have time for this."

"Your romantic words send chills through me," said the naked female beside him. "Or maybe it's from lying on this cold floor. Your phone's ringing again," she added.

He was wrecked—he had never felt more alive or satiated—and he really did have to get back to work.

"Saving the world's a bitch," he said as he sat up and looked around for his clothes. "You ripped my shirt off," he complained as he picked up the ragged cloth and felt around for the pocket holding the chiming BlackBerry.

If he was a Clan Prime he'd have been helping the lady up now and assuring her how wonderful the experience had been. Maybe he'd already have flowers for her.

"I have to take this," he said, and put the phone to his ear.

Flare didn't sneer at him but got up and gathered her own shed clothing.

"Where are you going?" he asked when she turned toward her bedroom. "There's a bomb in there."

"Along with all my possessions," she told him. "The bomb's dead and I'm a mess. If you think I'm leaving here without fixing my makeup, you're crazy."

He let her go. He had a lot to do, reports to assess, orders to give. They did need to be on their way. He went about being brisk and efficient.

But the whole time, despite keeping his attention on business, he marveled at the fact that he was bonding with a female who had to fix her makeup after every crisis. How the hell was he supposed to survive that?


"What's this?" Strahan asked.

Francesca patiently didn't point out that the black garment she was holding up was obviously a shirt. "I raided Barak's closet. He's a big guy," she said of the bondmate of the Shagal Elder. "This ought to fit you."

Strahan didn't seem to make the connection that he was shirtless and that the garment was for him; his attention was obviously elsewhere. She doubted that this was simply his normal reaction to midmorning sex after disarming a bomb. But then, she hadn't known him long.

"Get dressed. Police your gear. Let's move it." She tried to sound as firm as any Matri or drill sergeant, which at least got a smile from him.

He took the shirt. "Yes'm. My mind's on two calls, a text message and a sip," he told her as he put on the shirt.

It was matte black silk and molded to his hard muscled body perfectly. Francesca appreciated the way he looked. Not that it was easy to make a Prime look bad, but he looked damn good.

She also appreciated Strahan's explanation, since he didn't owe her any. She'd assumed he'd be the strong silent secretive type, but he'd turned out to be open and vulnerable enough to pique endless curiosity in her.

She didn't want to be curious about him, or worried, but she was both. *Stick to business,* she told herself. *Stick to important stuff.*

"Did Ed sniff out any more bombs?" she asked.

He shook his head. "We're clear."

"Damn!" she complained. "Because that makes me solely responsible should the house have blown up," she explained at his curious look.

"You would have gone with it," was his stoical answer. Which made her laugh. "Save your temper for whoever planted the bomb on you," he added.

"I like that thought."

He took her hand. "Let's go tear the clinic apart, shall we?"

"Sounds like a plan."

The fact that he automatically included her—Clan female and heiress—in his Dark Angel op pleased her more than words could say. She'd been offered every luxury the minds of Primes could think of, but nothing thrilled her heart like this chance to kick some butt at Tobias Strahan's side.


She kept quiet on the drive, afraid he'd recall who she was and she'd lose this chance to be of some use in her world. She took out her e-reader and tried to concentrate on a book while rain continued to pour outside. Tried, but she was too physically and psychically aware of Strahan to pay any real attention to words. The Prime took up a lot of space both ways.

*He ought to make me claustrophobic,* she thought.

*I'm told I give off comforting vibes.*

This was their only exchange during the entire drive. After this one thought from him, Strahan's mental shields slammed up and his gaze never once left the road.

Francesca thought she knew why he was keeping his distance. He was upset because they'd had sex. Not that he was regretting the act—no Prime ever regretted having sex. He hadn't been completely in control. Not just of her but of the situation and himself. It had definitely been the wrong time and place. She was in complete agreement. She wouldn't even have blamed Strahan if he was furious with her for initiating the first kiss.

He was on duty. She hadn't respected that. She'd reacted on instinct—the pure lust-inducing joy that he was alive, that she was alive, had carried her into his arms, and she'd had her way with him.

It had been wonderful.

Her body told her it was still wonderful and

urged her to do it again as soon as possible. She fought down a smile, along with the craving to cuddle up against him with her head on his broad shoulder.

She wondered how he'd look in leather pants.

Then she reminded herself that not a single member of the Dark Angels had been in sight when they left the Citadel. Maybe immortals didn't have the same inhibitions as mortals, but Strahan's Crew couldn't have approved of his behavior in the middle of an emergency.

All right, the specific emergency had been over, and his people were likely to put all the blame on Flare Reynard's femme fatale seduction of their beloved boss—at least this time. And they'd be right—at least this time.

And they'd shared blood! This had to stop before they had more than a drop or two mingling in each other's hearts, for the sake of keeping the bonding at bay. More importantly, to keep Strahan focused on his duty. She wasn't going to be the cause of his becoming careless, of his doing anything stupid or fatal.

She'd come to Los Angeles to get pregnant, and she'd stubbornly refused to leave when the other females were sent to safety because Francesca Reynard wanted what Francesca Reynard wanted. She'd stomped her foot and the leader of the Dark Angels had been coerced into being her bodyguard.

She hadn't considered that her selfishness would put a Prime in danger. Maybe she wouldn't even have cared if famously heroic Super Prime Tobias Strahan hadn't turned out to be—so damned *real*. Nice. Wonderful.

*Oh, hell!*

She was going back to Idaho as soon as she finished talking to Rose Cameron for Strahan. She'd do that for him because he'd asked it of her. Then she'd go back to her gilded prison, get out of his way, because she needed to do that for him.

She'd have vowed to never set eyes on him again, but that was too teenage and melodramatic for even her current mood.

She managed to pull her thoughts away from the situation and remembered she was holding a book, but she'd gotten only a page read by the time they arrived at the clinic.

# Chapter Twenty-eight

The head of the clinic was waiting in the reception area when Tobias walked in with Flare.

"Casmerek, I want to personally interview every mortal on your staff," Tobias said.

"So your text message informed me," Casmerek answered. "Good morning, Francesca."

The scientist was even less enthusiastic about the Dark Angels' involvement in local affairs than the Primes and werefolk. He'd been adamant from the first that no one who worked at the clinic could be involved in the attacks. He hadn't been openly obstructive or refused protection, but he sure as hell hadn't welcomed any investigation into the workings of the clinic. It didn't help that Casmerek worked with ailing vampires all the time and was totally unimpressed by threats or demands. He had to be tougher than his patients to be able to boss them around.

"I have proof that someone here planted a bomb at the Citadel," Tobias said.

"He does," Flare assured the blank-faced mortal. "It was planted in my bag, and this was the only place where I brought the bag. I'm really sorry, Cas, but someone here is a bad guy."

The effect Flare's sympathy had on the mortal surprised Tobias. Casmerek's shoulders slumped and disappointment showed in his expression.

"Someone tried to kill you?" Casmerek asked Flare.

She nodded.

"Nobody tries to kill one of my patients," he said. "Not after all the work I put into keeping you people healthy."

"It would be a waste to lose us after all the work you've put in," Flare agreed.

To Tobias's surprise Casmerek smiled, which was something he hadn't thought the dour doctor even knew how to do. Flare in charming and sympathetic mode could prove to be a useful asset.

"Dr. Casmerek—" Tobias began.

"I'd like to have a talk with you, Francesca," Casmerek said, cutting him off, then gave him a significant look. "Alone."

Flare noticed that Casmerek was about to explode and thought at Strahan, *Don't push him. Just do what you need to with the staff and I'll keep him out of your way for a few minutes.*

Her way made more sense than having an argument with the clinic director. Tobias nodded. He waited until Casmerek and Flare left the reception area before activating his Bluetooth. "Ali, I'll be in the break room. Bring me some humans."

Dr. Casmerek closed his office door and faced Francesca. "How many times have you mated with that Prime?"

She'd never been more surprised in her life. Too surprised even for outrage. "What are you talking about?"

"Sex. Copulation. Mating. Bonding, too, I suspect. What were you thinking? Are you trying to completely ruin your chances at getting pregnant?"

Francesca took a step back. Her legs hit a chair and she sat down hard on cold, unyielding plastic. She looked up blankly at the scientist and said, "What?" again. Which was a ridiculous way to react to his inappropriate statements.

"Are you sexually and emotionally involved with Strahan?"

"You're a mortal. How can you even tell that?"

"The pair of you walked in holding hands."

We did? She remembered noticing that the rain had stopped as they entered the clinic and cloud shadows scudding over nearby hills. She recalled seeing guards patrolling the grounds. She remembered how the fresh breeze had lifted her hair and the sense of . . . being protected and safe in the warmth of . . .

"Oh, please!" Francesca shook her head in disgust.

"See what I mean?" Casmerek demanded. "You don't even realize it's happening. Get away from that Prime if you want to be impregnated by me. Of course, if you want to do it the old-fashioned way . . ."

"What are you talking about?" Francesca rose to her feet. "You told me yesterday that I probably couldn't get pregnant. That there's something wrong with my blood."

"That's not what I said."

No, it wasn't. Not exactly. But it was what she had heard. She'd been so upset and tried so hard to hide it that the actual information hadn't filtered into her brain.

She sat back down and forced herself to be calm. She looked at the scientist. He was still annoyed. "Sorry I screwed up," she told him. And got a brusque nod. "But I don't understand how, Cas. I thought that my rare blood type was going to interfere with my getting pregnant."

*If I hadn't thought that I wouldn't have let myself go so completely with Strahan. I needed to feel like a female. Part of letting myself have sex with him had to be a need for physical comfort, didn't it?*

That was a good excuse, but Francesca dismissed it as self-serving. She'd wanted him, and he'd made her want him more.

Casmerek said, "I told you that we were doing very thorough testing to make sure you would be compatible with one of our sperm donors to increase the chances of your carrying a fetus to term. I didn't say you couldn't get knocked up."

"But—"

"I believe it would be difficult for you to become pregnant by just any Prime," he said. "But bonding changes everything. I'm a scientist and a mortal. Bonding doesn't make sense to me. It's magic. I don't like the idea of magic being a real form of energy, but I've had too much proof to deny the existence of magic."

"I don't want to bond with Strahan," she said. She wasn't lying, but it wasn't completely true.

"I don't intend to get pregnant by Strahan."

That was true. That would be losing. The game, not just an important move. She'd been fighting too long to let instinct mess up her game plan now.

"I guess I better stop sleeping with the Über-Prime."

A loud voice from deep in her soul screamed angrily at her decision. She didn't want to stop!

Tough.

She'd made this decision already but guessed she was going to have to consciously remind herself of it every moment until she took herself several states away from his overpowering presence.

"You may already be pregnant," Casmerek said.

She jumped up again. She was beginning to feel like a yo-yo. She'd been bounced all over the place since encountering Strahan.

"How can I tell? Is it too early to pee on a stick to find out?"

"I can do a pregnancy test, if that's what you mean. I don't appreciate your being crude, young lady."

Francesca laughed. "You're the one who said *knocked up*. And didn't I used to pick you up from grade school, young fella?"

Mortal or not, Casmerek was still a member

of the Reynard Clan. They'd known each other a long time, and she was the elder.

"It was from my math tutor's, in junior high, Aunt Frannie."

He gave one of his rare smiles, the one that made him look so much like her oldest brother. Casmerek was very much like his late father. Maybe he wasn't a Prime, but he was bound by duty and honor. She understood why it galled him that Strahan suspected the children of Primes as traitors. The Clan children were as protective of immortal-kind in their own way as the Clan Primes were of fragile mortals. They just weren't as flashy about it.

Francesca shook her head. "I don't want to know. Not yet."

"If you pretend it isn't true, it won't be?"

She ignored his sarcasm and this reminder that he knew her very well. "I'm tired of medical tests. You've taken enough fluids out of me in the last few days."

From now on she was saving her blood for Strahan. *No, no, no. Stop thinking—feeling—like that.*

"I promised Strahan I'd talk to Rose Cameron for him. Is that okay?"

He rubbed his jaw. "I'd like to spend some

time with Rose Cameron myself, but Tony is keeping her pretty busy. You can try knocking on her door, and if there's no moaning and thumping going on, he might let you in."

She understood how the mortal could be frustrated with vampires' obsession with sex. She was frustrated with it herself most of the time.

Or had been until Strahan came along. *Damn it*. Now a wave of gooey sentiment came over her at the thought of Tony Crowe's long wait for his bondmate.

"They have a lot of time to make up for," she said.

"And Tony's trying to pump as much of his blood into her as he can to keep her young."

"What did her kidnappers do to her?"

"Ask her yourself. And take notes for me, while you're at it." He opened his office door for her. "Good luck, Francesca. With everything."

# Chapter Twenty-nine

Francesca knew exactly where Strahan was when she walked out of Casmerek's office and would have made a conscious effort to ignore him if she could have. The problem was, after everything that had gone on since he'd asked her to talk to Rose, she couldn't recall exactly what it was she was supposed to learn from the mortal woman.

She had no intention of getting the wrong information and being told to do it again. That would only give her an excuse to spend more time in Strahan's company.

She headed for where her every sense informed her that would-be bondmate was, but she soon came across the werewolf Ed standing in an open doorway with Chiana, the medical technician. Ed was a big guy, and a wolf a good part of the time, and Chiana was a little thing. She looked thoroughly intimidated to have the werewolf looming over her. Francesca's impulse was to tell Ed to back off, but she managed to hold on to her temper. She thought maybe she should find out what was going on before she pounced protectively.

Chiana settled the confrontation for herself when she looked up, tears brimming in her eyes, and said, "No! My boyfriend doesn't want me to."

When Chiana fled down the hallway, Francesca stepped up to the werewolf. "What was that about? Were you asking a selkie for a date?"

Ed looked appalled. "Hell, no!" He cleared his throat. "I mean, no, ma'am. She's a seal, I'm a wolf. That just wouldn't be . . . right."

"My best friend is with a werewolf," Francesca told him.

Ed tried to make his expression and emotions blank. "I wouldn't know about that, ma'am."

She pointed after Chiana. "Then what was that about? Why was she so upset?"

Ed shrugged. "I was just trying to give her some advice." He touched his nose. "I noticed that she's stressed out. At first I thought it was because this place has been under attack. But when

I got close to her, I noticed that she—this is hard to explain to a vampire, ma'am."

"Try."

"She smells bad." He looked uncomfortable, like he thought she was about to bite his head off at such rudeness. When she waited for further explanation instead of killing him outright, the werewolf explained. "She's been in her skin too long. It's not good for a shifter to stay in human form for very long—you have to stretch out, change—"

"Be all you can be?" she suggested.

He nodded eagerly. "We have to shift and be human to be us. I hear your folk can go a long time without blood before the thirst gets to you. We werefolk can't do that, wait a long time between shiftings, I mean. It makes us nervous, anxious—nuts eventually. Chiana's definitely gone too long between swims."

"You could smell that?"

Ed nodded again. "I told her she ought to get back to the water. She didn't appreciate the advice. I guess I should have minded my own business."

Francesca was pleased at the werewolf's concern for a fellow shifter. The conversation also brought home to her how little she knew about the other immortal races. She wondered how Strahan did it, how he'd banded so many different types of immortals together into a cohesive, purposeful unit. He seemed to understand and respect them all, despite their differences. He was quite a guy. No wonder the Dark Angels loved him.

*Listen to yourself, Francesca,* she thought. *You're nauseating.*

"I heard her mention her boyfriend," she said to Ed. "Maybe there's some sort of selkie mating ritual they're waiting for and they can't go into seal form until then."

And why were mating rituals all she could think of?

"That's probably it," he said. "Excuse me, ma'am. I've got orders to check out more buildings for bombs."

"Lucky you," she murmured after the werewolf walked away, and she was left with the necessity of another meeting with Strahan.


"Just who the hell do you think you are?" Kea's angry voice reached Francesca just before she reached the entrance to the break room.

Francesca walked in smiling, knowing exactly what she was going to see. Kea stood belligerently in front of Strahan, hands on hips, head raised, not in the least intimidated by the big Prime's impressive height and width.

Kea went on. "You come in here acting like god almighty to the rescue and expect us to fall all over ourselves doing whatever you say. And when we do that isn't enough for you, you arrogant son of a— No, I shouldn't say *bitch*. That would be insulting werefolk and I won't do that. Or insult the Matri who gave birth to you."

Francesca knew that Strahan's mother had to have been a Tribe Prime's sex slave. Whether that Prime had brought the female with him into the Strahan family when he defected from his Tribe she didn't know. She'd be free and honored by the Family if she was with them, and hopefully head of her own House. But she'd never be a Matri.

Still, it was nice to hear Kea's respect for her fellow females, be they furred, fanged, or mortal, even if she was thin on the details.

Francesca noticed the Dark Angel Prime named Ali watching this confrontation on one side of the room. He was watching Kea, rather, and trying to hide a smile as the young woman gave his commander hell. More romance blooming in these dangerous times? It seemed that the air was full of pheromones. She didn't think she was noticing it only because of her own situation.

"I think what you're trying to tell me," Strahan said to the glaring woman, "is that you're refusing to allow me access to your thoughts."

"Damn right, that's what I'm telling you. I have rights."

"No one else has complained," Strahan said ominously.

Francesca noticed several other mortals sitting around the break room, all looking pale and dazed. They didn't look like the Prime had given them a chance to complain.

She fought the impulse to interfere. She really didn't want to undermine Strahan's authority, though it was damned tempting.

"Military types," she grumbled.

Strahan's angry gaze automatically snapped to hers. She'd never seen brown fire before. His expression was fierce.

"What?"

She held up a hand. "Nothing."

"Are you trying to undermine my authority?"

Her plan had been not to do that. "What's the matter with you?" she asked. "Are you trying to use me as a scapegoat because you're feeling guilty?"

"Guilty for what? I do what needs to be done."

"Is it necessary to be a bully?"

"A what? Is the spoiled princess upset that someone else is in command?"

Her own temper flared. She stalked toward him.

"Why, you overbearing, tin-plated dictator—"

"With delusions of godhood?" he said, finishing her sentence as she reached him. Kea had wisely scrambled out of the way.

Then he laughed, while his eyes gleamed with recognition and amusement.

*Oh, great.* Not only were they sexually attracted to the point of obsession, they also could quote from the same old television shows.

Strahan put his hands on her shoulders. "I shouldn't have gone off on you like that." His lips lightly brushed her forehead. "I'm sorry."

The warmth that filled her was more affectionate than lustful, though lust played a part too. Affection was the more dangerous reaction. "I bet I can guess why your temper blew, Tobias."

She looked around and saw that the room was empty; even the Dark Angel Prime had made an escape from their confrontation.

"Getting inside peoples' heads isn't that easy for me. And the thoughts I encountered were pretty resentful. I took the stress out on you."

He didn't find telepathy all that easy? Then why was it almost automatic for him to slip inside her mental shields?

"I was going to say you were feeling guilty for picking on perfectly nice people."

"No one is perfectly nice."

"Don't you have people to do interrogations for you?"

"I do," he said. "I brought in Sid Wolfe because she's such a fine telepath. But she's not here and this needs to be done right now."

"May I make a suggestion?"

She was used to giving orders and making pronouncements to Primes, but she already knew who gave the orders with this Prime.

He lifted an eyebrow inquiringly.

"Why don't you ask Anthony Crowe to help with the telepathic interviews? He knows these people, and they know him. It will cut down on the resentment factor. Besides, it might be a good idea to keep him distracted while I'm talking to his lady."

He gave her a smile that sent sparks zinging through her. He pulled her closer.

"What a good idea," he said. "I'm going to kiss you for that."

His mouth covered hers before she had a chance to protest. Then she didn't want to protest and her lips clung to his with all the hunger and longing she couldn't deny. Some logical part of her tried to point out that she'd made love to Strahan not two hours before. Need drowned that voice out. She could never get enough of this Prime, never be satiated.

# Chapter Thirty

They started out kissing and ended up grappling on the floor, their hands all over each other. Again.

He needed this, needed the taste of her. The feel of her fitting against him was perfection. The heat of her flesh warming his made him whole. The stimulus that came from their fangs pressing against each others' lips—needle points almost but not quite pricking extremely tender skin—drove him crazy.

The touch of her mind was the sexiest thing about her—open and waiting, willing, wanting to touch thought to thought. She was eager to share all the lust that—

*No!*

Necessity took control of him.

*Not again. Not now!*

His rejection flashed through both of them, hurt both of them. She flinched as he pushed himself away from her. The pain that flashed through her was more than he could bear. He reached for her, but Francesca sprang to her feet. He caught her before she could run away.

"I swear to the goddess it's not you," he told her. "I want you and I'll have you."

She struggled to break his hold. "But you have to be in control."

"Yes. I have to be in control of myself."

She cupped his face in her hands, no longer fighting him. "That wasn't a complaint, Tobias."

He was so surprised at what Francesca said, all he could do was stare, mouth open.

"You're in the middle of running an op," she said. "Your attention needs to be on the job or people could be killed. I get it. I agree. There are things more important than sex, even for vampires."

She kissed him before he could close his mouth. A gentle kiss. The taste of her was sweet, comforting, promising. They stepped away from each other after a few seconds, letting the kiss be enough.

*I hurt you before,* he thought. *I'm sorry.*

*I only felt rejected for a moment. Then I understood you weren't abandoning me. I'm vain, but I can get past it.*

*Apology accepted, then? Please?*

Her amusement sparkled through him. *Accepted. For that.*

*You are so wonder—*

"By the way, what did my mother offer you to get me pregnant?"

The matter-of-fact question hit him in the gut.

Tobias stepped back and studied Francesca carefully. She looked at him steadily. For once, he didn't have a clue what her mood was, what she was thinking. This was a hell of a poker player he was facing, a female who would be a queen. How he answered her was going to be very important if he wanted to keep her.

Being bonded was far more complicated than merely being in love. He knew he was treading on eggshells even as he decided on telling her the truth.

"Matri Anjelica threatened to destroy the Dark Angels if I didn't agree to sire your child."

"That sounds like her."

He couldn't offer her an apology for the bargain he'd made with Anjelica. He did what he had to do for the Dark Angels without regrets. He certainly didn't regret making love to Francesca.

He still couldn't tell what she was thinking. "You've known all along?"

A faint smile flashed across her features. "It was easy to guess what she was up to when she asked you to come to the clinic with us. We've been playing this game for years; it was time for her to start another round."

"Game?"

"It's been one game after another between us."

"I get the feeling you don't have a good relationship with your mother."

"I don't have a good relationship with my Matri. There are some decisions about her heir that I can't forgive my Matri for. It's a pity my Matri is also my mother."

"She does what's best for the Clan, but you know that already," he added at Francesca's cynical grimace.

"She used you," she told him. "Of course, so did I."

"Really?" he asked. "How? As a sex toy?"

She ran her gaze over him so hotly, he almost blushed. "You started the seduction, Tobias. As you were commanded to do."

"I wanted you."

She shrugged. "I'm so unimpressed by being wanted. So bored with it."

"Oh, you poor thing."

"I know I'm jaded, but I'm not bored with you," she added. "My mother sensed I wouldn't be. She knew I'd want you as much as you want me. I thought I could avoid falling for her trap because I knew it was there. And I wanted the chance to play at being a Dark Angel for a while."

"One of the reasons I went along with Lady Anjelica's plan was because I had my own plans for you."

"So we all used each other."

"I'm not upset about that. Are you?"

She shook her head. "We're all grown-ups. We thought we knew what we were doing. Only it turns out that instinctual mating drive thing is very real."

He was caught off guard by her bitter attitude. "You don't want to believe in bonding?"

"Who would? It takes our freedom of choice away from us, doesn't it?"

"But bondmates are perfect for each other."

"That's what all the boys believe."

"I thought the Clans made a cult out of the search for bondmates."

"Yeah, it's part of the chivalry games Primes play. We females aren't allowed to be all that romantic. We're encouraged to have children with several Primes before bonding. And if we never find a bondmate, that's even better."

"The continuation of the species rests with you."

She held up a hand. "Please! I've heard that speech daily since I hit puberty. Try walking around in a female's sling-back stiletto pumps for a few days, and you wouldn't find that call to reproductive duty so easy to swallow."

"I'd also have terrible blisters."

"Wimp."

Tobias nodded in concession, but they'd wasted too much time on personal matters. They'd deal with this, all right, but not now.

"We should go." He took her by the arm to lead her out of the room. "It's time you had that talk with Rose Cameron for me."

She tried to give him a casual smile, but he sensed a deep, resigned sadness behind it. "Yes," she agreed. "Let's get this over with. You can brief me on what exactly I'm supposed to ask this woman on the way."

# Chapter Thirty-one

"So, are you coming?" Saffie's roommate asked.

No, she was going. Why was she suddenly so sad about the decision? *It's only a few days until the holiday break and I've been asked—*

*Don't think before you jump. Plan. Prepare. Do it.*

Saffie stopped staring at the whiteout snowstorm outside the bedroom window long enough to say to her suitemate, Ayslyn, "I'm not feeling very well. Maybe I'll come later."

The event was the annual school Christmas Tea, given by the students for the faculty. Everyone dressed and acted like a lady, down to wearing a hat and white gloves. It was kind of fun, really, in a costume-party sort of way. It was so not part of the world where she belonged.

*Nice try at making me normal, Dad,* she thought. *Not compatible with human DNA.*

Saffie's hands bunched into fists as those words rolled over and over through her head. What was she, then? Did her father know? Had he lied to her all her life? She found that so hard to believe. She hadn't been able to bring herself to ask him. She had to see him face-to-face for that.

*Not compatible with human DNA.*

"You don't look good," Ayslyn said.

Saffie let her shoulders droop and sighed. "Flu, maybe?"

"You're awful pale. Do you want me to walk with you to the infirmary?"

Saffie held up a hand. "What if I'm contagious? You go on to the party. If I'm not here when you get back it'll mean I've been quarantined."

There had been an outbreak of H1N1 early in the term and everyone was nervous about it happening again.

Ayslyn's eyes grew wide. "I'm out of here. Don't touch anything," she called as she closed the door. "I am not getting stuck here over Christmas break because of the flu."

Saffie grinned at the closed door. Her suitemate had unknowingly helped in slowing down the inevitable search for her. She posted the excuse that she'd decided to head home early to make sure she didn't infect anyone else on Ayslyn's Facebook wall and sent it to her as an e-mail for good measure.

"I suppose leaving a note on her bed would be a bit of overkill," Saffie said as she began looking through her closet.

*Stupid snowstorm.*

Not that it didn't have its uses. The whiteout would mess up the security cameras and cover her footprints within minutes. But it was cold and nasty out there. Saffie considered stealing a school car but decided it would be more trouble than it was worth. She'd have to get the car through the gate, which would require messing with the security system. And all the cars were equipped with theft recovery devices. Better just to sneak past the dogs and climb the wall.

But she didn't have to like it.

Once she had a pack filled with the few absolutely necessary items she couldn't leave behind, Saffie checked her phone one last time. No sips, no texts, no voice mails. She swore in frustration, turned off the device, and tucked it into an inside pocket of her coat. She was on her own now and she could take care of herself.

But why'd it have to be snowing so hard?

*        *        *

Nothing about this day had gone easily, and Gregor was seriously considering killing something to make himself feel better. He despised being given an assignment that had nothing to do with the Master's real business. It was a waste of time, energy, and the valuable resource that was himself. Worst of all, it appeared to be merely a regression into the Tribes' old, fatal feuding ways. It made it hard for Gregor to believe the Master was really the one in control of the intricate long-term plan to take over the world. Was he working for the wrong player?

*Mine is not to reason why,* he told himself with a cynical smile.

He'd been told to fetch the girl, and fetch her he would. Although he regretted that he'd insisted the private jet pilot land on the icy runway of the small Cageville airport. No one had died, but the skid into a hangar was going to attract media attention he would have to elude. He had planned to kidnap the girl and fly away with her. Now something more inconvenient would have to suffice.

He was currently driving a stolen SUV at a crawl along a narrow lakeside road that was drifting over in the blizzard. The windshield wipers were fighting a losing battle against the heavy, wind-driven snow. He could see in the dark, but what he saw in the dark was a whole lot of white.

*Why couldn't the school be somewhere warm and easily accessible?* A week before he never would have had to take weather into account in carrying out his orders.

It was a good thing he could see in the dark when he spotted the figure in the center of the road trudging toward the vehicle.

The brakes didn't want to stop the car. The wheel whirled in his hands and the big SUV slid sideways and spun once around as it continued to move forward. Gregor caught a glimpse of a young mortal wearing a sky blue coat. The person looked out of a fur-trimmed hood with huge dark eyes but didn't try to move out of the way.

The vehicle came to a stop sideways on the road; the driver's-side window was inches away from the girl. Gregor put the window down to get a clearer look.

"Nice save," the girl said. "Did my dad send you?"

"I was sent," he answered. "You are Saffron?"

She grinned and nodded. He unlocked the car doors. She clambered over rising snow and into the passenger's side, sighing with pleasure when she settled into the heated seat.

"I knew Dad wouldn't let me down," she said.

"Who are you? Clan or Family? How long have you been with the Crew?"

Gregor put the vehicle in gear and slowly turned it back the way he'd come. Having the victim cooperate with an abduction was a first and the best thing that had happened to him all day.

"Call me Uncle Greg," he told her. "And be quiet while I drive so I can concentrate on the road."

# Chapter Thirty-two

With Tobias standing close behind her, Francesca leaned forward and put her ear to Rose's door. "It's quiet in there," she reported in a whisper after a moment.

Tobias put a hand on her shoulder. "There are three vampires in the vicinity," he whispered back. "We're all aware of each other."

She turned her head to look at him. Amusement lit his dark eyes. "Yes, but physical eavesdropping is more polite than telepathy."

He nodded. "But less fun."

Francesca could not stop her giggle. He began to laugh.

The door opened, and Anthony Crowe said,

"What is the matter with you two? We're trying to sleep in here."

"It's late afternoon," Tobias said. "Time for you to come out and make yourself useful, Tony."

Tony glanced back into the room. He blew a kiss to the woman inside. A faint laugh drifted back. "I'm busy, son."

Tobias's hand stroked sensuously down Francesca's arm. She almost blew him a kiss. *Damned bonding.*

"My lady and I would like to be busy in a similar manner, Tony, but duty calls."

"There are plenty of empty rooms in the clinic if you want to take some time off, Tobias."

"It's the clinic I need your help with, Tony. You are the security chief around here?"

"I'm on vacation," Tony said.

Francesca didn't like the escalating energy bouncing between the two Primes. They sounded friendly for now, but she sensed that aggression could flare at any moment. At least with each of them immersed in the bonding pattern for his own female, they weren't likely to get into a nasty fight. Or so she hoped, because she was standing right between the two dangerous males. There were good reasons that the females ruled the Clans and Families. Somebody had to be able to keep their head when psychic energy and pheromones started bouncing around among their kind.

"Excuse me," she said to Crowe. "May I have a word?"

Always the perfect gentleman, Tony Crowe switched his complete concentration to her. "Forgive me, Lady Francesca. What can I do for you?"

Only now that she had Tony's attention did she notice what he was wearing. "Why are you in a pink bathrobe?"

This time the feminine laugh from the room was more raucous.

"It's a long story, Lady Francesca."

"I'd love to hear it. May I come in?"

She stepped closer, but Tony didn't budge from blocking the doorway. "Rose really does need her rest, Lady, and—"

"Let the girl in, Anthony," Rose Cameron called. "I wouldn't mind having some company."

He gave Rose a crestfallen look. "But you have me."

"And I will love you forever—because you are a gallant gentleman," the woman added pointedly.

At this, Tony stepped out of her way and gestured for Francesca to enter. "Stay where you are," he told Tobias, and closed the door in Strahan's face.

Unlike the high-security rooms in the clinic,

which were set up for violent and dangerously sick vampires, this was more of a guest room. The walls were a pale blue, and the furniture was of light wood. There was a floral rug by the double bed and there were pictures on the walls. A sliding glass door opened onto a small patio, with a view of the clinic's grounds beyond. A huge vase of red roses on a chest brought vibrant color and scent to the room. Francesca instantly thought of it as a honeymoon suite, and almost as instantly wondered what it would be like to have time alone with Tobias in a room like this.

*Focus,* she told herself.

"The Dark Angels really could use your help," Francesca told Tony before she turned to Rose. "And so could the clinic staff."

"Fine," he grumbled. He couldn't resist a female's request. He grabbed up some clothes off a chair and left the room.

"There's always a lot of coming and going around here," Rose Cameron said, and Francesca finally turned toward where the mortal woman sat on the edge of the bed, a sheet decorously wrapped around her body. "Welcome. Flare, isn't it? I saw you during all the commotion yesterday. How's your friend Sid doing?"

"Fine. She's werewolf hunting at the moment." Francesca stared intently at the mortal, feeling that she'd somehow walked back into the past.

Francesca had seen Rose during the meeting at the Shagal Citadel, but only now did the identity of this red-haired, freckled, beautiful young woman finally sink in. "You really *are* Rose Cameron."

Rose gave a smile made famous in many old films. "You're a vampire. I'm only a movie star. Which one of us should be more surprised about the other?"

"But you're—"

"Old. Yes, I know. I suppose that's what you're here to talk to me about." She pointed to a chair near the bed.

The woman seemed calm yet radiated nervousness.

"I'm sorry," Francesca said as she sat. "Talking about what happened to you will be painful for you, I know, but I've been asked to find out what you recall about the people who experimented on you."

Rose flinched. "I've already told Anthony everything I know."

"That's very good, but what about the things you remember rather than know?"

Rose looked confused for a moment, then Francesca's meaning sank in.

"I've told Anthony about the last few days, when I knew I was being experimented on, but this has been going on for a long time—at least a year." She shook her head. "I have been so screwed with."

"You have," Francesca said in agreement. "But why you?"

"That one I know. Gregor explained that I was chosen because of my connection with Anthony. My blood was already somewhat changed, and I think they knew Anthony would someday taste me again. They used that as a catalyst. And we turned out to be a pair of romantic fools who did exactly what Gregor thought we'd do."

The woman's tone spoke volumes about this Gregor.

"Gregor's a Tribe Prime?"

"Oh, yes. He took a great deal of pleasure in telling me that. He told me all about the Tribes' evil experiments on me with all the relish of a bad movie villain. Anthony and I think—but you want me to start at the beginning, don't you?"

Francesca leaned forward in her chair. "I could telepathically—"

"Hell, no!" Rose scuttled away to the end of the bed, radiating anger and fear. "Nobody but Anthony gets inside my head. I've been mind-wiped by that bastard Gregor a few times, and it isn't happening again."

Francesca was furious on the woman's behalf.

"I do not like this Gregor." She folded her hands in her lap and tried to look as harmless as she was sympathetic. "Just talk about what happened to you, Rose. You never know what will be a useful detail for tracking these monsters down."

Rose looked out the patio door. "It's only the middle of the afternoon, but it's already getting dark. I hate how the sun goes down so early in December, don't you? No, you wouldn't mind, since you're a vampire. Anthony and I met in December—a long time ago." Rose looked back at Francesca. "Maybe not so long ago for your people, but a lifetime for me. Now I'm trying to fight the urge to be grateful to the ones who used me as a guinea pig in a rejuvenation experiment because they've given me back time. It looks like we're going to have the happily-ever-after Anthony's Matri denied us after the war.

"You know exactly what I'm talking about," Rose said, noticing some small reaction from Francesca. She moved closer and put her hand on Francesca's clenched fist. "Your Matri's giving you grief about something too, isn't she? Is it something to do with that Prime Anthony wouldn't let in?"

"No—and yes." Francesca looked away until she had the urge to spill her guts to this mortal woman under control. Rose looked young, but her air of experience reminded Francesca that Rose was well into her eighties. Rose also had the kind of presence that invited confidences.

"Let's get back to you," Francesca said to Rose.

"Anthony and I were lovers long enough for a bond to begin forming. I returned to the States in early 1945 and waited for him to come home from the war. I didn't see him again until a few days ago. Oh, we kept track of each other, secretly, but never met face-to-face.

"Eventually I moved into a retirement facility. I was still fairly healthy when I moved in and I enjoyed the place for the first couple of years. Then the management changed, and soon after the new guy took over I began to get ill. Except I wasn't sick: they were feeding me drugs to alter the chemicals in my blood, to bring out whatever it is that keeps vampires from aging. It hurt like hell," she added. "The pain got worse and worse for nearly a year. All because somehow the bad guys found out about Anthony and me and tried to ruin everything we shared for what was in my blood."

"Bondmates shouldn't be separated," Francesca said, knowing it was hypocrisy because she planned on leaving Tobias before things between them could get any worse.

Better.

More complicated, at least.

Rose gave her a worried look. "Anthony and I loved each other our entire lives and look what happened when we weren't allowed to be together."

"Your bitterness is understandable."

Rose touched Francesca's hand again. "Don't let that happen to you."

"I won't."

Francesca realized how sentimental this moment was and concentrated on the job. Besides, she'd been bitter for a long time; it was scary to be getting over it now. Disappointment was easier to live with than hope.

"Gregor gave you drugs for a year?" Francesca asked.

"Well, he wasn't the only one involved, was he? I think the entire staff at the home was involved—complicit, at least."

"Do you think they might have been telepathically tampered with?"

"I know I was. When I recognized that Gregor was a Prime, he told me that I'd realized it before and he'd made me forget. And he wasn't the only Prime in the place. Gregor told me he was leaving California, but that doesn't mean that the other one—"

"Other one?" This had to be important. "Who was he? What do you remember about him?"

Rose sneered. "Big blond guy. Called himself Dr. Stone. Gregor thought he was an arrogant idiot." She scratched her head. "Where did that memory come from?"

"What else?" Francesca said urgently.

"Dr. Stone was in charge of the staff. He—No, wait, I have an idea." Rose got off the bed, adjusted her sheet, and went to throw open the bedroom door. "Anthony, could you come back in here, please?" she called psychically and vocally.

# Chapter Thirty-three

"Why can't you leave Rose alone?" Tony Crowe's question came out muffled as he pulled a black T-shirt over his head. He glared at Tobias when his head emerged. "She's been through enough."

"She has," Tobias said in agreement. He waited until Crowe had finished dressing before he went on. "I'm trying to prevent the torture happening to her again—and to anyone else."

Crowe's eyes blazed with fury. Protectiveness radiated from him. "What do you mean 'again'? Gregor told her she'd served her purpose."

"And you believe him?"

Crowe considered that for a moment. "The

bastard laid out a whole scenario to Rose. Maybe some of it—maybe all of it—was to cover his own ass in case she was rescued."

"Do you think it's over because you rescued her?" Tobias asked. "This Gregor might even have thought he was telling the truth, but I don't buy it. She was a valuable experiment to them. They'll try to get her back."

"We took out everyone in the place where they were holding her prisoner."

"But more of the enemy is still out there."

Crowe gave a grim nod. "I don't want to think about it, but you're right." Once Crowe finished dressing, he and Tobias walked back down the hallway. "Where are we going?"

"Your office."

"Why?"

"It'll be more official if you call people in there."

"Who am I calling into my office? Do you really need me for anything?" Crowe asked him. "Or is this a diversion for Rose's sake? A diversion so Flare can question my Rose, I should say. Thanks for using her instead of my Sid," he added.

"I knew you wouldn't let me or any other Prime talk to her, and it needs to be done."

"I'll kill anyone, including Flare, if they mess with my woman's head."

"Ah, but if you felt the need to harm Francesca I would feel compelled to rip your head off," Tobias answered.

Both Primes knew that the other wasn't joking.

Crowe chuckled. "And you wouldn't be doing it to keep a gentle female from harm."

"She's not gentle, and I'm not a Clan boy," Tobias pointed out.

"It's better to leave chivalry to the professionals," the Clan Prime said in agreement. Crowe gave Tobias a speculative look, and Tobias knew what was coming. "You and Flare are bonding, eh? Who'd have thought it?"

"Her mother," Tobias growled.

"You're glowing with bonding energy, son. That can't be good for your concentration."

Tobias eagerly grabbed at the opening. "That's one of the reasons I need your help interviewing all mortals on the staff. One of them planted a bomb in Francesca's purse two days ago and she unknowingly brought it into the Citadel. She could have been killed." The thought of it made his blood run cold. He would have the one who'd done it.

Crowe came to an abrupt halt. "Someone

planted a bomb on Flare? Here at the clinic?"

"Someone set a bomb *at* the clinic that went off," Tobias reminded him. "There's a conspiracy to open up our world to the outside. You know what will happen when that happens."

"Yeah. You believe there's a spy at the clinic."

"A traitor."

"Not among my people," Crowe said. "I don't like it that you want me to telepathically interrogate everyone who works here for you."

"I'm not asking you to be happy about it, Crowe, but it needs to be done."

Crowe was furious. "I've already vetted everyone who works here. If they want the job they have to let me into their heads. Our people are all loyal."

"People change. Have you gotten into anyone's head lately?"

"Anthony, could you come back in here, please?"

Speaking of getting into anyone's head, they heard Rose Cameron's voice telepathically as well as faintly audibly from down the hall.

"She's getting better at communicating," Crowe said with pride and relief. He headed back toward Rose's room.

*You better come too.* This time the telepathic voice was Francesca's.

*I hear and obey.* He followed Crowe.

\* \* \*

Rose had put on a silk broomstick skirt and tunic and now sat on a chair in the middle of the room, the center of attention. She seemed to be the most relaxed person in the room, but she had been an actress for a long time. She was used to audiences.

Anthony Crowe stood behind Rose, his hands protectively on her shoulders. Francesca sat beside Tobias on the bed. They watched the other couple, and Francesca noticed when her fingers twined with Tobias's.

She sighed but made no effort to pull away. This touch was only a small comfort, as much for him as for her.

*If we give in to the little things . . . ,* Tobias thought.

*Yeah, yeah,* she thought back. *Just put your arm around me and shut up.*

He chuckled and pulled her closer as they kept their gazes on Rose and Tony.

"Go ahead," Rose said to her Prime. "This will work."

The plan was for Tony to tap into a moment Rose faintly recalled and bring out the details. He would touch Rose's memories, keeping the mind touch between them, and then he would broadcast what he learned to Tobias.

Frankly, this seemed a little complicated to Francesca and she wasn't sure it would work. But she thought, *I understand Rose's hesitation to—*

"*Can we take her now?*"

"*I'm not sure she's out yet.*"

She couldn't open her eyes, but she heard Gregor's voice, though it seemed a mile away.

"*What difference does that make? You've always been too gentle with her, but she's all mine now.*"

That was Stone. She hadn't seen him for a long time. Couldn't see him now but the memory of his face flashed through her mind. She'd never liked his smile; it was too much like a sneer. There was something snaky about his pale eyes. Like a reptile looking out of a human suit. A reptile with a drug problem, at that.

"*Not yet, she isn't,*" said Gregor. "*I'm taking her to the safe house. You have your own assignments.*"

"*It's my op. Everything and everyone is in place. The Clan bastards will be howling in outrage by this time tomorrow.*"

"*As long as your diversions cover moving our operations the Masters will be satisfied.*"

"*The Masters will be overjoyed!*"

"*Have you set this place on fire yet?*"

"Don't tell me my job. You've been in my territory too long already, Minotaur."

They kept talking, forgetting about her as they stood on either side of where she lay.

Or were those words? Maybe it was rain. Soothing, soft rain. Everything was so soft.

Dark.

# Chapter Thirty-four

"It worked, didn't it?"

"Oh, yeah, Rosie, my love. A lot better than I thought it would—from the totally stunned looks of those two, they joined us all the way."

"It occurs to me that I am not Rose Cameron."

The voice was deep and masculine and came from very close to Francesca. She was leaning into the side of a hard body and the warmth of it was pleasant and comforting after being so alone and lost in the dark. She sighed as she snuggled closer. And it began to occur to her that she wasn't Rose Cameron, either.

Francesca opened her eyes and saw Rose and Anthony looking at her and Tobias.

"That was . . . different," Tobias said.

"But it worked," Anthony answered.

Francesca took a moment to straighten out what had happened, what she'd seen and felt of Rose Cameron's memories, and firmly reminded herself of who and what she was.

"That was different," she said. "We were all there with—as—Rose. We heard what she heard."

"More importantly, we experienced her memories of Stone," Tobias said.

"I've never felt telepathy used like that before," Francesca said.

"I've never tried anything like that before," Crowe said. He rubbed his temples, then massaged Rose's. "Are you all right, love?"

"Can you imagine what the entertainment industry could do with something like that?" Rose asked.

"No," all three vampires said at once.

Rose gave them all a disgruntled look, then she shrugged. "Come to think of it, we wouldn't need actors if people could just be plugged in to story lines. Was anything you picked up from me helpful?" she asked.

"Yes," Crowe and Tobias answered.

"I picked up a major hatred for those two Tribe boys," Francesca told her. Not that disliking Primes had ever been hard for her, but what Francesca felt for all Clan and Family boys was love compared to her feelings about the arrogant evil of their Tribe cousins.

"Sounds like Gregor's a Minotaur," Tony said. "I didn't think there were any of that Tribe left."

"There're one or two who are still renegade," Tobias said.

Francesca noted the tenseness of the exchange and that Tobias's expression was blank when she looked at him. The emotions pulsing from him were anything but blank. They were some confusing combination of sadness, wistfulness, and anger. Regret?

"You were born into Tribe Minotaur?" Francesca asked.

*We'll talk about me later.*

Francesca nodded in answer to his thought, but she wasn't sure his feelings had anything to do with himself. How many secrets did Tobias have?

"I recognize Stone," Tobias said. "He's one of the unaccounted for Tribe Primes we have a file on. He hasn't been spotted for a couple of years."

"Well, now he's accounted for," Anthony said.

"We'll track him down soon enough. I'm sure you'll want to be there, Anthony."

"Wouldn't miss it for the world."

Tobias stood and tugged Francesca up with him. He nodded to Rose. "Thank you for your

help, Lady Rose. I could still use yours," he said
to Crowe.

"Go chase vampires and leave me alone with
my—"

"Oh, go on, Anthony," Rose said. "You know
you'll feel guilty about not doing your duty if you
spend every waking minute with me."

"Yes, go on," Francesca said as she slipped
away from Tobias. She smiled sweetly at the
Primes. "Let us girls entertain each other for a
while. In fact, why don't you and I go shopping,
Rose?"

Tobias and Crowe stared in astonishment.

"I don't have a thing to wear," she added.

"Are you out of your spoiled-brat little mind,
Flare Reynard?" Tobias demanded. "There are
people out there who want to kill—"

"We're supposed to be going about our normal lives, aren't we?" she reminded him. "Wasn't
that your idea? To let the Dark Angels hunt the
bad guys while we go about our daily lives and
pretend there's nothing wrong? Everyone knows
that most of my life is devoted to shopping. And
you have to be dying for a wardrobe update, don't
you, Rose?"

Rose was smiling and gave an understanding nod, while Crowe stood next to her, looking

aghast. "I think getting out of here would be a lovely idea." She added, "I will not spend my life imprisoned, even by you, Anthony."

He said, "But—"

"I used to go to a place off of Melrose that specializes in vintage clothing," Rose said. "I don't know if it's still there. I've been wearing granny gowns for a few years now."

"If you're thinking of Orion's Belt, it's still there," Francesca said. "I'll borrow a car and we can get out of the way for a few hours. I think we should ask Kea and Chiana to come along. Kea's pissed off and Chiana's stressed out. They could use some time off."

Tobias moved to stand in front of the door. He was a big guy and used his size to loom dangerously in the way. He gave them a weapons-grade glare. "I will not have anyone under my protection putting themselves in danger. Am I understood?"

"I'm with him," Anthony said.

Rose put her hand over her mouth and giggled. She shared an amused look with Francesca. "Is it the bonding that's making them slow, do you think? I'm sure your young man is normally quicker on the uptake than right now. Anthony is usually very clever."

"*Diversion*," Francesca finally told Tobias. "Honestly, I thought you were supposed to be a military genius." She stepped close to him and grabbed the front of his black silk shirt. "I am spoiled. I am a brat. I am an adder-tongued bitch. But my name is *not* Flare!"

He gave her a considering look. "Diversion."

"Bait in a trap," she said. "You've turned this place into a fortress. Time to take the battle to them."

"I know."

"I don't know if they'll be stupid enough to fall for it, but getting their experimental subject and bagging a vampire female has got to be very tempting to the bad guys."

"It won't be safe."

"I'm a vampire," she said. "I don't want to be safe."

He smiled, sharp as a blade. "You're going to get me in trouble."

"Of course I am. Can you handle it?"

He gave the slightest of dismissing shrugs and eased her hands away from his chest. He didn't let go of her, and his hands were so very big and warm and hard holding hers. They looked into each other's eyes for a few seconds.

Finally, Tobias said, "Rose is mortal."

"I won't put Rose in harm's way," Crowe announced.

"I'm old enough to make my own decisions,"

Rose informed her bondmate. "You had me cause a diversion once before, Anthony. Do you remember?"

"That was different!"

Rose looked past her bondmate to Francesca and Tobias. "He told me to distract the crew of a German tank long enough for him to get inside it. It worked." She smiled sweetly at Crowe. "Being part of this won't be anywhere near as dangerous as what we faced in the Battle of the Bulge." She took his hands in hers. "And this time I promise not to flash my titties at anyone."

# Chapter Thirty-five

"I knew I should trust my instincts when I got up this morning. This tingling feeling all over told me this was going to be a bad day," Saffron said.

"Panic attack."

"That's what Dad said. It wasn't *just* a panic attack, but Dad doesn't always get that I have intuition because I'm mortal. Or at least he thinks I am. For a while after I found out the bad news I was pissed at him; I thought he must know all about what my DNA showed."

"Which is?"

"That my paternal DNA isn't human. Weren't you briefed on this?"

"My instructions were to fetch you; I was not told why."

"Typical. But being pissed at him was the real panic attack part because he has never lied to me about anything. Ever."

"Are you sure?" Gregor asked.

He'd told her not to talk, and she had been quiet for a while. For over an hour there had only been the growl of the engine, the howl of wind, the heavy slap of the windshield wipers, and his occasional swearing as invisible ice patches tried to run the SUV off the road.

The big engine and four-wheel-drive transmission were willing, but the snow piling up made it harder and harder to drive this rural, infrequently traveled road. Maybe the locals were too smart to venture out in such bad weather.

At some point she'd brought out a cell phone. She'd ignored his, "Don't."

But she had discovered that the battery was low. He refused to let her plug it into the dashboard outlet, telling her they needed all the power for driving. The girl had settled back in her seat with an annoyed sigh, stared ahead, and crossed her arms.

Then she'd started talking.

He'd tried to ignore her, tried to block her voice out, considered throttling her. Then he realized what a fount of information she was about Strahan's organization.

"You're not questioning Tobias, are you?" she asked protectively. "Has he ever lied to you?"

The girl was upset, chattering because of it, and dying to find an outlet for all her tension. She was wearing pink gloves on her tightly coiled fists.

"Tobias Strahan has never lied to me," he told her.

She reluctantly relaxed.

"Disappointed that I won't argue with you?" he asked.

"You sound like Dad."

"Really? We aren't that close."

"You're new to the Crew, right? I don't recognize you, Greg."

"You recognized that I am Prime the moment you saw me. How did a mortal girl manage that?"

The girl laughed. "I've been around Primes all my life."

*Making her trusting of all Primes? Tobias should have trained her better than that.*

"You didn't answer me," she said. "How long have you been with us? I don't remember the name Greg in our database."

"Not everyone shows up in the official records."

She was impressed. "Dad sent one of the black ops guys to pick me up?"

He fought down the urge to smile at her

sudden look of hero worship. "I was in the area."

"Where are we heading?" she asked.

"New York."

"Dad doesn't want me in Los Angeles?"

"The op there is still hot."

"If he thinks I'm going off to London with my friend's family after what I found out today, he's crazy."

"You're not going to London."

Saffron accepted this information with a satisfied nod. She even settled back in her seat to watch the headlights forming a tunnel in the driving snow.

After a few minutes of silence, Gregor asked, "Who's Dragomir?"

"A Tribe Prime," she answered. "Harpy Tribe, I think."

Gregor hadn't expected her to recognize the name any more than he had when the Master mentioned Dragomir. Not only hadn't the mortal girl not shown any surprise at the question, she gave him the information as if she was used to being quizzed about all sorts of esoteric facts. *What an odd education the Dark Angels are providing this mortal mascot of theirs.*

"You *think* Dragomir's a Harpy?" he asked.

"You don't have to be sarcastic," she answered. "Harpies have been hiring out as mercenaries, but their master Dragomir's one of the Primes who have dropped out of sight since the Bosnian raids."

"So he is," Gregor answered.

He knew about the Dark Angels tearing apart a Tribe alliance with the Eastern European underworld, but he wasn't as up on the details as Saffron, and he should have been.

He didn't show how frustrated he was that this kid was crammed full of information he lacked. Knowledge was power; knowledge could save your life or get you killed.

Saffron was a pawn in some game the Master had decided to play, but Gregor recognized how valuable she would be because of all she knew. The Master wouldn't appreciate her except as an adolescent sex toy. Gregor gripped the steering wheel tighter, furious at what insane bastards Tribe Primes were. Saffron was no pawn as far as he was concerned.

"Tell me more about Dragomir," he said. When she gave him a puzzled look, Gregor added, "I need you to help keep me awake while I drive through this shit."

"Dad wouldn't like you swearing around me."

Gregor smirked. "I beg your pardon, Lady Saffron. Dragomir?"

"Why is everything always homework?" she

complained. "Dragomir is suspected to have had ties to some mortal terrorist groups in the nineties. But taking sides in politics turned out not to be profitable and he dropped that hobby. His Tribe is probably still involved with dealing arms to any mortal groups that want to fight each other."

"Probably?"

"The Tribes have started making much better use of mortal front people than in the old days. It's getting harder to follow their movements." She gave him a curious look.

"Very good," Gregor said, praising her. "I think I'll keep you around."

"Thanks. What's that up ahead?"

"That" was the whirling red lights atop a police vehicle parked sideways across the narrow road. They were almost to the nearest town with an entrance to a main highway, and now this.

Gregor considered barreling through the roadblock, but that wasn't the sort of thing a Dark Angel would do. Besides, with the road so slippery there was no telling what could happen.

As it was, Gregor was barely able to stop the SUV before he hit the other vehicle.

An officer dressed in a heavy quilted coat got out and approached through the storm. Gregor reluctantly lowered his window, letting in the biting cold.

"Yes, officer?" Gregor asked, speaking loudly over the wind. He prepared to catch the cop's gaze to manipulate his thoughts as necessary.

He turned out to be a she. "All the roads are closed," she shouted back. "You'll have to remain in the area."

"But we have a plane to catch," Gregor said in protest. "We're trying to get home for the holidays."

"Not tonight, sir. The blizzard has the whole state closed down, including the airports."

"I was planning on taking a train," Saffron muttered beside him.

"The roads are closed," the police officer repeated. "Power's out too. But the motels by the interchange outside of town are taking people in. Follow me, I'll take you to the turnoff."

Gregor watched the cop make her way back to her vehicle. He only remembered to put the window back up when he heard Saffron's teeth begin to chatter. The weather wasn't fit for mortals to be out in, that was certain.

"What are we going to do?" Saffron asked.

"We're following the officer to the nearest motel," he answered.

"But—how am I going to tell my dad where I am if the power's out?" There was a trace of panic in the girl's tone.

"Don't worry." He touched his temple. "Remember that Uncle Greg's a telepath."

He took his foot off the brake and eased the SUV forward, following the flashing red lights of the cop car down the dangerous road.

# Chapter Thirty-six

*This is a bad idea.*

*You're only thinking that because it's not your idea, Commander Control Junkie,* Francesca replied.

*I did think of it, princess mine, and I knew it was bad. Necessary, but bad.*

Francesca smiled, sending the emotion of it through the connection between them. He was on guard outside the building. She was inside Orion's Belt with the other women from the clinic.

Then she consciously stopped paying complete attention to the presence of Tobias in her mind, built up the barriers that were trying to dissolve and make them one. She reminded herself that the connection was harder on Tobias's ability to remain rational than it was on hers.

Like every vampire, she'd been trained since she was a baby to wrap a barrier around her private self while still being aware of every other telepath around her. Bonding put a strain on that barrier, made it fade and blend.

She'd never been convinced bonding was a good thing, and now that she was experiencing it she still wasn't sure. Hormones and endorphins and orgasms and psychic highs made the victims crave it. Clan and Family vampires were convinced bonding was the pinnacle of all they were. Tribe vampires considered it a perverted evil and used perverted, evil practices to fight it. Francesca acknowledged the instinct was implacable and impossible to deny, but impossible to ignore? Maybe not.

Weren't Rose and Crowe's years of living apart evidence that it was possible to . . . cope?

"Are you all right?" Rose asked. "You seem distracted."

Rose had just stepped out of the dressing room in the back of the shop. She was wearing a sage-green cocktail sheath from the early sixties.

"I was thinking about you, actually," Francesca answered. "That suits you."

"It ought to; I used to own one just like it."

She ran a hand down the heavy matte silk of the bodice. "In fact, I think this might be mine." She smiled wistfully. "I keep reliving my past, apparently."

"Well, if you like your past, why not?"

Rose turned away from the full-length mirror she'd been gazing into. "I can see my past on TCM anytime. It's the future I'm looking forward to. Aren't you?" she added. "After all, that big Prime of yours is something else."

"That he is. But then, so am I."

"I thought it was Primes who were so . . ."

"*Arrogant* is the word you want, Rose. And no, vampire females are worse than the Primes." She chuckled. "We have to be considering the way the Primes are. Tobias is nicknamed the Über-Prime, by the way."

She heard the pride in her voice and tried to be at least a little annoyed with this reaction to Tobias.

Rose gave her an understanding smile. "How long have you been together?"

"Two days."

Francesca waited for shock, but the mortal laughed instead. "Maybe being in danger speeds up the bonding process," she said speculatively. "After all, people were shooting at us when Anthony and I met and our connection was . . . amazing."

Francesca asked quietly, "Do you mind if I ask a question about that connection?"

"Celibacy—that's how I handled it," Rose answered before Francesca could ask. "You were going to ask how I managed to live away from Anthony for so many years, weren't you?"

"Uh, yes."

"Why?" Rose gave her a sharply assessing look. "You aren't simply curious, are you? Why would you want to be separated from your bondmate?"

"There are lots of reasons, although the only one that counts is that I want to do what's best for Tobias—for the Dark Angels. For the defense of our people."

"That's very noble."

"It sounds that way, doesn't it? Noble enough to make one gag." Francesca's lips twisted into an ironic smile, which faded into a pained sigh. "I am so conflicted, Rose."

Rose touched her arm. "Please don't even think about doing what I did. It's a lonely life."

Francesca knew that well enough. She'd been celibate herself since Patrick's death—until Tobias came along. Now the spark of life he'd lit inside her threatened to flare up all the time.

*Flare.* She hated that word.

"Anthony didn't remain celibate," she said to Rose.

Francesca knew that he'd sired her best friend, Sidonie Wolfe, and he'd certainly hit on her, just like every other Prime, at Convocations. Of course, he was an old-school gentleman Prime who'd likely seen trying to seduce her as being polite.

"I know Anthony was with other women," Rose said. "He and I will probably have some discussions about that. But I suppose it's very difficult for Primes to go without."

"Probably impossible," Francesca said in agreement. Even the thought of Tobias with another female caused her to burn with jealousy.

Rose added to her distress when she said, "I always *suspected* when Anthony was making love to another woman, and it hurt like hell. You are far more telepathic than I'll ever be; you'd surely feel it deeper than I could."

These words cut so deeply into Francesca she had to turn sharply away from the mortal. When she did she almost tripped over their shopping companions.

"Sorry," she mumbled, and wondered how much they'd overheard.

Kea and Chiana had drifted through the racks of expensive old clothes to join them during this conversation and she hadn't been aware of them until now.

Telepathic suggestion had made certain that the four of them were the only ones here despite it being the height of the holiday shopping season. The clerks and cashier were taking an extended break in the back room.

Kea held up a strapless black dress. "Do you think Ali would like me in this?"

*Are you going to be much longer?* Tobias's thought intruded as Francesca began to answer Kea.

*You told me to take my time so everything and everyone could be in place.*

Chiana spoke up. "I'm thinking about buying a bathing suit."

Francesca and Kea looked at her in utter surprise.

"That is the strangest thing you have ever said," Kea told her friend.

"Why?" Rose asked.

"Because she's a selkie," Kea replied. "Why would a seal need a bathing suit?"

"I was joking," Chiana said.

Francesca didn't think the wereseal was capable of joking at the moment. Chiana was pale, thin, and nervous. She definitely needed more than an evening out with the girls for what was ailing her.

"It's that boyfriend of yours, isn't it?" Kea

asked Chiana. "He's put another crazy notion in your head."

"You have no idea," Chiana answered, her voice barely a whisper.

"I've been keeping my mouth shut, hon," Kea said. "But you have got to dump this guy. He bullies you. Things always have to be his way. We'd all like for interspecies dating to work, but both sides have to make compromises and he—"

"Interspecies dating?" Francesca asked.

"She's been living with a mortal for months now. I don't even think the guy knows she's a selkie."

"He knows," Chiana whispered.

Tobias's thought filled Francesca's mind before she could ask any more questions. *We're ready for your close-up now.*

It wasn't nerves that suddenly tightened Francesca's muscles, it was the anticipation of coming combat. She slid her tongue over her throbbing fangs.

These feelings were so wrong. She was going to get herself locked up in a tower someplace if she kept it up.

She could hardly wait to get into a fight. That was what Tobias Strahan did to her. It was going to bring the Matri Council's wrath down on him if she didn't remove herself from the dangerous life he lived. But in the meantime . . .

*Lordy, sir, but you do bring out the vampire in a girl,* she thought back at Tobias, and tried to transmit the image of her fluttering her eyelashes at him.

His laugh filled her with champagne sparkles. *Move it, and bring the ladies with you,* he thought.

## Chapter Thirty-seven

"They must know that this is a trap," Crowe said.

"But they're here anyway," Tobias answered. "And someone from the clinic called our visitors to this spot."

"I concede the point," Crowe said.

They were sitting by the window inside a coffee shop, cups in front of them, attention on the movements on the street outside. They watched all of it with eyes adapted for night vision.

"Why would anyone walk into a trap?" Tobias asked.

"Desperation," Crowe said.

"Precisely. Desperation, and dissension. I've got a feeling they've reached the point of trying to impress each other to mask the fact that they plan to betray each other. *They* meaning the mortal commanding the Purists and the vampire commanding the overall operation. They don't trust each other and are trying to prove that they do to each other."

Crowe took a sip of coffee. "None of that makes any sense, you know."

"Probably not," Tobias said. "Their hidden intentions aren't important; only what they're up to at this moment matters."

He finished his own coffee and turned his attention to the Angels strategically stationed in the area. He had a werecougar on a roof, a pair of vampires in a small park opposite the clothes shop, and a shifted werewolf curled at the feet of a fae sipping tea at a table outside the coffee shop. Other Crew members were in parked cars at either end of the block. The Dark Angels had waited patiently and let their prey drift into the area while telepathically shooing anyone not involved away from this part of the street.

He spoke into his headset. "What do we have?"

"Three mortal lifeglows in the alley behind me," the fae reported. "Side door to the store there."

"Truck engine idling behind the shop," another Angel reported.

"Primes inside the truck," the werewolf reported. "Can't tell how many." Vampires tended to fracture werewolves' psychic senses.

"Three Prime heartbeats in the truck," the werecougar said, filling in the information for the werewolf.

"I think they're running out of Primes," Tobias said.

"Let's help them get rid of some more," Crowe said.

"In a moment." He'd already given Francesca a telepathic heads-up; now he thought to her, *Move it, and bring the ladies with you.* He stood. "Places, ladies and gentlemen," he told his team. He left the coffee shop and crossed the street to the entrance of Orion's Belt.

Francesca brought the other females out of the shop. "Now what?" she asked him.

"Now you stay out of the way and let me work," he answered, and watched the explosion of temper flare in her green eyes. Fury made her even more beautiful.

Crowe shepherded the other women away while Francesca stood her ground in front of him, squarely blocking the entrance to the store.

"Oh, no you don't," she told him.

"That's the plan." He had several types of psychically gifted folk working to make the Purists and Primes believe the women were still inside. He had to get his people in while this window lasted.

"I can help," she said insistently.

"You already have. You aren't allowed to do any more."

"But—there are still mortals in there. I could get them out while you—"

"Already planned for. They won't get hurt."

"They better not."

He picked her up and set her aside, kissing her forehead while he did so. He managed to avoid her fangs when she snapped at him.

Ali, Ed, and Crowe went through the shop door. Tobias went in behind them.

"Fine!" Francesca called after him. "Just don't expect me to be here when you come out."

"Those boys did not bring their A game," Crowe commented as he came out of the store behind Tobias.

The Purists had rushed into the store first, to find the Crew waiting. They'd been taken prisoner, even the one who'd managed to slice Ali across the arm with a silver knife. Ali had been a bit testy about that, but at least his attacker was still breathing. The Primes had not been treated so gently. All that had been learned from the vampires was that they were Harpies, but that was no surprise.

"I think they're running out of players," Tobias answered.

"That means we're winning," Ed added.

As far as the attrition rate of the other side, Ed was right. But Tobias had a feeling . . .

The mortal women Francesca had been worried about were fine and were being escorted to their homes. Their memories were altered and all the damage to the shop would be taken care of before the women were allowed to return. The Dark Angels had the expertise of thousands of years of immortal-kind dwelling invisibly among mortal-kind to call upon in making it all seem normal.

Tobias looked up and down the street. Members of the Crew went about their assignments. All was as it should be in his world, except he already knew Francesca wasn't there. Her absence was an ache.

"Damn it! Where did that woman go?" he demanded of the first street guard he spotted. "Lady Francesca," he said, elaborating for the young Prime who stared at him in confusion. "Where did she and the women with her go?"

"She took them in one of our cars. She said she was going to Idaho, boss." He handed over a handheld GPS unit. "But she went here. The location's already guarded."

Crowe peered around Tobias's shoulder. "I know that address."

"So do I." Not that he and Crowe wouldn't be able to follow the psychic call of their bondmates, but it was nice to have specific directions in the traffic-snarled hell of the L.A. area.

"It's too bad vampires can't fly," he complained.

"Want me to call in a chopper, boss?" Ali asked as he joined them.

Tobias gave the enthusiastic young Prime a quelling look, then asked, "Where do you think you're going?" when Ali climbed into the backseat of the nearest vehicle as he and Crowe got into the front.

"Kea's with your ladies, right?" Ali answered. "She's from the clinic, and I'm wounded. She'll find fixing me up romantic."

"Ah, romance is in the air for one and all," Crowe said.

"Yeah." Tobias pulled the SUV out onto the street. "We're all just full of it."

# Chapter Thirty-eight

"Francesca!" Tobias shouted.

The group of women seated in Domini's kitchen jumped as the door slammed. Chiana was the only one seated around the kitchen table who didn't look amused at this obvious sign of Primal annoyance.

Rose giggled and stood, facing the doorway into the living room. "Anthony's with him."

"So's Ali," Kea said, equally pleased at this vampire invasion.

"Francesca!" Tobias's shout was louder this time.

"At least he didn't call you Flare," Domini said.

"That is a point in his favor," Francesca said

in agreement as Tobias came stomping into the room, Crowe and Ali right behind him.

Domini touched her forehead and smiled. "I can tell Alec will be home any moment. We'll have Primes falling out the windows if we try to pack any more in."

Domini and Alec's house was small but had a large yard. It was set in a canyon in the hills above the city. There was nothing lavish about the place. Francesca was glad her brother had insisted on adding a couple of rooms when he'd settled into the house his bondmate owned. The Reynards were a luxury-loving lot.

Domini collected Navajo rugs and art that featured condors. Francesca didn't understand her sister-in-law's fondness for overgrown buzzards, but she was amused by the idea that Domini planned to start a new Clan and name it Condor when she finished the slow transition from mortal woman to vampire female.

Francesca rejoiced that Domini was one of the rare women who actually could make the transition into a different type of being through the bondmate link. The more female vampires the better, Francesca thought. It was especially good to have the Matri of a new Clan joining the ranks who wasn't burdened with all the baggage piled onto females born into Clan culture.

"Are you going to go see what Mr. Grumpy Pants is yelling about? Or would you rather this be a public argument?" Domini asked, interrupting Francesca's reverie.

Francesca's heart was racing and everything in her was pulled toward Tobias, even though her thoughts had tried to veer away from him.

She gave Domini a smile and accepted a fresh mug of coffee from her before she walked from the kitchen into the living room. Anthony and Ali moved past her into the kitchen as she came in, but Tobias stayed planted in the living room, glowering at the sight of her, his arms folded across his broad chest.

He looked good when he was angry. She sensed the excitement in his blood, stirred by combat and now focused on her. She fought not to go weak in the knees in reaction. How could they ever get anything done with all this mutual attraction flashing between them?

Francesca came close and held out the coffee. "It's fresh."

He glanced at the mug. "Do you think that having my hands occupied will stop me from throttling you?"

"You have no intention of throttling me. Ravishing, maybe," she added, going for an ironic tone but wondering if her words came out sounding a little more hopeful than she'd intended.

*Bonding. Damn.*

He took the mug, and heat that had nothing to do with the hot coffee coursed between them. They both took a step back, though neither moved very far.

"What are you annoyed about?" she asked while he gulped down the coffee.

"What are you doing here?" he asked when he was done. "I thought you were going to Idaho."

"Uh . . . yes . . ."

"Then why are you here?"

His words hit her as much in her pride as in her heart. She had to leave him, but the last thing she'd expected was for Tobias to actually want her to go. He was supposed to argue about it, at least take a lot of convincing to agree that she was doing the noble, necessary thing. He could at least have praised her selflessness.

He wasn't supposed to accept that she needed to get out of his hair, what little there was of it, without being at least a bit brokenhearted.

She wished she hadn't given him the hot coffee, because now she couldn't fling it into his face.

Primes did not reject Francesca Reynard!

*Calm down, girl,* Francesca told herself. *You're not really that shallow and selfish.*

"This house isn't as secure as—"

"It's guarded. I'm here because it's my brother's house." She sneered. "Oh, and I'm sure we're all in the safest spot in the world because you're here now."

Maybe she *was* a little bit shallow and selfish.

Apparently he was wearing sarcasm armor, because he didn't so much as blink or budge or give a hint of a thought away. He could read her thoughts so much more easily than she could his.

"Lots of practice dealing with different types of telepaths," he told her.

And he was smug about it.

"Yeah, yeah, you're the best at what you do."

"I need to do what I do right now. You wasted my time bringing everyone here."

"I knew what I was doing. She needs—"

"Which one—"

"What the hell are you doing here?" Alec demanded. Her brother slammed the front door, all righteousness, with a Dudley Do-Right chin and laser-etched cheekbones. "Get away from my sister, Strahan."

Tobias thrust the empty mug back into her hands. He turned to the enraged Reynard Prime come to defend her honor and delicate sensibilities.

"Now, that's what I'm talking about," she murmured.

Alec went on. "You've put her in enough

danger, Strahan. I've heard all about last night."

"We were rather noisy," Tobias replied with laconic indifference to Alec's outrage. "But since you weren't there you don't have reason to complain about my and your sister's mating waking you up."

Alec looked between her and Tobias. "She can have sex with whoever she wants. I'm talking about your using her as a decoy at Wilde's house. And I've heard about the bomb at the Citadel. And the latest shopping escapade–slash–kidnap attempt."

"How do you know about that?" Tobias asked. "We just wound that op up."

"My bondmate called me on my way home," Alec answered. "What were you thinking? Don't you care that you've been putting a female in danger?"

*All right, I've had enough defending now.* Francesca put herself between the two Primes, facing her brother. "What are you going to do, Alexander? Tell Mom?"

"Precisely."

"Mom's already pulled the magic-ruby-ring ploy on me. She can't evoke obedience by sending that to anyone more than once."

"Mom will not condone your fraternizing with Strahan."

She laughed. "Mom's the one who put him up to everything that's happened."

"Not the dangerous stuff," Tobias said. "She only wanted me to get you pregnant."

Alec's boiling rage immediately turned down to a low simmer, but his curiosity level rose. He started using all his senses as well. "You're bonding with my sister?"

"You make it sound like a bad thing," Francesca complained. "Which it is, but it's also none of your business, Alexander."

Alec laughed. He gave Tobias a friendly punch on the arm. "Welcome to the family."

"Thanks." Tobias turned back to her and to business. "Which one of your girlfriends is it?"

"The who is pretty obvious once you take a good look at Chiana's emotional state, but I haven't asked her why."

She tossed the empty mug to her stupidly grinning brother. "I'm going to be an uncle," Alec said.

That wasn't what he'd been told, but there were more important things than babies to think about at the moment. "Come on, Tobias, she's waiting in the kitchen."

# Chapter Thirty-nine

*Be gentle with her, Tobias.*

*She's a traitor,* he reminded Francesca. *She tried to kill you with a bomb.*

*She planted a bomb in my bag to explode at the Citadel and attract mortal attention. That's not quite the same thing.*

To Tobias it was. He didn't care how stable C4 was before being set off, the traitor had used Francesca to deliver the bomb. She could have died and he couldn't be gentle with anyone who put her at risk. Alexander Reynard was right to be angry that his sister had been in danger. Tobias was angry with himself for his part in putting her in peril, no matter how much she liked it.

"She's not getting away with—"

"Gentle." Francesca put her hand on his shoulder before he stepped through the kitchen doorway. Her concern and compassion flowed through the connection between them. "Just look at her, Tobias."

The wereseal was alone in the kitchen. Sitting at the kitchen table, drawn in on herself, the small woman seemed to be shrinking away to nothing. She turned huge dark eyes on him that were full of terror and confusion, but Tobias didn't think she was actually looking at him, actually afraid of him. Her fear was for something, someone, else.

"What the hell happened to you, girl?" he asked.

Chiana turned sharply away. "I can't talk to vampires. I can't."

As Tobias came closer the little woman slipped off the chair. She curled around herself on the floor, moaning.

When Francesca started to help the selkie, Tobias put his arm out to stop her. "Listen to what she said," he said in response to her outraged look. "Ali!" he called. "Where are you? Bring Kea in here."

The pair emerged from a bathroom off the kitchen. Ali's shirt was off and Kea held a tube of anti-silver medicinal cream.

"What are you doing?" Kea dropped the tube

and ran to kneel by her friend. She glared up at Tobias while Chiana clutched at her. "She's sick."

"I know," Tobias answered. "You can help her."

"Help me!" Chiana cried between sobs.

Kea held the selkie close. "What's wrong? Tell me."

"I've been trying for months and nobody listens! He hurt me and took . . . me, and nobody sees or feels or cares." She buried her face against Kea's shoulder while the woman held her tight, looking angrily up at Tobias.

"Not me," Tobias said. "Ask her who took her self away. Ask her why she's working with the Purists."

"Purists! Don't be ridiculous. She's—"

"Ask her. I can't."

Chiana turned her head and looked past him rather than at him. "You all think like mortals. You don't think you do, but you do. Nobody *listens.*"

"What don't we listen to?" Tobias asked gently. "Ask her, Kea."

"All right," Kea said, conceding. "What haven't I listened to you about, Chiana?"

"Him!" Chiana shouted. It was a cry of pain. "Them," she added in a faint whisper.

"Oh my goddess!" Kea looked up sharply.

"Her mortal boyfriend! She has a mortal boyfriend."

"Werefolk mingle with their own kinds," Tobias said. He recalled that he had a bonding werewolf and vampire serving in the Dark Angels, but neither was mortal, were they? "Why would she even tell you she's with a mortal?" he asked Kea.

Kea closed her eyes for a moment. She stroked Chiana's hair. "Oh, honey, you were trying to tell me something, weren't you?"

"What did she tell you about this mortal?" Tobias asked.

Kea gathered her thoughts for a moment. "She met this guy while she was on vacation and he moved in with her. Not long before the attacks started," she added thoughtfully.

"He doesn't like her to shift to her seal form," Francesca added. "Ed told me it's making her sick."

"A selkie needs to swim," Tobias said. "Swim or die."

"Why don't you shift, honey?" Kea asked. "No mortal's opinion could mean that much to you."

"I can't! I can't!" Chiana pulled away from Kea and rose to her knees, screaming. "I'm going to die!" She looked around wildly. "They made me do it, but I deserve to die!"

Francesca turned Tobias to face her. "The Tribe vampire—Stone—he's brainwashed her, hasn't he? I don't know where the mortal boyfriend comes in, but only a vampire could mess her up like this."

"The mortal will be her controller," Tobias told Francesca. "The one she reported to, the one gave her orders."

"The one I'm going to kill," Francesca said, looking at the suffering Chiana.

"That's my job." He put a hand on Francesca's shoulder. "Your job is to help her."

Surprise flashed through her, and fear. "I—"

"We don't have time to discuss this." Tobias settled on the floor next to the selkie and brought Francesca down with him. "You want to be useful, my love. I've never met anyone who needs to be useful more than you do. A Matri's heiress has plenty of telepathic training. Here's your chance to use it."

Francesca looked in horror between him and Chiana. "I don't want to hurt her."

"I'll hurt her if I try," he said. "You told me to be gentle with her, and this is the only way. Do it."

Francesca glared at him for a moment, but at the same time he watched her get her temper and nerves in check. "Get out of my way," she said when she was under control.

# Chapter Forty

Chiana tried to lunge away when Francesca approached. "Don't touch me! Don't touch me!"

Kea managed to hang on to the struggling selkie until Francesca could take her place. Francesca had never probed an unwilling mind before. How to do it?

Chiana begged not to be touched by a vampire. The best Francesca could do was let Chiana go.

"I'll do as you ask. You have rights, Chiana. You're not a prisoner."

"I am! I am!" Chiana pounded her small fists on the floor as tears streamed down her face.

Francesca waited to see if the selkie would bolt, but Chiana curled into a tight ball under the table. Her breathing was ragged, her sobs growing weaker.

Francesca twined her fingers tightly together, refraining from physical contact. She closed her eyes and concentrated all her psychic attention on Chiana. She let her shielding down, moved her consciousness toward—

Darkness. Pain. Angry shadows writhing . . .

Francesca pulled back. She fought through a fierce pain pounding in her head to find herself.

Desperation. It was a sharp pain howling and clawing inside Chiana's mind. Fear was a second beast that guarded Chiana's hell.

Francesca went with these monstrous images conjured by her own thoughts to define Chiana's suffering. She was Clan, right? Monster fighting was the family business.

*Come and get me!* she shouted, and threw her being at the creatures stalking the gates of the selkie's prison. The beasts could not withstand the violent, thirsting, hungry, domineering vampire nature Francesca wielded against them. She used her natural weapons to tear through the barrier with barely a thought.

Fog swirled around her. Turned to darkness. Turned to water.

Cold, salty, wonderful water.

Rising to the surface, flowing toward the rocky shore.

*Last day of vacation. I want to go home, but I don't want to leave. The sea here is cleaner, more alive. But I have to leave. The bachelor seal who's been courting me is going to be disappointed . . .*

Laughter fresh as the water rippled through her.

Her body found the beach. Water flowed off her fur. She lifted her muzzle to sniff the—

*Who? What?*

"Hello, little girl. You're mine now."

*Claws. Ripping. Raping.*

*Pain, pain, and ever more pain.*

"You took my skin from me! My skin! Please, no! I can't shift without my skin!"

"You'll get your skin back if you do what you're told."

"Whatever you say. I must do whatever you say."

"Not me, little girl. Look at this mortal. Obey him. He's as close as your lover now. Closer. Obey him. You have no choice."

*No choice.*

*You have a choice,* Francesca told Chiana. She hunted for the spark of rebellion that found ways to give hints of her imprisonment. *They didn't take all of you away. You don't really believe the myth. You don't need a sealskin to change— the ability is there. He lied. Deep down, past all the pain, you have to go there. You can shift again. It's in your blood, bones, heart, deep down in your DNA.*

*That's right. Down the spiral path. Scream as much as you need to. Don't stop. You have to find the way. Feel the softness of the sealskin. See the beauty of it. Wrap it around you. That's right. That's good. You're beautiful. Whole.*

"Francesca? Francesca, come back to me. Chiana's okay. I need you to come back to me. Now!"

She was being shaken and she didn't like it.

"Ow! Damn it, woman, keep your claws out of me!"

"Tobias?"

"Of course it's Tobias! Are you going to open your eyes and look at me?"

She liked looking at him. "All right. You need a shave," she added when her eyes were open. They were face-to-face. He was a lot taller than she was. "Why am I dangling off the floor?"

"It seemed safer that way." He slowly lowered her and let go of her arms when her feet were on the ground.

She rubbed bruised upper arms and vaguely remembered her claws sinking into skin. The smell of a drop of his blood sent heat through her. Tobias had only been defending himself. "Sorry about that."

He kissed her forehead. *You did good, kid.* Tobias turned his attention away from her, but his arm came around her shoulder. "Ali, get that poor selkie into the ocean ASAP. Take a couple of Angels along on guard duty."

"Right, boss. Can Kea come too?"

"Fine. Make a party of it. I owe Kea a good time for suspecting her."

Francesca snuggled beside Tobias, securing her shielding while admiring the way Tobias so decisively gave orders. She loved the way he was making up for mistreating Kea.

*Get over it,* she told herself. *He manipulated you and he's happy to pack you off to Idaho.*

But Francesca couldn't keep up her cynicism for more than a moment. Besides, running off to Idaho—for his sake—had been her idea.

If she could only stop touching him, she could think clearly about him, but she didn't want to move. She wanted to turn her head into his shoulder, breathe in the scent and warmth of Tobias's hard body, put her arms around him, and . . .

*Bite me and I'll take you on top of the kitchen counter.*

Lust shot through her. She ran an extended

fang against the inside of his arm, thrilling as blood heated his skin. *There's a spare bedroom. If Rose and Crowe aren't using it at the moment.*

*They're on the back porch,* Tobias answered. *Billing and cooing.* His frustrated groan was a subliminal sound only she could hear as he eased away from her. "Hold all your naughty thoughts, for now. I have to go to work." He spoke into his headset. "Let's go get the Purist hiding at Chiana's. I'm considering skinning him alive. And no, you can't come with me," he added to her.

"Maybe I'll catch a plane while you're gone," she answered, trying to assert herself now that she was free of his embrace.

"You won't."

"I might."

Once he was gone, she murmured, "I won't."

# Chapter Forty-one

"You failed me. Hardly unexpected."

He listened to the snide, sneering voice of the vampire and considered tossing the cell phone off the edge of the balcony where he stood. The wind off the water was cold and salty, and noisy Christmas parties spilled out onto the terrace below and onto the sidewalk in front of the bar across the street. Bright lights strung on every building and wrapped around tree trunks added to the festive air. Everybody was happy—because they didn't know the truth.

He had no wish to join the merriment or to be talking to the vampire. But some conversations could not be escaped.

"The failure was not only mine. My people

didn't have enough backup from your mercenaries to defeat the Dark Angels."

"Mercenaries are expensive. And their numbers have dwindled a bit in the last few days." The vampire gave an exaggerated sigh. "I wish I could trust in the effectiveness of you weak mortals until replacements arrive."

"My people are depending on yours for rescue. They'll continue the fight."

"My auxiliaries would rather wait for a full moon to attack, but losing so many Purists so quickly forces me to change that plan. We don't want Strahan looking too deeply into their shallow little minds, do we?"

What difference did it make if he and the monster wanted the captured humans freed for different reasons? As long as they were rescued he'd be grateful to the Tribe Prime—who would someday pay.

"My people at least fight for what they believe in," he said.

"Don't be so prissy," the vampire said. "You haven't succeeded in a single attempt to roust your enemies from their lairs. You promised me the females and couldn't follow through."

"Bickering about that is pointless. The selkie hasn't returned to me," he confessed.

"She won't," the monster answered. "My

control's been stripped from her. I've got a bitch of a headache from that."

He'd suspected as much and now he knew. Fear twisted in his gut. "They'll be coming for me."

"Better you than me. Time for you to make the ultimate sacrifice to protect me. Ultimate sacrifice," he repeated. Then Stone hung up.

*Ultimate sacrifice.*

The words rang through his head until they became a painful shout that drove him to his knees. He fought it for a while, fought the will imposing itself over his. Then it all became clear. He raised his head, full of purpose. The ultimate sacrifice it would be.

It was time to die.

But not before the world knew the truth.


Circling helicopters sweeping searchlights over the buildings up ahead were the first bad sign.

The second was Tsuke's voice in his headset. "There's one police copter up there and all the rest are TV news teams."

"Damn."

And he wasn't swearing about the police involvement. Nor did he think for a moment that the excitement ahead wasn't connected with his Purist prey.

"Patching through a news report," Tsuke said.

". . . at least twenty hostages held at the Surfview Bar and Grill . . . We have a report that several hostages managed to escape from the building . . ."

". . . the guy kept yelling that vampires are real and the world needs to know," a man said. He spoke between ragged breaths, like he'd been running. And he sounded scared. "He shot someone when he walked in. Said that was to show he's serious. He was holding a gun to a girl's head when I got out. I heard him telling her he was going to kill her if she didn't admit that monsters are real."

"That's a witness interview on a police channel," Tsuke explained.

"I know what it is," Tobias said. "That's trouble."

"L.A. SWAT reports their perimeter is set up," Tsuke said. "Snipers working their way into place across the street from the bar."

*Hell.*

Tobias wove in and out of traffic, accelerator pressed to the floor, heading for the nearest exit. He could get to the scene faster if he got out of the SUV and ran. He gave the order for all the other cars converging on the Purist to do the same. Never mind doing anything to avoid media attention. It was time for all the vampires and shifters to run free.

Even then they might be too late.

This was not how it was supposed to go down. The Angels had been so successful in blocking the Purists' efforts up until now, and they were so close to wrapping it up. . . . Now this.

They'd missed the chance to keep the media from being alerted this time. There were cops. There were hostages. The Purist had taken his crusade into the mortal world—where there were always some people willing to listen to warnings of monsters, doom, and conspiracies.

And the last thing he wanted was to get the police involved. Memories could be adjusted, but the curious, suspicious, tenacious nature that produced a good cop made it harder to keep those changes permanent. These practical-minded types were the last to believe in supernatural beings, but they were the most likely to discover the reality.

Too late now. But maybe there was a way to work with them. Not everyone on the police force was what he or she seemed.

"Here's the plan." He spoke into his headset while sending the information telepathically at the same time.

\*   \*   \*

There were two bodies on the floor. The scent of blood was in the air, calling the monsters to feed.

The crowd he'd herded against the bar was terrified, each one fearing they'd be the next to die. He couldn't kill them all; he had to save at least one bullet for himself. For the ultimate sacrifice.

He didn't want to kill *any* of them. They were his kind. Humans weren't the enemy, and he mourned their loss. He'd let some of them escape. To spread the truth.

"The world has to know."

The police were outside, red lights whirling on their vehicles. White lights stabbed down and circled from overhead. Television news crews were gathering. The cell phones he'd made the hostages pile on the bar kept ringing in a myriad of different musical ringtones. All the lights and noise were really very festive, very in tune with the season.

But where was the vampire?

"Where are you?" he shouted. He watched the entrance, where the door gaped open. "I know you're coming for me. Show your face. Show your fangs!"

"That won't be necessary."

A woman screamed, but the man standing just inside looked like a perfectly ordinary human. He'd been hoping to see the monster.

"You're a vampire. He's a vampire!" he shouted.

"If you say so." It held out its arms, pretending to show that it was unarmed. "You've got me," the vampire said. "Let them go."

"Tell them the truth," he demanded.

The vampire looked at the hostages. "He wants you to know that I'm a vampire. Come outside with me," the vampire said to him. "We'll talk to the media together. I'll tell them."

He sneered. "To save the mortals?" The vampire nodded. "You must be a Clan boy."

"Clan boys don't lie."

He grabbed a woman and pushed her toward the vampire. "Feed on her. Drink human blood. Show them what you are and I'll let them go. I'll come outside with you."

"All right."

The vampire grabbed the whimpering woman's arm, raised her wrist to his mouth, and bit. She screamed and fainted. The vampire let her drop to the floor. Her blood was on his mouth.

"I've done what you wanted. Come with me."

Clan boys didn't lie. They were crazy that way. The monster would tell the world. He would go with him.

He had a gun in one hand, but the important weapon was the knife he pulled from its sheath. He came closer. The vampire was very tall and muscular, with huge hands. There was a dangerous stillness about it, but he didn't fear the monster's imposing size or attitude.

"The blade is silver," he told the vampire. "I'll be holding it at your throat. Understood?"

"Understood."

The vampire turned to leave. He came up behind the monster and pressed the tip of the blade to the base of the creature's spine. Its back was a wide, protective shield. He followed close behind when the vampire stepped outside.

Tobias gave one swift glance to the third-floor balcony across the street before he threw himself to the ground.

The Purist had quick reflexes and was good with the knife. A line of pain ran across Tobias's back as he went down. It was worth the pain to give the SWAT sniper a clear target.

Two shots sounded even before Tobias hit the ground.

Tobias rolled onto his back as the Purist fell, bullet holes in his forehead and chest. The sniper had taken no chances.

The sniper was Colin Foxe, and he was a Clan boy. He was also a cop, and saving mortals was his job. Tobias was glad the Clan Prime had been on the scene when he sent out a telepathic call with what he had in mind. Foxe and a werewolf cop had answered the call.

The werewolf helped him sneak past the police barrier. Foxe assigned himself the sniper's role. Tobias lured the Purist outside.

So much for that part of the plan.

Tobias moved behind a row of outdoor tables, into the shadows by the wall of the bar. Cops rushed up to the body. More rushed into the building to help the hostages. They would find one woman with a bitten wrist, but the EMTs would find only a human bite mark. He'd found that it wasn't that easy to draw blood without using fangs.

More police across the street tried to hold back the gathered reporters.

Dark Angel Primes moved among the throng of mortals, telepathically planting a story about a madman who'd accused a hostage of being a vampire and forced the hostage outside, where the SWAT team saved the day. One of the real hostages would remember being the one pushed outside and to the ground. He'd become a celebrity. The Corbett twins would make sure no media images of the incident showed Tobias. It was *all* good.

Tobias rubbed his smarting back. Maybe not all good. But at least it was over.

# Chapter Forty-two

*N*ot *compatible with human DNA. What the hell does that mean? Really? And I hate being stuck here. I need to talk to—*

"You're thinking far too loudly," the vampire beside her said.

"Sorry," Saffie answered, her voice muffled by the pile of bedclothes covering her.

Greg had stripped the other double bed in their motel room and spread the coverings on hers, insisting that she was the one who needed to stay warm. The building's furnace was as dead as everything else that used electricity in the area. The temperature was dropping by the moment and the howling wind was hard on her nerves. It was a hell of an unpleasant night. Inside and out.

"I can't sleep," she said.

"I noticed."

Greg was on the bed with her but lying on top of the covers. It wasn't the most practical way of sharing body heat, but it was chaste and proper. Saffie thought her father would appreciate this Prime's gentlemanly behavior.

"Aren't you cold?" she asked.

"Yes."

She let it go. Inviting him under the blankets might sound like she was coming on to him, as Primes could easily misconstrue any comment or gesture as having a sexual meaning. It had been a few months since she'd been in the company of vampires, but dealing with their weirdness was as automatic for her as breathing.

Saffie turned onto her back, though it took some effort. The cocoon of blankets was heavy. She felt imprisoned even though she was warm and the bed was soft.

"It's been a long day. Sleep now."

Greg's voice was soft, persuasive. His thoughts teased suggestions around the edges of hers.

"Telepathy doesn't work on me," she said. She could recognize the flux of mental energy, but she couldn't use it. Her thoughts could sometimes be read, but telepathy certainly couldn't be used to give her orders or alter her memories. "Haven't you read my file?"

"I forgot that detail," he answered. "I'm only trying to help. You need to rest."

She needed to get home. She needed to talk to her dad. But there was no Wi-Fi available, no landline working, no cellular signal. She wished she was a telepath, because she couldn't bear to ask Greg to interrupt her father again. Greg had contacted him already and told her that Tobias was very busy saving Los Angeles right now and would be in touch later.

She understood.

But she also needed answers.

"What do you think I am?" she blurted out. "What am I?"

There was considerable silence before Greg said. "I think you're a who, not a what."

"But my DNA—"

"Is a bunch of twisty squiggles that are almost the same as any other primate's. It's not like you don't already know you're adopted and that the world is full of weirdness."

"I'm not human!"

"You're as human as I am."

Saffron didn't fall for the obvious retort that

he was a vampire. She didn't say anything, as she realized she was pulling what Dee called a Needy Greedy, and had been for days. She reminded herself that the mortal members of the Crew had to be ten times tougher than everybody else. *Don't bleed on the outside, it attracts sharks,* Dee always told her.

"I'm going to go to sleep now." But before she did, she added, "I've got a bad feeling about what's going on out there."

Gregor didn't think the girl was talking about the weather, and he agreed with her.

It wasn't the howling of the wind that set his senses on nervous alert. Nor was it the uncomfortably cold room that made him restless. *Something wicked this way comes,* he thought, and that didn't make any sense. He was the official wicked big bad wolf in this Red Riding Hood's life.

*Bad analogy,* he thought, recalling what had happened to the original Red's BBW. Still, he had a feeling that the huntsman was on the way.

Once the girl's heart rate told him she was deeply asleep, Gregor slipped from the bed. He pulled the curtain back from the window and gazed outside. His eyes searched through the storm, but more importantly, he concentrated his other senses on everything around him.

He counted the mortal heartbeats in the building and sensed no threat from their fellow stranded travelers. He stared out into the darkness with eyes tuned to all available light. He listened to the silence beneath the wind. He hunted for sparks of thought beyond mortal consciousness.

Oh, yeah. There was something out there.

Who? And why?

Dark Angels? No, the heroes were busy. If it wasn't the good guys, it must be the bad. Reinforcements sent by the Master? Whoever it was, he didn't fancy the company. The girl had been entrusted to him and he was keeping her to himself.

He went over to shake Saffron awake. Her eyes opened instantly. She allowed herself to be afraid for only a moment.

He nodded in acknowledgment. "Get dressed."

"I am dressed," she mumbled, struggling to throw off all the layers of blankets. "I went to bed dressed."

"We're leaving."

She didn't ask questions but quickly put on her shoes and coat and picked up her bag. There were advantages to raising a child in a military unit.

He waited by the door with the car keys in his hand, admiring her ability to move efficiently in what was near-total darkness for her, not letting her mortality get in the way.

He ushered her outside. The parking lot was full of vehicles, and they were covered in snow. He wasn't even sure which SUV was the one he'd stolen earlier in the day.

It was the girl who led him forward through the heavy drifts.

Gregor kept Saffron in sight through the swirling snow, but he was surrounded by a growing sense of danger. Vampires were coming.

"They're here," Saffron said. They'd reached the middle of the parking lot. She turned back to him. "Even I can feel them."

"They aren't friendlies."

The angry, hungry mental pressure told him that. Tribe Primes, but not anybody he knew.

"What the hell is going on?" he demanded.

"Don't ask me," the girl replied.

"I wasn't told to rescue you. I was told to bring you in."

They were shouting at each other above the growing roar.

The already fierce wind was picking up, turning the snow into a hurricane. They looked up.

"Who the hell would fly a helicopter in this?" Gregor asked.

"A vampire," Tobias Strahan's daughter replied. Nothing seemed to surprise her.

The chopper that came down onto the parking lot was huge, some sort of military transport. The Primes who jumped out carried weapons, the sort that fired silver bullets. One of the Primes grabbed the girl. The others pointed their guns at him.

"No, no," a voice called out from the entrance of the copter. "Bring him along. I know who he is, and I never pass up the chance to recruit a Tribe boy."

The Primes gestured for him to move toward the helicopter with their guns.

Saffron looked sharply back at him, her expression full of betrayal and fury. "Tribe?"

He shrugged.

"Are you telling me I've been kidnapped *twice* today?"

# Chapter Forty-three

"So, a vampire walks into a bar . . ."

Tobias smiled as Francesca came up behind him at the patio door in Ben Lancer's kitchen. He could see a trio of werefolk guards patrolling the grounds out in the darkness. A Prime was on watch by the front door. Everyone else in the house was asleep.

They were alone—a situation more dangerous than his encounter with the Purist.

"At least I walked out of the bar."

"You saved a lot of mortals."

"You Clan girls get turned on by heroics, don't you?"

She wrapped her arms around his waist and pressed herself against his back. Heat shot

through him, and something much more powerful than lust permeated him as well.

He was . . . *complete* when they were together.

"Ouch," he said. "I was stabbed in the back,
you know."

"I felt your pain when the silver slashed you
and ran to your side."

He glanced over his shoulder, eyebrow raised
skeptically. "Really?"

"No. My cousin Colin called to say you got a
tiny cut." She pressed her forehead between his
shoulder blades. "I did feel a little twinge."

"I was very brave."

"It's your job."

"Aren't you going to kiss it and make it all
better?"

"Probably." She stroked her cheek across his
shoulders. A cat claiming territory? "Whatcha
doing?"

"Trying to reach Saffie." He held his Black-
Berry up. "Not a sip, not a voice mail, nothing
for hours. It's not like her not to keep in touch,
especially when—"

"Have you checked the weather lately? You
do know there's a major snowstorm on the East
Coast, right? Power outages have to be rough on
people without telepathy."

"Maybe that's it. But—"

"You've got a bad feeling?"

"I do."

She sighed, and he felt her suddenly sharing his worry. "Have you tried telepathy?"

"Not yet. She's resistant to it. She's probably asleep," he added. "I don't want to give her nightmares."

He put the BlackBerry away and turned to face Francesca. She kept her arms around him. He put his hands on her shoulders. They looked into each other's eyes, and Tobias had no idea how long that went on. They didn't share thoughts or do anything but be together.

He hadn't realized how tired he was until Francesca's closeness gave him back some energy. He'd deliberately come back to his headquarters instead of going to her. Of course she'd taken matters into her own hands. He hadn't consciously known she was coming to him, hadn't consciously called her—yet here they were. Together.

"Damn," he muttered after a while. "We are so screwed."

"I know," she said.

"Are you accepting it?"

She was the infamous Flare! She'd never accepted a Prime in her life. Now she had her beautifully manicured claws deep in his soul.

*Why me?*

*You ought to be flattered.*

Maybe he was. Then again, if he hadn't been so forceful about claiming her that first time they wouldn't have been together. He couldn't regret that and ached to do it again.

*Together.*

What a frightening word that was.

"I don't know what I'm doing," she said. "I'm just—here."

"Why?" he asked. "How?"

She threw back her head and laughed. *Damn, her throat is gorgeous!* Her green eyes gleamed with a sexy hint of red when she looked back at him.

"They let us Clan girls drive, you know. That's *how* I'm here. The answer to *why* is multipart."

"Is life a quiz?" he asked.

"It's a test." She sighed. "Always a test. Of loyalty. Of friendship. Of honor. Of will."

"Of survival," he added.

They agreed on so much, he and this Clan girl who was oh-so-inappropriate for what he thought he wanted. That was how it was supposed to be with bonding, wasn't it? Two minds, souls, bodies meshing perfectly. How could anyone not want such perfection?

How could anyone not be terrified of it?

"Do you know how the Tribes deal with

bonding?" he asked, and felt the shiver of horror that went through her mind and body in response. "Tribe females belong to the strongest males. They exist to be bred. They are bought and sold and fought over. Mortal slaves are used for sexual pleasure, but every Prime knows never to become involved with a vampire female. Use their bodies, stay out of their minds. Breed them, then pass them on to their next master as quickly as possible. Try not to taste them; never let them taste you. Never even look into their eyes. There are all sorts of superstitions about how females drain Primes' strength, many examples of their evil ways. The whole point is to keep Primes from bonding with females."

"And look how well that's worked out for the Tribes. They're all crazy!"

"From a Clan princess's point of view, I suppose you're right."

"It should be right from a Family Prime's point of view, as well."

He shrugged. "I was born into Tribe Minotaur. Deep in my gut I still believe females need to be controlled."

"You need to work on that."

He grinned. "You love it, woman."

"What I love in the bedroom is completely—"

"My business."

She didn't deny it. "Are you taking this history lesson somewhere?"

"My sire owned a breeder and fought all the time for the right to keep her to himself. He kept her too long. She got her fangs into him."

Her green eyes flashed with anger at his ugly description of Tribe life. She sneered. "What happened? Did they live happily ever after?"

"They did," he answered. "They still are. But their bonding destroyed the Minotaur Tribe."

"And this was bad how?"

Her rising anger licked hotly at his senses, turning fury into an aphrodisiac. There was good reason she was known as Flare.

How very like a Clan female not to see that there was a tragic side to the triumph of his parents' love story.

"Their bonding changed my world," he went on. "Most of my growing up was done in a Family crèche. My adult life is spent actively opposing what's left of the Tribes. But should the Tribes' way of life be completely destroyed? Are they completely wrong? Would I have found better solutions for them if I'd remained within the Tribe structure? I have some doubts about the wonder that is bonding. You're not the only one facing the inevitable with some issues."

She pulled away and stomped across the

kitchen but stopped at the doorway and grasped the frame so hard the wood cracked beneath her fingers. The pull they had on each other stretched painfully tight between them.

She couldn't leave him. He wouldn't let her if she tried.

"Damn it!" She whirled back to face him. "I vowed to leave you for your own good, before this . . . *instinct* took complete control. I wanted it to be my contribution to the Dark Angels. I didn't want to do anything to jeopardize your leadership."

"I appreciate that."

She took his words as sarcasm. Her temper continued to blaze. "I believed you were trying to save the Clans and Families—from mortals, from Tribes, from ourselves. I want to believe in your mission, Tobias. Now I'm not sure what your mission is. To make us like the Tribes? To rule the immortal world?"

*What the hell is she talking about?* "How can someone I'm bonding with completely misunderstand what I meant?" he asked, bewildered.

"You dissed your *mother*! You praised the Tribes' treatment of women."

"No, I didn't."

She repeated back to him, verbatim, everything he'd said about his family history.

Ouch.

He had to admit that coming from her, it didn't sound good.

He held up his hands. "Maybe I didn't explain myself properly. Aren't we supposed to just *know* everything about each other?"

"I guess not," she said.

In a way this was a hopeful sign. It showed that they were individuals who could confuse and annoy and misunderstand each other.

"Listen," he said. "I'm worried about my kid, there's a Prime still out there we have to find, and my back hurts. Sometimes I get a little . . . maudlin, confused, about the past. My parents' bond was wonderful for them. I'm proud to be a Strahan Prime. In the long run joining the Family was good for many of the Minotaurs, but there were deaths, and there's still plenty of hatred and sworn vendettas. Their bonding didn't help promote peace, didn't help bring a reasonable solution to the Tribes' problems. I want peace."

"Even if you have to kill to get it?"

"Yes. I'll fight the Tribes because they make it necessary, but I want the Tribes to survive. They aren't nice people, but they are a pure expression of our ancient predator nature."

"Twisted. Evil."

"But we need to acknowledge their culture

and persuade them to want to change. Historically bonding is the worst sin to them. I don't know how that came about, but I also know it's caused plenty of problems among us *civilized* vampires too."

She nodded. "The mortals have no idea how mild the fight for Helen of Troy was compared to some of our bonding tales."

"So maybe I'm a little scared of bonding."

"You see it as a weapon? Something that can turn on you?" she asked.

"Maybe. A little."

"Point taken." She eyed him suspiciously. "Are you scared of bonding in general or of bonding with me?"

"Yes."

Francesca threw back her head and laughed.

The sight and sound nearly drove him to his knees. He loved her laugh. It sent sparks flying through his blood. Her lovely, long exposed neck when she tilted up her chin was the most erotic sight in the world. Primes would kill for the chance to pierce that soft, warm skin, though he'd strike first if anyone tried. He ached for the chance to fight off a challenger, to prove to her and the world whom she belonged to.

Tobias rubbed his fingers across his mouth, his aching fangs. His vision was trying to switch into the spectrum where he could see lust as heat and blood. He had to keep himself under control. "Stay on target," he muttered. "You were leaving to keep from jeopardizing the Angels? To help me? I do appreciate the thought—but didn't you think I'd have to come after you?"

"I hoped you'd be stronger than that."

"In other words, you wanted to torture me?"

She laughed again. "It doesn't matter. I'm not going to the Reynard Citadel. Not tonight. My mom gave our pilot the holidays off. She did that on purpose to keep me here, you know."

"You said you have a pilot's license."

"Am I supposed to steal a plane?"

"A Dark Angel would."

"I'm not—"

"You are."

"You don't know my Matri."

He took a step toward her. She took one toward him. They weren't able to stay apart even though they tried.

"Your Matri has made you scared of bonding, angry at being with a Prime, angry at being part of our world."

All of her deep resentment, her anger as thick and hot as lava, throbbed through her, into him. It was a barrier between them, and he had a temper of his own.

"Tell me," he said.

"I don't want to talk about it," she said.

He was on her in a heartbeat, his hands gripping her, his gaze boring into hers. "It wasn't a request." His voice was raw with jealousy. "Who is he?"

# Chapter Forty-four

Francesca didn't want to talk about this. This was her private soul, her secret heart. This was the pain that kept her fighting, kept her alive, kept her strong.

"Strong for what? Strong for who?"

"Get out of my head!"

"I can't. Damn it, you know I can't."

He was there, stalking around the walls of her consciousness, looking in the windows. "Sneak thief," she snarled, curling tightly around her memories. She wouldn't go there. Let them lie dormant.

*Let them turn to poison inside you? Let the poison permeate everything we could be?*

She hated her hunger for that word—*we.*

She and Tobias together, forever. Images flashed through her of their hands entwined, their bodies entwined, their beings, ambitions, and lives entwined.

She fought the images that built a barrier around her memories of a mortal lover.

"I'm here. He's not. You've wasted enough time, Francesca."

Her conviction wavered. Had it been a waste? The waste of her life, her love, her time—

Patrick could never be everything she needed, wanted. She couldn't give herself freely. She'd held back. She'd *had* to hold back, for her species' sake. For her Clan's sake.

The pain came out in a banshee howl.

"Oh, goddess, I never even tasted him! Not once. I loved him but I didn't dare . . ."

"Loved who? Talk to me, Francesca. Let me help."

Tobias was holding her tightly yet somehow tenderly as she clawed and fought to get away. She tasted blood but couldn't tell if it was his or her own. Was that some trick of bonding?

It was Tobias's blood—yes. His pleasure still reverberated through her, pushing back her panic. He'd let her sink her fangs into him.

It made her crave what she could share with him.

She spat onto the floor. "Damn you! You're trying to make me forget him."

"I'd like to," he answered. "Ow!" He shook her. "Keep your claws in, woman, and listen to me."

His hands closed hard around her wrists, trapping her like the silver manacles the Tribes used on their females.

Francesca went completely still. Her voice was as cold as ice. "I will not be your prisoner."

"You've been a prisoner all your life," Tobias retorted. "I can feel all the invisible chains winding through you. Let them go."

"You mean let him go!"

She struggled, snapped at him, kicked him, but Tobias would not let her go. All the time his thoughts caressed her.

"You are my prisoner," he told her. "But I'm yours too. You have as much power over me as I have over you. We don't have to be crippled by it. Loving this mortal has left you crippled for years."

*No! No! No! You don't understand! You can't understand! No Prime can understand—*

*Love? Don't be ridiculous. Calm down.*

Strahan's thoughts closed around hers like a vise. Velvet darkness shrouded her pain.

When the soft darkness faded, Francesca was

lying on the guest room bed, sheltered in Tobias's arms. *Just as it should be, damn it all to hades.*

She lifted her head from his shoulder to meet his dark gaze. "I don't want your help," she told him. "Not like that."

He stroked her hair away from her face. "I only knocked you out because your hysteria was going to wake up everyone in the house."

"How kind of you to think of everyone else."

He ignored her sarcasm. "It's what I do."

"I wasn't hysterical. I was . . . all right, I was, but it was your fault."

His fingertips traced her cheek, her throat, between her breasts, back up the side of her face in a slow, sweet circle. His touch lingered on her skin.

"I don't understand how it's my fault, Francesca."

His complete honesty kept her temper from flaring again. "You want me to forget him," she said. "That's infuriating, humiliating, wrong—"

He put his fingers over her lips. "It's arrogant for me to want you to forget someone you loved. And it is wrong. But I can't help wanting everything you are to myself. It's a Prime thing."

She snapped at his fingers. "Is it any wonder I hate Primes?"

He kissed her with just enough fang to draw a drop of blood from her lower lip. His tongue tasted it and twined with hers. A shudder of pleasure went through them both. *No mortal can do this for you.*

So very true. *I never wanted him the way I need you.* Francesca hated to admit it but couldn't deny it.

"How did you want him? Tell me about him, Francesca," Tobias said. "I need to know why you hurt for him. I won't try to take away the pain if you don't want me to. I won't try to take him from you. Your memories, your history, belong to you."

His sincerity touched her very deeply. "Thank you."

"You know a lot more about me than I do about you."

It was true enough. Francesca took the hint, but it was incredibly difficult to let go of the secrets she'd kept to herself for so long.

"His name was Patrick." The words came out as a rough whisper. "He was a big, blond jock, a hell of a lot smarter than he looked. So funny, and kind, very comfortable with who he was. He never knew I was a vampire."

"You didn't believe he'd be comfortable with what you are?"

"I never wanted him to know. We met in

college. I was this snooty rich girl. He was on a sports scholarship." A sound rose in her throat, half sob, half laugh. "We did homework together. He taught me how to cook. He was a vegetarian when we met, but a vampire and a vegetarian could never work out. At least I managed to get him to eat fish."

"Why didn't you want him to know who you truly are?" Tobias asked. "Vampire females have taken mortal lovers before, even had children with them. Ben and his lady had a son."

They were in Ben Lancer's house. Ben had been lovers with a Corvus female for decades before she was called home to her Clan because she was the Matri's heir. Francesca knew that story very well. The story of the Corvus female's mortal romance was her story as well, but she hadn't had decades with Patrick. She hadn't had children with him.

She went on. "He went into the marines as soon as we graduated. He was the son of hippies whose hobby was making candy, but he always wanted to be in the military."

"You didn't answer my question. Why did you pretend to be someone you aren't with this Patrick? Didn't he deserve the truth? Why do you want to be mortal?"

"How many questions do you want me to answer at once?" she demanded. "You asked about my mortal lover; I'm telling you about him." She swallowed the aching urge to cry. "I know you deserve to know about him. But all these other things are more than I can deal with right now. And I don't want to be mortal," she answered. She closed her eyes but couldn't keep the tears from leaking out. "Maybe I did pretend to be one for a while, with him. We were married in Las Vegas just after he got his first posting. My family wasn't invited. His wasn't, either."

"Your Matri accepted that?"

"I never told her. Besides, as long as he never tasted my blood, our being together meant nothing to her, at least for a while. If we'd had more time together, I would have told him. But since I could never let myself bond with him—"

"Females can't bond with mortal males," he said, interrupting. "It's not biologically possible."

She laughed softly. "A couple of days ago, no one admitted that female vampires and werewolves can bond, but look at Sid and Joe. I don't know if I could have bonded with Patrick—"

"You were born to bond with me."

He was so sure of himself, of the truth of what he said. His hands moved possessively over her. His lips touched her throat, his tongue flicked over her pulse. She felt a brief caress of fang, a few sharp pricks. Pleasure reverberated from him, through her, and back to him. The erotic cycle was like nothing she'd felt with anyone else.

"See what I mean?" he asked.

# Chapter Forty-five

Primes were so damn romantic.

And maybe he was right. Maybe the Über-Prime was the only one the Bitch Queen Flare could share her life with.

"I don't know if we can bond with mortals," she said. "I do know that we don't dare."

"Survival of the species."

"Lie back and think of the next generation, as we're taught in vampire school."

He laughed at her bitterness. "No vampire female ever just lies back."

He kissed and nipped a line across the top of her breasts. It felt so very good. She tried to stay still, but her breathing quickened and her craving body rose to meet his skilled touch.

"All right, we enjoy sex," she admitted. "Do you want to have sex or talk right now?" she asked.

Because she could not do both at once, especially not when the subject was Patrick. That she could talk about Patrick with this Prime and also want to make love to Tobias amazed her. This moment had been impossible to imagine a few days before. She was happy for this moment, and that too would have seemed impossible before now.

There was a glow of lust in the big brown eyes that gazed into hers, but he tamped down the hunger. His expression became calm and steady, though the lust wasn't completely gone. From either of them, Francesca acknowledged.

"Ever," he said. And they both laughed. "Tell me what Patrick has to do with your war with your mother," he said when they were serious again.

She discovered that she was dying to explain this to him. "You're a casualty of our war yourself now. I can't apologize for that."

"No need. Because I'm no victim. Was Patrick?"

"No." She shook her head. "Not really. I made the choices about our relationship, and I was happy with them. With him."

"Could it be that you were a little too much in control with your mortal?"

Francesca winced, but she answered honestly. "Probably. I didn't think about it at the time, but we Clan females are used to having everything our way, aren't we?"

"Not with me."

Time would tell. A bonding usually ended up as a relationship between equals. The battles in between would be interesting. But before they could work through the future, Tobias deserved to know about her past.

"I moved in with him off base when he was assigned to train on helicopters at Twentynine Palms—"

"He was a jarhead, eh? Good for him.

She stroked Tobias's cheek. "Damn it, I did not want to be attracted to another war fighter."

He turned to kiss her palm. This simple brush of lips sent lightning through her.

"How am I supposed to tell you anything if you keep making me want to mate?" *And stop looking so smug!*

*Patrick and your Matri. Show me.*

Her memories opened to him without any more prompting.

*Francesca had no memory of putting down the phone, but there it was on the table, buzzing at her like an angry wasp. The light outside the windows was fading. Odd. It had been noonday* bright when she answered the ringing phone. She hadn't put it down, had she? She'd dropped it. She put her hand on the phone, and it all came back to her.

"Your husband's been in an accident. Two copters crashed into each other on a training flight. He's hospitalized with a broken neck and third-degree burns."

Why hadn't she known? Why hadn't she felt it happen to him?

Why had her being filled with hopeless grief and everything else gone blank around her? How long had she been this way? She had to get to Patrick! She had to help him!

A knock came on the door as she snatched car keys out of her purse. She knew who was there before she flung the door open on Primes. They'd never approached her, never spoken to her, but these Reynard Clan Primes had been shadowing her for years, guards assigned to protect a precious female. This time she was glad to see them.

"We have to get to the base hospital," she told them. "Something awful has hap—"

"Come with us, Lady Francesca."

They stepped forward, blocking the door. Their senses were tightly guarded, their presence suddenly ominous. One grabbed her arm when she tried to dodge around them.

One of them held a thickly padded envelope out to her. "From Matri Anjelica."

She didn't give a damn. "Let me go. Let me out of here. I have to get to Patrick!"

She fought the Prime holding her, but her mother had picked her guards well. There was no getting away from this one.

"Don't you understand? He's dying!"

Shouting didn't do any good. Telepathic orders did no good. They showed no sympathy for her tears.

The one with the envelope finally ripped it open. A folded piece of paper and a ruby ring spilled out onto his palm.

Francesca saw the ring through her tears. It belonged to her mother.

Oh, shit.

The Prime took her hand and made her take the ring, forcing her fingers to wrap around the horrible thing. It was heavy and cold—with symbolism and threat.

He unfolded the paper. She caught a glimpse of her mother's handwriting as he did. He read, " 'By order of the Matri's Ring, I, Anjelica, Matri of Clan Reynard, require that Lady Francesca Reynard return immediately to Citadel Reynard to accept her duties as heir and daughter of the Clan.' " He let this sink in, then read on. " 'I *mean it, Flare, or I wouldn't have sent the ring. It's time for you to pick a Prime and give me grandchildren.'"*

"No! Patrick!"

*She wasn't going anywhere except to her husband.*

*But the Primes held her. They forced her out the door and into the back of a car. They held her down while the car drove away. She screamed and thrashed, bit and clawed. But it did no good.*

"To this day she swears her calling me to the Citadel as Patrick was dying was a horrible coincidence and that those damned Primes exceeded their authority." The memory of the life she'd been forced to abandon clawed at her soul. "Goddess damn it, I hate that woman." Her voice came out raw from her aching throat.

"You've been screaming." Tobias's voice was close to her ear. His breath brushed her cheek, and he wiped tears from her face.

He was stretched out beside her, his arms around her. His size and warmth comforted her as she worked her way back to the present. She stared at the ceiling and breathed in reality. Reality was Tobias. His touch. His presence, physical and psychic, equally strong, equally seductive.

*This is now,* he whispered in her mind. His hands moved over her, not gently, not comfortingly, but stirring hunger stronger than the pain. *Live in the now. With me.*

He wasn't promising to take the pain away, not offering an alternative or a perfect future. He was simply offering himself.

It meant everything in the world to her.

*All right,* she answered.

Francesca turned into Tobias's embrace and sank her fangs deeply into his flesh.

# Chapter Forty-six

At least she wasn't cold. She was scared, exhausted, totally pissed off, but Saffie was no longer freezing cold now that they'd switched from the helicopter to the private jet. The helicopter ride had been hellish; the Prime pilot was a cackling crazy, riding the storm like it was a wild horse. She'd crouched on the cold metal deck and wrapped herself up in a ball until they landed on an airfield beyond the storm front. There'd been heavily armed Primes pressed in all around her, but worst of all was that Greg stayed close beside her with his hand on her shoulder. She'd wanted to jerk away from him and burned to rip him to shreds.

But she was a mortal surrounded by hostile

vampires. She'd been carefully taught that in such a situation the best thing for her to do was to stay passive, keep silent, keep her head down, her manner hopeless, and give absolutely no indication she might have some skills. *I'm just a helpless little mortal female, lalala . . .*

The Primes other than Greg completely ignored her. She appeared to ignore him even though she was acutely aware that he had possession of her backpack with all the gear that held Dark Angel intel. He was a smart one and knew what he had. What exactly was his role in this? During the helicopter flight she suspected he was also a prisoner, even though Dragomir didn't have this other Tribe Prime restrained in any way.

She recognized her kidnappers' leader as Dragomir, the Prime master Greg had asked her about. Greg gave no indication of knowing the mercenary leader. It was all very strange. She was dying to find out what was going on, and now that she'd been brought into the luxurious main cabin of the jet along with Greg, Dragomir, and a couple of bodyguard types, she hoped to find out information she could use to plan her escape as well as feed her curiosity.

She got pushed into a seat on the side of the cabin. Dragomir gestured for Greg to join him at seats around a table. After the jet took off one of the guards set drinks down on the table for them.

"We are on our way to California," Dragomir told Greg. "The weather is much nicer there." He took a sip from his glass. "Blood vodka. Have you tried it, Gregor of the Minotaur?"

"And why are we heading to California?"

"Business, of course. My principal has need of Harpy Primes' expertise."

Saffie hid a smile. She hoped their destination was Los Angeles. The Crew was there. Dad was there.

Greg took a sip of the pale red liquid, making it look like a ritual. "Pleasant," he said. "Thank you—Lord Dragomir?"

The Master Prime laughed, a deep, booming, falsely cheerful sound. "That's right, we haven't been introduced. I am Dragomir, and I have heard about you. I was glad to hear that your former Master sent you to retrieve my property."

Saffie pressed her lips together hard to keep from gasping at the word *property*. She didn't doubt Dragomir was talking about her. She wanted to demand to know what he was talking about, but she kept her mouth shut.

Greg asked the question for her. "How is the female your property? My Master told me to bring her to him."

Dragomir's smile didn't go anywhere near his

eyes. "So that she could be returned to me. Your former Master called to tell me she still lived. Since I was passing through the neighborhood, I decided to reclaim her myself."

*Still lived?* That hit her like a punch to the stomach. What did he mean by that?

As much as she wanted to know, Greg didn't ask. "My *former* Master?" he asked. He looked more curious than concerned.

Of course the Tribe boy was going to turn the conversation to himself.

"I've heard that you are smart and an opportunist. Your former Master doesn't appreciate your talents the way I will. You can work for me, or you can die. Yes or no?"

Greg lifted his glass in a toast. "Happy to be on board, Master."

Another false laugh from Dragomir. "Welcome, Gregor. Tribe Harpy is always looking for qualified Primes."

*Because you're a bad leader who keeps getting your boys killed,* Saffie thought. Her father would never have put the Crew at risk with that crazy helicopter stunt. Apparently there was some personal vendetta involving her, but you didn't put your troops in danger for your own private agenda.

Of course she hoped Dad wouldn't see rescuing

her from this bunch as a private matter. She'd be perfectly happy if he brought the whole Crew along, despite the teasing she'd get for having to be rescued. If she didn't think of a way out of this on her own first.

Nothing she could do but listen until the plane landed.

Francesca had never been so happy. She couldn't imagine anything better than to be where she was right now, or anyone better to be with.

Tobias's body covered her, a hot, hard-muscled blanket that kept Francesca pinned to the bed, and she didn't mind it a bit. Blood and sex had come together so perfectly between them that she didn't know where she ended and he began, and didn't care. Her body was so sated she was ready to melt into the bed. If this two-ton boulder of a male wanted to sleep the night away on top of her, she was happy to oblige.

She rested her hand on the base of his spine, pressing him even closer to her. There was something so endearing and enduring in the way his head rested on her breasts. It was where he belonged.

She nipped the top of his ear affectionately for one more small taste of him. "Good night," she whispered. Feeling the approaching dawn in her bones, she closed her eyes.

A knock on the door wrecked her peace a moment later.

"Goddess damn it!" Francesca swore. "Go away!"

"Get used to it," Tobias grunted, and kissed her shoulder before he got up and opened the door. Francesca sat up and saw a large werecoyote sitting in the hallway. She wondered how he had knocked on the door in his shifted shape, but she was no expert on the skills of werekind. She supposed she'd better learn if she really was going to stay with the Dark Angels.

A thrill went through her at the thought—of excitement, anticipation, and trepidation. There could be trouble for her and Tobias ahead—with her Clan, her Matri, the Council.

"The political maneuvering will give you a purpose," Tobias said, cutting into her thoughts. "Here's your opportunity to free the females of the Clans by freeing yourself."

She liked the idea. "You're smart, and sneaky. I like that about you."

"But this isn't the time to worry about the future. What is it, Eleanor?"

*Sorry for the interruption, boss,* the waiting werecoyote thought. *We've got company heading up from the beach*. Message delivered, the shifter padded away.

She listened in on Tobias's telepathic conversations with other Angels while they both hurriedly got dressed. He found out details and gave orders. When they were ready Francesca accompanied him to the kitchen, where members of his team were already waiting.

Along the way he gave her a look that said he was surprised she'd let a little emergency spoil her beauty sleep.

"I'm getting used to it, as you ordered, boss," she said. "Even if my hair does look frightful." He gave her an encouraging pat on the head. She snapped at him, and they grinned at each other.

Ben Lancer stepped forward. He was wearing a blue terry-cloth bathrobe, but the old man looked as dangerous as anyone else in the room. He seemed put out. "What are you doing letting werewolves onto my lawn, Tobias?"

"Housebreaking them."

The old man snorted. "You damned well better pick up after them when you're done. And don't wake the neighbors."

"Why would werewolves risk attacking Primes?" Francesca asked. "Are they crazy?"

"They're ferals," one of the Crew werewolves sneered. "That says it all, ma'am."

She'd already gathered the hostile shifters weren't from the local werewolf population but from the growing minority of humans who had deliberately gotten themselves bitten and learned how to shape-shift as easily as born werefolk. The natural werewolves hated these abominations, and it was always fatal for anything but a vampire to be on the bad side of a werewolf.

"They've come for the Purist prisoners," Tobias said. "Figured this would happen." He sounded happy about it. "I wasn't expecting werewolves, though. I do not know where they came from."

"You set this up as a trap for the rest of the Purists who'd try to rescue them?" Francesca asked. "Or were you hoping for the last Prime to show up?"

"I'd be happy to get the Purists out of my media room," Lancer said. "When I let you use my place as headquarters, Toby, I didn't expect you'd turn it into a jail."

"Toby?" Francesca asked. She noticed several of the Crew fighting to hide smiles.

Tobias ignored her questions. His attention was now intently focused on the combat situation. He spoke into his headset to the guards outside. "Remember what I told you about putting up minimal resistance and falling back."

Francesca bet that Ben wasn't going to like it if the werewolves were allowed indoors, blood-stains and broken furniture and all that. But as he'd already said, it would be better than waking the neighbors—alerting Malibu police and the media.

A chorus of howls sounded in the distance.

"Keep it quiet," he told his fighters.

"That's not us, boss," someone outside replied.

Tobias stepped onto the back patio to get a better look at the situation.

"And it's not the ferals," another voice reported.

Francesca stepped out beside him and studied what was happening with all her senses. She saw the world as heat signatures, heartbeats, blood scent, and circulation. Shadows became bright; the moonlight gave a burning diamond blaze to the nearby ocean.

There was a Prime by the house to her left. Someone with invisible wings to the right of the patio. Werefolk moved over the lawn toward the house. She saw four werewolves moving stealthily at the edge of the property, where the land sloped down sharply toward the beach.

But there were other werefolk moving up swiftly behind them: wolves, foxes, a coyote, a mountain lion—and a vampire. She recognized the vampire. One of these werewolves let out a long howl.

"That's Joe," Tobias said.

"Sid's with him," Francesca said. "Who are—?"

The feral werewolves were overtaken before she finished.

*Do it quietly!* Tobias shouted telepathically.

*Of course, boss.* The answer came back from Joe.

The ensuing battle was savage and to the death but accompanied only by low growls and snarls.

Sid Wolfe walked through the carnage nonchalantly with the sort of cool indifference only a vampire could carry off, her hands in the pockets of her leather jacket. She came to stand by Tobias on the patio, causing Francesca a momentary stab of jealousy until she remembered that Sid was bonded to Joe Bleythin. She still put her hand possessively on Tobias's arm.

"You told Joe to bring the local werefolk to the party if we found ferals in their territory," Sid reported. She tilted her head toward the fighting. "And here they are."

# Chapter Forty-seven

Tobias had long ago learned to block the intoxicating effect of spilled blood, but when he became aware of Francesca's gaze fixed on the darkness and saw the gleam of her fangs, he took her arm to lead her back into the house. He wasn't surprised when she fought him. He was surprised when Sidonie grabbed Francesca's other arm and helped him get Francesca into the house.

"I've been hanging with werewolves for years," the former private detective told him. "I've had to get used to their copious bloodletting."

"At least that's one thing I won't have to train you on." He concentrated on Francesca, who was gazing with a glazed expression out the patio door. *You're not tasting anybody's blood but mine, sweetie.*

He held his wrist up to Francesca's mouth, and that got her attention. It got Sidonie's too.

"What the hell have you done to my best friend?" she demanded.

He felt a rush of pleasure as Francesca drew a sip of blood from him.

"What do you think he's done?" Francesca asked. That she sounded smug pleased him no end. It pleased him even more that she'd gotten hold of herself so quickly. Everything about Francesca pleased him. He had himself one damn fine female.

"Oh," Sid said after giving them an intense physical and psychic looking-over. "I guess congrats—"

Tobias held up his hand for silence, and he took his vibrating BlackBerry out of his jacket pocket.

Before he could say anything, a voice whispered faintly, "Listen." Powerful jet engines purred quietly in the background.

Tobias put the phone to his ear and was silently brought into an ongoing conversation.

"Listen to what?" a gruff Eastern European voice asked.

"May I ask some questions, Master Dragomir?" another male voice asked.

"It's a long trip. I'd welcome intelligent conversation. I'm told you're very intelligent and I plan to use it, Gregor. There are things you need to know. What do you wish to know first, who my principal is?"

"May I make the assumption that you are working for the same group my former Master doesn't think anyone knows about?"

Dragomir laughed. "I'm not sure your Master realizes that he is not the one totally in charge of our operations. He tries, but just under the surface he's as foolhardy as every Tribe Prime used to be." Another brief laugh. "You and I realize we are being manipulated by others, but I'm interested in making a profit. Let others try to take over the world as long as they pay me very well to provide the muscle they need."

"And why are you taking your soldiers to California? I thought that operation was winding down."

"So it was, but your friend Dr. Stone requested reinforcements to deal with the Dark Angels."

"His assignment was to create a diversion, no more."

"So he was reminded. But he saw an opportunity to end Strahan's interference for good. I sired him and trained him and he ultimately answers. I seriously considered his plea for help, but I was putting together an op for Brazil I didn't want to postpone. Then fate intervened when your former Master called to taunt me about the female. When I learned about Saffron, I knew I had a chance to wipe out Strahan's group once and for all."

Fear clenched deep inside Tobias's guts and soul as he heard his daughter's name. *Saffron? What about Saffie? Is she in trouble?*

It took all Tobias's self-control not to shout his questions into the phone. He found that Francesca's fingers were twined with his free hand, a solid link to sanity. She gave him strength he'd never known he needed before.

"By pitting your mercenaries against Strahan's mercenaries?" Gregor asked.

"Yes. I've wanted Strahan dead for a long time. A seer with military training makes a dangerous adversary. I tried getting rid of him even before he formed his Dark Angels, just after he stumbled across the beginning of the plan."

"He survived."

"He's lucky. But now I know he has a weakness I can use against him."

"The girl? Saffron?"

Another laugh from Dragomir. "*Saffron* is not the creature's name. I don't know why she survived or why Strahan kept her, but she's my property. I have her back to use as I see fit."

"You have completely confused me, Master Dragomir. I got the impression Strahan has had the girl since she was a baby."

"You don't understand why I had an infant slave?" That damn laugh came again.

*Slave? Property?* Tobias's temples throbbed with fury. Nobody spoke about his baby like that! Tobias was ready to jump through the phone to rip Dragomir to bloody pieces.

Francesca squeezed his fingers tightly. *Steady.*

"The slave came into my possession in a simple enough way. I sired her on a mortal female." Laughter. "You are good at hiding your emotions, Gregor, but even you cannot hide your revulsion."

"I mean no disrespect, Master. But—"

"It was an experiment. I bred the bitch on purpose to see if she'd have a vampire baby. The mortal was a half breed, mortal but with a vampire mother."

"A Clan or Family female? I've heard they sometimes take mortal male lovers."

"My mortal pet's mother was a female of an Asian Clan. I captured them both when we raided their Citadel. I experimented to see if I could get a vampire offspring from the half breed. It didn't work; she had a mortal baby. But I found a use for them. A double use, really. Very profitable."

"This had something to do with Strahan?" Gregor asked.

"I was contracted to dispose of Strahan at the same time I agreed to help a group of political radicals make a violent statement. They wanted to blow up an airplane. I decided to use my pet to carry the bomb. She was the bomb, with a simple telepathic trigger. It wasn't likely that a woman with a baby would be suspected of sabotaging an airplane. We called it Operation Saffron. My terrorist clients got themselves killed before we could carry out their plan, but it was still a good idea. I used it on Strahan."

*All those people died because of me? He forced Saffie's mother to kill herself?*

*Microscopic bloody pieces. There won't be a molecule left of this Dragomir when I'm done with him.*

"Strahan survived the bombing. With the child," Gregor said.

"I'll never understand how. But he's as emotionally soft toward mortals as any of his sort. This *Saffron* is a weapon to use against—"

Silence as the connection cut off.

Tobias took the BlackBerry from his ear and stared at it for a moment before heaving it as far across the room as he could.

\*　　\*　　\*

Francesca winced as the phone shattered against the kitchen wall. Joe Bleythin and Shaggy Harker had to dodge ricocheting plastic shrapnel as they came in from the patio. Wide grins were wiped from the werewolves' faces as they hurried up to Tobias.

"Boss?" Joe asked.

Tobias's muscles were as rigid as stone. The look on his face was the most frightening Francesca had ever seen. His huge brown eyes swirled with hatred, fury, and terror. Francesca wanted to help him somehow but knew trying to hold and comfort him wasn't the answer. He needed to kill.

"His daughter's been taken," she told Joe and Shaggy Harker. Everyone else in the kitchen had easily overheard the voices from the phone. Low murmurs and angry telepathic comments were zinging around the room.

"Who's taken the kid?" Shaggy demanded.

Sid explained what was known to the newcomers.

Tobias came out of his frozen rage as she finished, and he said to Harker, "The fight for your territory isn't over yet. The Tribes are sending in fresh reinforcements. If I have to tear up this city and reveal the existence of our kind to find the bastards with my kid, I will."

Harker threw back his head and howled. Francesca worried that this was a protest until the local werefolk leader said, "You don't need to hunt for them. We can lead you right to them."

# Chapter Forty-eight

Tobias looked to Joe Bleythin for an explanation.

"My hunch that we should start tracking our bad guys where the original ferals hung out was right. They were dead, but their scent was overlaid with fresher traces of ferals that had been there over the years. It took a while, but we traced them to their den at a small airport. I gathered the local troops for a raid, but the ferals took off before we got to them. We followed them here. The scouts we left behind all report vampire headaches. There's a vampire in the hangar at the airport all right," Joe added.

"Why did a pack of werewolves show up

here?" Ben Lancer asked. "They had to know it was suicide to go up against Primes."

"That's easy to answer," Shaggy said. "Stupid and sad, but easy." Everyone looked at the local shapeshifter leader. "Even ferals have a twisted loyalty to the pack ethic. These curs made a pact with the Purists and Tribes and they got themselves killed fulfilling the pact. Their mortal *brothers* were prisoners. It was their obligation to try to rescue them."

"I bet the vampire talked them into it," Sid said. "If he was cutting his losses, it was the perfect way to get rid of them."

Tobias wasn't interested in the why or the who of the plotting right now but waited impatiently for the explanation out of respect for Shaggy.

And it was intel. He made himself remember that he needed intel when he wanted to run off right then. He was interested in only Saffie's safety. He wasn't going to do her any good if he didn't do this the right way. He had the Crew. He had an ace inside that airplane. *Saffie*—

"She's going to be fine." Joe broke into Tobias's thoughts.

Tobias nodded. He squared his exhausted shoulders and gathered in his Crew with a decisive glance. "Listen up, people!" he announced.

\*    \*    \*

Francesca took a few steps back to get out of the way as Tobias did what he did.

While Tobias gave crisp, precise orders to his attentive soldiers, Sidonie moved to stand next to her. Sid kept her gaze on the Dark Angel leader, but she spared part of her attention to ask, *You and Tobias? Bonded?*

*It was a whirlwind courtship.*

*Do you want this?*

*Did you want to be bonded to a werewolf?*

*It's not a matter of what I wanted or what Joe wanted. Oh, okay. Sorry,* she added after a bit of mental silence. *Does Tobias know about . . .*

*Patrick?* Sid was the only one who'd known about her marriage. *He knows.*

*Does your Matri know about Tobias?*

*I'm staying with Tobias,* was Francesca's answer. She smiled as sudden intense belief hit her. *He needs me.*

*Tobias is the Dark Angels, and the Dark Angels are a combat unit. Do you think the Matri Council will allow both of us in a com—*

*The Matri Council will have to learn to live with not always getting everything their way. My mother set me up with Tobias. She's going to support me in Council whether she wants to or not.*

Sid gave a low whistle and looked at Francesca

admiringly. *I've always been good at scheming, but you're the political genius of our generation. This is going to mess up your writing career, though.*

Tobias turned to her before she could protest that she wasn't a writer. He took her arm and led her back to the guest bedroom. Her spirits sank with dread along the way.

She went on the offensive even before the door closed behind them. "Don't you dare tell me I'm not allowed to come along on this op."

"I wouldn't dream of it."

She was in his arms an instant later. He held her so close, so desperately tight, she thought she was going to break. But she loved it.

"You're too strong to break," he told her. "You're a Clan girl. Clan girls and Family girls don't break." He kissed her so hungrily that her head began to swim, his hands on her hot and hard.

She moaned against his lips but pulled her mouth from his before it could easily lead to something else. She ached with wanting him, but they were both aware that this was not the time, bonding urge or not. She put her hands on either side of his face. His cheeks were rough with beard stubble. "Saffie is strong too," she said. "She's your child—no one else's. She's a Family Prime's strong, tough daughter. As well as the daughter of the regiment," she added with a smile. "Think of what she's already come through with you. She'll survive all those horrible, hideous revelations, and so will you."

He closed his eyes for a moment. He looked incredibly sad and weary. But he hid those emotions away when he opened his eyes. "Saffie and I will survive," he said. "But working through that is in the future. Right now we have to get her back. And in the past . . ."

He pulled her closer. His hands rested on her waist, big and competent and full of latent violence that warmed a vampire girl's heart.

"In the past I tried to defend the way Tribes think about females to you. Then I listened to that monster talking about Saffie's mother, about Saffie, and I realized the bullshit I'd fed you earlier was a nostalgic kid's view. I'm sorry." He rocked back and forth with her in his arms. "I am so sorry."

He was apologizing to the dead woman and the child he loved as much as he was to Francesca. She pulled his head down to her shoulder and held him and let him work through it without thoughts or words. Sometimes just being there was more important than all their psychic talents.

He lifted his head when a knock came on the door. He gave her a gentle kiss on the forehead and a brief smile that melted her heart.

"I'm ready," he called. "Let's go," he said to her.

# Chapter Forty-nine

Francesca glared at the wide bracelet circling her right wrist. It contained a tiny electrical device called a mini-zap. Everyone in the van was wearing one, as it blocked telepathic signatures from other telepaths. It was the Dark Angels version of stealth technology. The silent humming was driving her mad.

"It's giving me a headache," she complained. "And I think I'm getting sunburned."

The early morning sunlight coming through the windshield didn't fall directly on where she sat near the rear of the vehicle, but she could *feel* it even though she knew it couldn't hurt her. It was her imagination fed by the physical reaction to the mind shield.

Seated across from her, Sid held up her own arm. "You'll get used to it."

Counting the driver, there were four other Angels crowded into the van heading south toward their destination. The plan was to secure the bad guys' hideout for themselves before the private plane landed.

"Oh, like you've worn one before," she snapped at Sid. The irritating mini-zap was not helping her mood. She was also a little queasy from having ingested at least a quart of cow blood. This was another part of the Dark Angel battle prep for vampires. Being sated was supposed to help keep them from going into a blood frenzy when fighting other vampires. It cut down on the fun, but also on reckless mistakes, she'd been told. There was a lot to learn about being a Dark Angel. She and Sidonie were learning on the job instead of going through basic training.

"You're as new to this gig as I am," she reminded Sid.

"Yeah, but I was around when the original zapper got field tested by the vampire hunters who are supposedly our allies. That prototype hurt like hell."

This reminder that Sid had gotten to have adventures for years as a private detective upped Francesca's irritation.

Sid recognized it and put a calming hand on Francesca's shoulder. "It's not the low-level pain that's bothering you the most. This is really the first time you've been completely alone in your own head. For someone just beginning to bond—"

"Please be quiet now," Francesca told her. "Or I will kill you."

Sid only snickered. But she concentrated her attention on inspecting the silver knife she'd chosen to add to her natural weapons, fangs, claws, strength, and speed. Seemed a bit like overkill to Francesca, but she'd accepted one of the knives just to make Tobias happy. She did like the piratical look of the sheath strapped to her thigh.

The headache was only an inconvenience. It was worth anything if it helped save that child. She rubbed her aching temples.

*"Where the hell is Tobias? Why didn't he let me go with him instead of assigning Sid to baby-sit me?*

*Because he has to,* the reasonable part of her pointed out.

"Not being able to feel him is . . . terrible. How can you bear to be separated from Joe?"

"I've had practice," was the bitter answer. "Relax. It's only for a little while. You can stop sulking now," Sid said as the van came to a halt. "We've arrived."

When she got out Francesca saw that the van, along with several other vehicles, was parked on a dusty roadside on a ridge. In a valley several miles away was the small airport, and another mountain ridge rose beyond it. The place boasted a hangar with an arched metal roof, a couple of small buildings, and one runway. A pickup truck, a sports car, and several motorcycles were parked by the buildings, and the property was surrounded by a razor-wire-topped chain-link fence.

Standing next to her, Sid asked, "See them?"

Francesca shielded her eyes with her hand and studied the bramble-and-brush-covered ground between the ridge and the fence. "Eleanor," she said when she spotted a werecoyote slinking behind a clump of scraggly trees. "Joe," she guessed when she saw a huge black werewolf deep in some bushes. He crouched beside a reddish brown werewolf with a graying muzzle. "Shaggy?"

"Correct. Now that the werefolk are in place, we vampires will join them." Sid moved to where the others were unloading equipment from the back of the van. "Are you going to help?" she called back to Francesca. "Or are you afraid of breaking a nail?"

Francesca laughed and extended her claws a

little. She wiggled her fingers as she joined Sid. "Jungle Red."

They laughed. It was an old joke between them. Despite the discomfort from the mini-zap, Francesca was suddenly very happy that she and her best friend were finally living the lives they'd always wanted.

*Thank you, Tobias,* she thought, sure he felt her even without telepathy.

Tobias waited until he got word on his headset that everyone was in position, concealing any sign of his impatience. He stayed perfectly still, and word came that the fence was breached, followed by the report that the ferals guarding the perimeter were out of the picture.

He nodded.

This was the preliminary round, the first step. He liked his ops carefully orchestrated, but this one had to go perfectly.

He scanned the slightly overcast sky, willing the plane to appear. They'd calculated their attack to almost coincide with the airplane's projected arrival. The less time the new arrivals had to sense any danger, the better for the Crew. The time projection had to be correct. He refused to worry about it now. Right now, there was a vampire in the main building, and Tobias was looking forward to killing him.

"Let's go," he said to the fae whose job it would be to magically construct a shell around him in the form of the soon-to-be-late Dr. Stone.

# Chapter Fifty

Gregor wasn't sure what was going to happen next, but he was anything but complacent as the private jet approached the landing strip. Those who directly opposed the Dark Angels had a tendency to die. Survival was high on Gregor's list of priorities. Being only one more grunt for Dragomir to throw into the fray was not on his list at all, but he bet he knew who the mercenary leader was going to order to be first out of the plane—the first casualty in case something went wrong.

He might not have liked that spot, but if he could get the girl to go with him on the exit, he could fulfill his own orders. Her going voluntarily wouldn't be in the cards, of course. He carefully gave her an occasional glance, and what he saw didn't look good. Where the kid had been feisty before, she looked completely broken now. She'd been crying quietly but steadily since Dragomir casually revealed her personal history. She was so drawn in on herself she was practically catatonic.

*Oh, well, it won't be difficult to pick her up and carry her.*

The airplane had been descending swiftly and now Gregor heard the landing gear operate. Outside the nearest window he saw a forlorn, dusty landscape. *Welcome back to California,* he thought. Had it been only a few days since he'd left? It seemed like a century.

There was the slightest of bumps as the plane wheels touched the ground. As the jet bounced down the rough runway to finally come to a stop, Gregor concentrated his senses on what waited outside. He detected one vampire and several werewolves inside the perimeter fence he'd spotted from the sky. Things seemed to be just the way he'd been told they'd be.

Despite being anxious for action, he waited until after Dragomir had gotten to his feet before he unbuckled his seat belt. One of the bodyguards came forward to grab Saffron.

"I'll take the female myself," Dragomir announced. He took Saffron by the arm. She flinched and whimpered but didn't try to pull away. The guard carefully remained on the other side of her.

"You go first, Gregor," Dragomir ordered.

At least this was no surprise. "Certainly, Master."

"There is supposed to be a limo waiting in the airplane hangar. Bring it round for me."

It was good to be on the ground. It was even better to have the door open and Gregor gone. Saffie welcomed the fresh air and having at least one scum-sucking parasite out of her face. She breathed in lungfuls of air, trying not to throw up. Dragomir's touch was obscene, hard to bear. And she kept crying! She couldn't stop and worried the weakness would screw up her vision when she needed it.

A vampire was waiting on the ground by the shallow stairs Dragomir led her down. She noticed more Primes exiting from a doorway up by the cockpit. Dragomir threw her to the ground before she could get a count. She knocked into the guard on the way down and got a push from him too. Pain shot through her knees as she landed on concrete at Dragomir's feet.

"My son!" Dragomir kicked her aside as he stepped forward to give the Prime a big hug.

"Welcome, sire." Stone stepped back and gave a deep bow.

Saffie couldn't figure out which one of the pair was less sincere. She was no psychic, but she didn't need to be to sense the tension beneath their false affection. Tribe Primes were competitive 24/7. She knew that whatever the vampires did, it was all dangerous for her.

Stone pointed at her. "What's that?"

Dragomir gave one of his cheesy fake laughs. He nudged her with his foot. She held very still, to keep from giving in to the impulse to bite his leg.

"That is, and always has been, Tobias Strahan's death. It's his weakness and the bait that will lure him into our trap."

Stone came closer to repeat Dragomir's foot nudging, hard enough to push her a few inches away from Dragomir. "Really?" he asked. Then his voice changed. "She looks like a scared kid to me."

Saffie took a quick look at Stone's face. She saw the killing fury in his big brown eyes—her dad's eyes—and ducked her head to hide the smile. The glamour was wearing off, but Dragomir hadn't seen it yet.

By now all the mercenaries were off the plane. They were gathered by the cockpit, waiting for orders. She heard the purr of the limo engine coming from the hangar. She kept her arms crossed tightly over the bulge in her hoodie and thought about the position of the guard behind her. The buzz and burn of anticipation raced through her. It was all Saffron could do not to hold her breath.

"Scared kid? What do you mean by that? Are you going soft?" Dragomir demanded.

"Yeah. She's always had that effect on me," her dad answered.

She heard his snarl as he leapt at Dragomir. She caught a glimpse of claws. Dragomir swore. There was the heavy thud of bodies grappling.

Saffie spun toward the guard. He was rushing to help Dragomir and didn't even notice her. He certainly hadn't noticed her pluck the small silver-shooter he wore in his waistband. The small gun held six bullets. She fired two into the vampire's head and two more into his chest.

Silver bullets don't do as much damage to a mortal body as regular ammunition, but vampires weren't *compatible with human DNA,* were they?

*Want my blood? Taste me if you can.*

Tobias drilled the thought into Dragomir's mind as they grappled with snapping fangs, sharp claws, and hard muscle.

*Come on. I'm delicious.*

*I bet you are,* Dragomir sneered back.

Tobias continued to taunt. He even let the other Prime rip a chunk of flesh from his shoulder just to get the blood scent into Dragomir's nostrils.

"I'm going to drain you!" Dragomir shouted.

He snapped at Tobias's throat.

Tobias danced away.

They circled each other, evenly matched, equally dangerous, equally determined to kill each other. For a few seconds Dragomir didn't recognize him. The fae had used his powers to throw a glamour bearing a strong resemblance to Stone over Tobias, and people see what they expect to see.

*My son! Where's my son?* Dragomir screamed the thought when he finally realized he wasn't fighting Dr. Stone.

The thought sent a shot of pain searing through Tobias's shields.

He ignored the mental blow. *Dead,* he answered. He sent an image of Stone's twisted, lifeless body toward Dragomir. *He didn't put up much of a fight.*

Dragomir snarled. He howled with fury. He made a lunge toward Saffie.

But she wasn't where he'd left her. There was a body lying nearby, fresh blood oozing across the ground. Tobias had known what it meant when he heard the shots.

"My girl's smart and tough. I don't think she got that from you."

All the other vampires in the Crew were now battling the mercenaries. They'd ripped off the mini-zaps and mental energy zipped dangerously back and forth. Francesca was over there, but he didn't look for her. He had to trust her to take care of herself. Both sides wielded silver weapons along with natural ones. Tobias was confident in his people and concentrated on his own fight with Dragomir.

He'd finally goaded the other Prime enough to send him into blood rage. Dragomir spun around Tobias and brought a double-handed strike down on his back. Tobias dropped to his knees from the heavy blow. He spun around and upward as Dragomir sprang onto him, not giving the other Prime the chance to sink fangs into the back of his neck to sever the spine.

Tobias sank his fangs into Dragomir's throat, ripping and tearing at the Prime's windpipe while Dragomir clawed and punched and kicked. He fought like a damned tiger. Tobias held on tight and ignored his own pain while snapping at Dragomir's neck over and over. He smelled and tasted blood as it spurted over his face and chest, but he didn't give a damn about it. This was about killing.

When Dragomir's struggling finally slowed, when there was no breath in him and his spirit only held on out of stubbornness, Tobias rose off his body to grab his head. One hard twist completely severed Dragomir's spine. No vampire could survive this. But just to make sure, Tobias used his K-bar to completely sever Dragomir's head from his body.

"Nobody touches my little girl," he said, and tossed the head to the ground.

As he did a bullet whizzed past his shoulder.

"In front of you, Dad!" Saffie yelled.

Tobias looked up to see a Prime slumping against the side of a car. There was blood on the vampire's chest.

"Greg!" Tobias rushed forward.

"Dad! He's—!"

"Don't shoot him again!" he shouted to his daughter. "He's your uncle."

# Chapter Fifty-one

When Tobias shouted Francesca couldn't take it anymore.

She'd fought every instinct screaming inside her but was able to hold off from rushing to help Tobias while he battled the other Prime. She'd been aware of his pain and his cunning, and reveled in his skill, but hadn't let the knowledge overwhelm her. She was part of the fight too. What she did to help keep the mercenaries from getting to their Master helped Tobias, even if she didn't get a chance to kill anybody. Primes with far more experience were always there ahead of her every time she tried to attack someone. She did manage to try out her knife when she stabbed upward under a Prime's raised arm. The Prime dropped the gun he'd been holding, and one of the Crew rushed in to finish him off with fangs.

Then Tobias shouted, and she ran to him.

He was holding his daughter in a tight embrace when she reached him. They were kneeling on the ground beside a wounded Prime. Francesca had to put her hands behind her back to keep from touching her bondmate, to keep from interrupting this reunion.

The girl was fighting hideous pain. She'd been betrayed, shamed, maltreated, and had learned far more about her own life than any victim should have to know. She was vulnerable.

But at least she was angry. Francesca felt the boiling fury and hoped it was enough to get the kid through these horrible moments.

And Saffron had her father's enfolding embrace to help her. He radiated comfort. He radiated love. He radiated protectiveness.

*You're mine. You're loved. Forget that bastard. You're fine. I love you, baby. I love you so much.*

The girl listened. She held on fiercely and let Tobias soothe her soul.

Francesca was glad of Saffron's reaction as the girl calmed, but she worried about the mortal's fierce, fierce anger. That wasn't likely to go away any time soon.

She'd do whatever she could to help Tobias's daughter. But now was not the time.

She looked down at the bleeding Prime.

The Prime looked up at Francesca, eyes full of pain. "Medic?" he rasped.

Should I finish him off or do as he asked?

"What do you mean he's your brother!" Saffie shouted, suddenly pulling away from Tobias. "He kidnapped me!"

"No, he didn't. I sent Greg to get you."

"I also kidnapped her," Greg said. "And made the call from the plane. It's complicated," he told Francesca as she dropped to her knees beside him. She pulled his shirt aside and probed the wound. "Ow!"

"You're damn right, ow!" Saffie snarled at him. "Who are you?" she added to Francesca as Tobias moved to Greg's other side.

Francesca gave the girl a reassuring smile. "We'll talk about me later." The kid had been through enough shock and changes for now. "Call me Fran."

Tobias raised an eyebrow at her but didn't offer any comment. "How's Greg?"

"I touched silver in there. If it comes out he'll

be fine. I've had some EMT training," she added. What was the use of having a nephew who was the main physician to the vampire world if she didn't learn anything from him?

"Fine." Tobias wiped blood off his knife and set to work on Greg's shoulder.

Greg swore. Loudly and creatively. When he wasn't howling in pain.

"You deserve it!" Saffie shouted.

Francesca watched the crude operation, glad that vampires were generally immune to infections. Greg passed out when the lump of silver was finally dug out.

Tobias flipped the bullet away and turned to his daughter. Saffie glared down at Greg. "He's my brother," he told her again. "More importantly, he's been working undercover among the Tribes for years."

Francesca came to a realization. "This guy's Gregor, isn't he? He's the one who tortured Rose Cameron!"

"I can explain that," Greg whispered. Tobias helped him up. He sat propped against the door of the limo. "I couldn't stop what happened to Rose. I couldn't break my cover. But I gave her the tools she needed to escape." Greg looked intently at Saffie. "I called Tobias when my Tribe Master told me to fetch you. I'd been trying to keep Dark Angel communication codes from being broken, but when the geeks broke the codes I did what I could to salvage the situation. I was bringing you home." He looked past Saffie to Dragomir's body, then back to his brother. "I really wish you'd let him live long enough for me to strip his brain. He knew a lot."

"I'm not in the least bit sorry." Tobias touched Greg's healing shoulder. "Welcome home, Greg. You've been under too long. I was beginning to worry you'd gone native."

The brothers looked intently at each other for a moment.

"You trusted me with your kid," Greg answered.

"Of course I did. I said I was beginning to worry. You've been undercover long enough."

"Almost long enough," Greg said. "I have to stay under long enough to save the computer geeks the Master's holding prisoner. I can't abandon those kids. And I haven't found out who our real enemy is. Getting close."

Tobias nodded his understanding; no one got left behind. "Don't get so close I don't have a brother."

"I have an uncle?" Saffie asked. The knowledge

finally seemed to be sinking in. She looked briefly back at the body. Her features twisted with distaste and hate. "And a—sperm donor."

Francesca spoke up. "You have a loving father!"

"You have Tobias," Greg said. "And all the aunts and uncles you can handle with the Crew."

Tobias put his hand on Francesca's arm. It was covered in drying blood, but vampires didn't mind that sort of thing. Saffie gasped when Tobias gave Francesca a gentle kiss on the cheek. "You have a mother too."

"What!"

Francesca sprang up to face Saffie. She gently grasped the affronted girl's shoulders. "You've had enough for now. Everybody here has."

Saffie looked her over warily. "You're a vampire."

Francesca nodded. "Francesca Reynard, Clan Reynard."

Saffie's already wide eyes widened even more. "You're Flare? *The* Flare?" She giggled. The sound was only slightly hysterical. "You and Flare, Dad?"

Tobias shrugged.

Saffie pulled away from Francesca. She shook her head as she backed up. "I cannot deal with this. I cannot deal with this right now."

She turned away. As she did a group of Dark

Angels came up to surround her, pouring out affection and relief at seeing the girl safe.

Tobias got up, but Tsuke and Joaquin came up to report and ask for orders before he could go to the girl.

Francesca put her arm around his waist. "Give her time," she said. "Give her some space right now."

"I'm going to rest now," Greg said, and closed his eyes.

He waved his people away. There was a hell of a lot to be done, but not just yet. Tobias was more aware of Francesca's nearness, of her support, than he was of anything else. "How did I ever do this without you?" he murmured. He was almost frightened by the strength of his emotions. Of his need for her.

"I have no idea," she answered.

He laughed and pressed his forehead against hers. "I want to make love to you all the time," he told her.

"Same here."

"I love you so much." He whispered the words close to her ear.

Her gaze flashed up to meet his; she was as surprised as he was at this very un-Prime-like admission to a vampire female. But bonding was supposed to be about love, wasn't it? Or else why did vampires crave this perfect closeness?

"It's not perfect," she said. "We aren't perfect. I don't want us to be perfect."

"Princess Flare and the Über-Prime?" he asked.

"We aren't those people."

"At least not all the time," he countered.

She laughed. "I love you," she told him. "When I never thought I'd be able to love anyone again."

He was equally surprised by her declaration. "You love me? You fell in love with me."

"Don't look so smug."

"I am Prime."

"Yes, well, we have years to work on that."

"When did you fall in love with me? Where?"

"You first," Francesca countered.

"I knew when you busted me over being mean to Kea. You were so righteous, so . . . the woman I loved then and there."

"Well, damn, isn't that romantic?"

"For me it was. You?" he demanded now.

"You had me the moment you first called your daughter."

"What?" He was flabbergasted. "How could you have fallen in love with me then? We hadn't even had sex yet."

"Primes." She stroked his cheek. Her smile was all the light in the world. "You better get to work now, boss," she told him. "Then as soon as that's taken care of, I want to get back to work on having your baby."

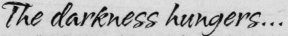